MATHSMAGICA
TAPESTRY OF SHADOWS

DANIEL STEFANOV GEORGIEV

ISBN: 9798322763253

Imprint: Independently published

Copyright © 2023 by Daniel Stefanov Georgiev Blentkills

All rights reserved.

No part of this book may be reproduced in any form or by any electronic or mechanical means, including information storage and retrieval systems, without written permission from the author, except for the use of brief quotations in a book review.

WITHIN THESE PAGES

SHINES *THE LIGHT* OF MANY.

FOR HOPE MAY REMAIN SAFE ONLY WHEN SEALED AWAY.

INTRODUCTION

ENDARIEL'S POINT OF VIEW

The void leaked.

Ornate metal doors lay defeated, the Darc Family's manor flashing with bursts of light.

How unbearable.

"The Luminari," Aetherial said.

"Quick. Before it's too late," I said, urgency claiming me.

Battle cries shook the staircase. The light beams grew brighter as swords clashed. The corridor turned and black thunder engulfed all the light, its force sending shivers down my spine.

"Black Magic."

Only our heavy steps could be heard now.

Beyond the corridor laid six Luminari mages burned into a blackened grey crisp. My gaze met with the man behind this sorcery. His pale face matched perfectly with his blond hair and noble robe.

Cracks took shape across my palms as the purple void glowed from them. *Time is sparse...*

INTRODUCTION

Weak and petrified, the man's tears ran down his cheeks, his wife slowly turning to ash at his feet. I expanded my right hand's thumb and pinkie, casting a void circle beneath him, thunderous sparks freezing my target in place.

Closing in, I placed my palm over his face. I inhaled, prepared for the ritual. My eyes closed, blocking out everything except my loyal sister's voice.

"Endariel, he's..."

I opened my eyes and noticed his skin turning dark. The blue colour in his eyes succumbed to the after effects of the foul magic.

With a click of my tongue, I dismissed the ritual. My hands shook. Suppressing the void had become a significant challenge; the cracks grew too big.

"Endariel, your vessel won't... last much longer," my brother came next to me. "Should we—"

"No need, Aetherial. Absolutely no need," I said, my voice low.

"Then what should we do?" my sister asked.

I released the void circle restricting the man and walked past him as his body crumbled to the ground.

"Forgive me... I couldn't... protect them," he said in a drained voice.

At the end of the corridor, behind the ashes of the woman, lay a small room with two children asleep in their cradle.

"Are you joking?" my brother burst out next to me, as my gaze fell on the young boy. "I know there's no time, but this is absurd!"

"Dear brother," I turned to him and gently pressed my glowing hand against his chest. "Close your eyes and focus."

Adhering to my guidance, they both ignored their eyesight and gazed deeper than what eyes could see.

"By The Wings, I see it," Aetherial said, his deep voice filled with awe.

"...And besides. I have little choice left," my hand radiated faint violet petals, disintegrating in the air.

"Endariel, your body," my sister gently caressed the large cracks on my back. "It's the first time this has happened."

"And the first time we failed to secure the vessel!" brother said.

"Lay foundations for my return. You have... twenty years," I said, putting my hand on the baby boy's forehead. Violet light radiated across the room.

"Endariel! You're disintegrating!"

"It's somehow different this time! But... it... will work!" I said, as my body dispersed, and at a steady pace, soaked into the boy.

"The girl," my sister picked the baby into her arms. "Do you sense it?"

"Yes, I do," my brother nodded and turned towards the boy. "The Luminari Faith will proceed with their execution."

"We must get them to safety."

"And we will do just that. Let us go, Lethalica. To lay the ground for our king's return."

CHAPTER 1
DARKNESS IN THE LIGHT

SOVA'S POINT OF VIEW

Arcane magic cloaked Mathsmagica in a tapestry of shadows.

The guards at the bridge pulled to the side, and I stepped into the border. The dark shroud faded with each step, and I could see the setting sun behind me.

"Come on, Nilah. We don't want to be late." My gaze shifted from the sunset to my sister, her golden locks reflecting the last light.

"Sorry! I'm just so fascinated with The High Arcanist's shroud spell every time!"

"The event happens once a month and we're always late for some reason!" I said, rolling my eyes.

"Ugh, fine!" she blurted and dashed forward. "Try to keep up!"

Her silhouette flew by me and shrunk at the colossal sentinel of Mathsmagica's centre - *The Academy*.

"You think you're so fast, do you?" I picked up my

tempo to match hers. She bounced from one wooden rod, lanterns hovering above it, to the other.

"Hey, watch out! God damn mages!" a man yelled, running out on the street, shaking a fist in the air. "You'll break the potions!"

"Nilah, you dashed so fast you shook the tables!" I laughed as I went past him, and my sister's chuckle also reached me.

My feet, nimble, stepped on the glowing cobblestone pathways, their soft light of residual energies absorbed by my black cloak.

The closer we got to The Academy, the more people there were. The idea of running past them was a bit too much, even for us, so we took a jump atop the roofs. On the other side of the street, Nilah dashed from house to house, the sound of her running feet filling the air. Passing by, we met the disapproving gazes and unmistakable gestures of head-shaking. That didn't matter. We were finally going to be on time for the "Day of Happening" festival The Shapers made.

The rooftops ahead were odd-shaped; perhaps a Shapers architect made them. It swirled oddly and the chance of slipping seemed high. I sought a less dense spot to land on and then walked from there further.

A wind rustle and the clanking of shoes meeting stones came right next to me. "So much for getting there faster," Nilah said, coat rustling as she landed.

"It's fine—"

"It is *not*," a voice interrupted me.

"Who—"

"You have caused quite the commotion," a man that seemed our age said, as he approached me with an aggressive push.

"We're sorry, sir." Nilah lowered her head and apologised.

I shifted my gaze to her and after a slight pause; I closed my eyes and lowered my head too. "We apologise."

"Hey, you. Raise your head," the man said. He had shoulder length curly brown hair, matching eyes, a wide jaw, and a concerningly angry look. The uniform under his coat hinted he was a student at The Academy, as well.

"I do not recognise you. Why do you bow your head before me if we're wearing the same uniform?" he demanded.

"You must be a noble," I said, fixing my eyes on him.

"So what? You are too, obviously."

I didn't respond, but Nilah did. "We are commoners. We just... have–"

"What!?" he grabbed her by the shirt and pulled her close, frowning. "What nonsense are you speaking, woman!? You can't wear these uniforms if you're—"

I grabbed the man's hand and pulled it to the side. He let go of Nilah. "We apologise for the commotion. Please, as classmates—"

As I spoke, a flame in the shape of a dragon circled the sky above us, a blazing fire heating the air. It made a few loops and then crashed into an icy sphere, which hovered in wait, transforming it into a water dragon.

"Come on, Sova! The show has started!" Nilah said, her voice filled with excitement.

I bowed my head, and followed my sister. The crowd had already become so dense; it seemed inappropriate for the man to further converse with us.

Three men performed a ritual dance on an elevated stage not too far in the distance.

The men kicked, the dragon took a turn in the sky, they

punched, and it changed elements. For what seemed to be the big moment, two of the men breathed fire, shaping two more dragons. They entwined into one another, changing into water, fire, and ice dragons, creating a spectacular sight to behold.

The people standing closest to the stage wore red capes, and they reached out to the sky, with palms open. Fire orbs manifested and slowly flew towards the sky.

"Sova, look! It's like the dragons are dancing in a sky of fire stars!" Nilah jumped.

I narrowed my eyes to see better. To me, half of what I saw looked like a blackboard with a bunch of equations on it. I shook my head, trying to free myself from this burden and just enjoy the light show.

"Sova, did you see? They melted into each other and shaped a phoenix falling! What in Nocturna's beauty was that!?" Nilah pulled my sleeve.

I felt my right hand's fingers flicking, Nilah's voice coming through to me. I looked at her and smiled at her cute pouting.

"Sova, did you even pay attention to it? Are you listening to me!?"

"Of course I am, Nillie."

"So? Did you enjoy it?"

"Sure. The Shapers are definitely those who perform the most spectacular of magic," I said and joined her as she followed the outgoing crowd. "Seems like it's over, then?"

"The rest of the ritual is for followers only. It's not public, so yes."

"Alright. To the dorms it is then?" I asked, shrugging.

"It was so short, Sova! So good! But couldn't it last longer? It's not fair!" she complained.

Poor girl, she seems disappointed. After that chase we had, she expected more; I suppose. I wish I could have seen it through her eyes, though.

"Hey, Nilah." I pulled her close. "Wanna see who gets to the dorms first?"

Her jaw went loose. "Bro, even after that? We almost got into trouble earlier."

I pulled away from her. "Chicken."

"What did you say!?"

"Chicken," I tempted her.

"I'll even give you a head start. You'll see how good I am. Don't make me use my Shadow Step!"

"Oh my, you would dare invite me to a Shadow Step challenge?"

"Three. Two. One. Let's go!" Nilah said and surged between the crowd.

My eyes lingered on her for a few seconds, but I could tell she wasn't using Shadow Step. I enhanced my body with mana and dashed to follow her.

This time, aside from brushing against a few commoners, we didn't cause any other trouble. It felt like in a blink of an eye we reached the Umbra district. The hovering lanterns sprayed their surroundings in a violet colour, and the cobblestones had a feign glow to them.

Nilah slowed down and approached a shop with potions and basic materials. I walked next to her and looked at the small vial in her hand, blue liquid splashing inside it.

She took a coin out of the pouch on her belt and dropped it on a special crystal, then she sipped from the vial. The coin vanished, a white smoke fizzling in the air out of where it used to be.

"You had to replenish?" I asked, looking at the empty vial on her belt. *I often forget she has this problem.*

"Sorry, Sova. Not all of us are as gifted," she smiled and put the vial in its rightful spot.

We continued down the alley and gossiped about The Shapers.

"I knew you were foul." A familiar voice spoke from behind.

I turned around to see it was the same guy who had showed up earlier before the show. He walked at a slow pace towards us.

"What do you want?" Nilah asked. "We've done nothing bad this time!"

"They're the ones, Father," he said, and a man, perhaps one head taller than him, stepped off from a white dake's back. It was normal for nobles to ride on these creatures' backs. Their sturdy musculature, thick fur, and three-toed feet with sharp claws allowed them to travel pretty much anywhere.

"Arthus, my son, you brought me here for this?" the towering man asked, his voice deep. I strained my eyes to make out his face, but the darkness concealed his features. Yet, there was an unmistakable aura of power surrounding him. Something similar to what I felt with some of our teachers at The Academy.

"I told you they look shady! And they probably stole from that shop just now!"

The man turned to face Arthus and paused.

"What's wrong? Father?"

The man slapped his son so hard he crumbled to the ground.

"Do you realise what would happen if a Luminari follower did something on Mathsmagica grounds against The Shadow Covenant, Arthus? For no real reason, at that," the man asked, and leaped on his dake's back. With a haunting howl, the creature galloped into the enveloping darkness.

"Nilah, let's go," I whispered and pushed my sister gently.

"Just you wait!" Arthus yelled as he recovered back to his feet.

We kept walking, ignoring the callout.

"Just keep walking," I said.

Before I knew it, a flash took my vision for a moment. Arthus pulled me by the shoulder, forcing me to face him.

"Leave us be and everything ends well," I muttered.

"It all ends well when I say it ends well, Covenant rat!"

He threw a punch at my face, but I blocked it, my left hand aiming at his face. He pushed it away, and head bumped into me, though I took it without receiving any real damage. Nilah pushed him and he stumbled to the ground. Enraged, he growled and bashed the ground with his fist. In a flash, he was already before me and his attack landed on my stomach. My breath escaped me.

Nilah punched Arthus in the kidneys, but he didn't budge. With a powerful push, he sent her sprawling to the side, her body crashing onto the unforgiving pavement.

"You will not bear witness to what just happened," Arthus said and threw me at the wall and simultaneously smashed his fist against my solar plexus.

In another flash, I could see numbers and equations. I shook my head, recovering from the blows, but only to fall on my knees and spit on the floor.

Thud after thud, I came to myself, my eyes opening wide as I realised the bastard was striking my sister with his filthy hands.

The shadows beckoned me. I rose to my feet, black

thunder gathering might within my palms. A breeze waved my coat as my eyes gazed upon my prey.

"One last chance," I said in a low voice.

"Brother, no!" Nilah cried, as the filth got off her and approached to face me. "Don't do it!"

As Arthus opened his palm towards the sky, a gentle breeze caressed his skin, carrying with it a shimmering dust that coalesced into the form of a sword.

"You dare threaten me, shadow scum!? So be it. I will let it be known that the scum has broken Mathsmagica's rules and attempted to kill an official's son," Arthus said and waved his sword before him. "After I kill you, of course. In self defence."

With each drop of mana that I poured into the sphere in my hand, its power grew exponentially, creating powerful vibrations that filled the air.

"Enough!" a female voice echoed across the street and a flash of light constructed a wall between me, Arthus, and my sister.

Long black hair weaved in the air, as the woman in white Luminari attire rushed to my sister's aid.

"Are you okay? What's your name?" she asked, casting a light inducing spell.

"I'm Nilah," she responded, her bruises recovering.

Arthus stood, his sword still raised at the sky. I couldn't help but notice his trembling hands and his bitten, chapped lips.

He slashed his sword at my sister's aider. The woman, in a flash of light, had a sword in her hand and blocked the attack, the sound of metal clashing resonating across the street.

She extended her palm at Arthus, and a beam of light threw him against the wall between us. He bashed into it and by the time he could react, the woman already had her blade centimetres away from his neck.

"Stand down, Arthus. This is *not* what we should do," she said.

Arthus clicked his tongue and looked to the side. The swords and the light-wall dispersed.

"Rats," he said, and walked away.

My fingers trembled as I dispersed the spell from my palm back to the shadows. Light engulfed me and my pains faded almost in an instant.

She is mighty.

"I am sorry for that. Are you two okay?" she asked and helped Nilah get back on her feet.

"Thank you. I feel so much better," Nilah said, smiling. *She appears to have completely healed. Like nothing happened.*

"Arthus is like that. I saw him bump into you guys earlier and I... well, I just know what he does."

"And that's all alright according to your religion?" I asked.

"It's far from that. But I'm sure that all of us have exceptions, right?"

"Right." I nodded and headed towards the dorms when Nilah pulled my sleeve.

"Hey! Thanks for saving us! May we know your name?" Nilah asked.

"Oh my, of course! How insincere from me. My name is Evie Stratovic. And what are your names?"

"I'm Nilah Ren, and this is my brother Sova Ren. Nice to meet you!"

I nodded.

"Ren?" Evie frowned. "I haven't heard of that noble family."

"Umm..." Nilah put a finger on her flushed cheek.

"Your knowledge is as exceptional as a noble's should be. You are correct," I said, smiling.

"Sorry? I," Evie rubbed the back of her head. "I'm not sure I understand what you mean."

"We're not nobles, haha..." Nilah shrugged and looked at me. "I told you it'll be awkward when we say this."

"It's not like we have another choice," I responded with a shrug.

"Wait, wait. What do you guys mean? Nilah, okay, but Sova, I saw you casting Black Magic just now. And you're still alive, so... you're noble, right? Wait! Are you stepsiblings?"

"Oh my, no," Nilah shook her head. "We're twins!"

I lowered my head. "I'm sorry, but it seems there is an unwritten exception where commoners also have an affinity to certain magic."

"This is very interesting. So then, does that mean that you too, Nilah, have an affinity to magic?" Evie asked, her expression a mixture of excitement and confusion. I could tell she wanted to believe us, but found it hard to do so.

"For better or worse, we both have an affinity for Black Magic."

"Alright... Okay, um. Well. This explains why you have The Academy's uniforms, then!"

"Are you a student as well, Evie?" Nilah asked.

"Yes, I'm a first-year student. I'm in my Luminari attire, as I had to perform a certain task at the church."

Right. As students at The Academy, we have to wear those uniforms to be distinguished. Annoying as hell.

"We too!" Nilah rejoiced. "Then maybe we can meet up when we go to our lessons!"

"I would find that most delightful," Evie smiled.

I put my arm around Nilah's shoulder and looked at her.

You altruistic little kid. We're supposed to lie low, not make friends with people we had been waging war with until a decade ago.

"Alright, I think I'll let you guys go rest. Excuse me for taking so much of your time!"

"It's okay. We're happy to have met you! Right, Sova?" Nilah said, and poked me with her elbow, forcing a smile out of me.

"Right."

"Okay, then, Nilah and Sova. It has been a pleasure talking to you. Light be with you!"

"Shadows consume you!" Nilah said, cheerfully.

Evie frowned at that phrase, but as she read Nilah's expression, shrugged it off and smiled.

"Thanks, I guess!"

Among the Archives

"With a head of a wolf, muscular body covered by thick fur, the dakes shape an intimidating figure. Their feet have three toes adorned with sharp claws to help them navigate any terrain with grace. They are used mainly for transport, both for people and goods. With fur much enjoyable to touch, it's also pleasant to the eyes, as depending on the dake, it could have a really nice colourful tint.
Despite the intimidating look, they can be friendly and bonding with humans.
Their diet usually consists of all kinds of grass, but should the need arise, they can devour flesh, though they fall sick a few hours after."

"Horses are used mainly for 'races' and sports. It is really rare that someone would use them for transport as they get tired easier than dakes."

- "Encyclopedia for kids" by Unity of Humanitarianists

MATHSMAGICA

CHAPTER 2
THE LIBRARY

Arcane runes waved magic, decorating the walls and ceilings of The Grand Arcanum Library. The numbers that only my eyes could see covered the whole place, boasting the endless magical knowledge living within the arcane tomes and mystical scrolls.

I tore my eyes away from the awe-inspiring sight of magical knowledge soaring up to ten floors high and extended my palm above the ashen crystal orb to proceed in. The barrier moved like waves of water steaming with white smoke as I passed through it. The first time I feasted my eyes upon this blissful sight, the countless equations gave me a headache, but thankfully I'd already gotten used to it. I could simply enjoy the grandness of it.

"Sovie, how long are you going to stare like that? Come on, let's go," Nilah's blond hair bounced before me.

I smiled at her and accompanied her over to the librarian. Behind a floating oak desk, red hair covered a youthful face with big circle glasses. Her fingers traced across a thick book's diagrams and runes, the scent of ancient parchment filling the air. She had blue robes with runes tailored into silver shapes.

"Sorry," Nilah approached her. "We're–"

"Yes, I'm aware. Third floor, section B," The Librarian pointed.

"Thanks," Nilah nodded.

Next to us approached a hovering magic circle. We stepped on it and it adjusted to be just big enough to fit us comfortably.

"Third Floor, section B," I said, as I extended my palm over the circle.

It spun, supposedly its way of saying, "Okay, I understand," and then it took us in the air.

The other floors seemed to boom with students researching their craft, yet I couldn't help but notice the lack of presence in ours.

"It's like always. We won't even need to use the chambers," Nilah said, shrugging.

"Yeah. So many lost opportunities, I suppose."

"What do you mean?"

"Well, we have a lot of libraries and tomes back at home, but in Mathsmagica, we have access to an entire world of knowledge. It's just strange that the other Covenants aren't making use of this," I spoke, as we treaded across the floor, scrutinising through the titles.

"Well, we both know why that is, don't we?" Nilah asked, after being silent for a while.

"That shouldn't matter. For Black Magic, knowledge and control are all that matter. If one values their life and the lives of the ones they hold dear, they should be here, improving," I said, picking up a title.

"That seems like a nice book," a familiar voice came

from behind me. "Which one would you recommend to me?"

Evie's black hair stood in contrast to her white attires, brown eyes staring with innocent curiosity.

"Evie!" Nilah jumped to embrace her. Evie chuckled, a joyful sound that filled the air, as she wrapped her arms around Nilah and hugged her.

"Really?" I asked.

Evie swept her fingers across the books and crouched to the ones at the bottom.

"Evie, what are you looking for on this floor? It's dedicated to Nocturna and Black Magic." Nilah crouched next to her.

"Ah, yes. I'm aware. It's not my first time here, you could say. I've got some idea about the magic itself, but I want to research more about the cultural aspects of the people."

I blinked rapidly. *Well, she fought Arthus to protect us. Strange.*

"Come. I'll show you some splendid titles for that." I extended my hand at her to help her up. Not that she needed it. I frowned at myself for doing this, yet Evie accepted my help and followed me, her gentle skin a light touch on my palm.

"It's astonishing how Nocturna's followers have an entire floor, yet are the most oppressed. You have a huge cultural heritage," Evie spoke, looking around.

"You said it's not your first time here. What were you studying before?"

Evie looked away, and after a brief pause, responded. "It was necessary that I studied theory on Black Magic."

I nodded and sighed. "Well, it makes sense."

The corridors on this floor were vast and there were

floating tables about every ten metres. I found them to be called chambers as each table had a magic circle which, should you want it, could isolate you from your surroundings.

"Here we are. I think you can start with this book. As children grow up, they use this book for guidance." I felt the weight of the book in my hand as I handed it over to her.

Evie held it in one arm and with her free hand ran her fingers across the book's cover. "Into the Shadow lore: Nocturna's footsteps."

Nilah, already holding onto two other books, waved at us. "Hey, let's read together! We can share a table!"

When did she take those?

"That would be a light-given!" Evie exclaimed.

"Sure," I said and walked over to the closest chamber. "Isolation on or off?"

"Well, I don't really see anyone around here, and I don't think–" Evie spoke, but Nilah's voice halted her.

"Brother, you dummy! What's the point of us sitting together if we go into separate chambers? Of course, isolation is OFF!"

"Alright, alright!" I raised my hands in the air. "Relax!"

Evie chuckled at our interaction.

"Here, this is for you!" Nilah said and pushed a book into my hands.

We sat down, Evie on my left and Nilah on my right.

Alright, what did you give me this time, Nilah? The title's silver letters were in a beautiful contrast to the black leather cover. "Nocturna's Moon Dance," I whispered.

Before I knew it, Nilah was already deep into reading, and Evie was tracing down the text with a finger. I looked at her eyes, absorbing the text of our culture with such interest that left me baffled. *How can you be so genuinely interested in what your country's been teaching you to be the mortal enemy?* Yet these questions arose just to distract myself from the fact I found pleasure in looking at her lips now and then, whispering a word. The way her hair stood behind her ear, revealing her pale skin. The sight of her perfectly sculpted chin left a lasting impression - sharp and elegant. *Is she an elf? No.* After studying her for a while, I concluded she was not that different. *Just born in another country. A country teaching you to hate us.*

"Sova?" she asked.

Her voice put me out of the prolonged gaze I unconsciously had been giving her. A sharp pain in my waist forced me to grunt. I turned to face the culprit.

"Stop making Evie uncomfortable. She's a fine lady, indeed, but you should behave! Bad Sovie, bad!" Nilah pouted.

I couldn't control the burning blush on my cheeks. "Nilah, what are you saying!?"

Evie chuckled.

I tried to control my shame. *Coming in the clear is my best move out of this situation.*

"Look. I just thought how unfair it was that our countries would make us hate each other, yet we are really not that different!"

"Right, right..." Nilah smirked and looked away.

I shook my head, yet I couldn't completely sweep off this unease. The chuckle was gone and Evie looked serious. I diverted to where she was looking at, seeing none other than Arthus himself.

With heavy steps and a deep frown, he passed by our table, clutching a book tightly in his hand. I scrutinised the title. *That's odd.*

"What brings you here?" Evie asked before I could.

Arthus' usual confident eyes sought corners before responding. "Same as anyone else who enters a library, no?"

"Know your enemy," I stood up, "am I right?"

He regarded the book in his hands and responded, "Right. The question is, Evie, what are you doing here?"

"I believe you answered that question yourself, just a few seconds ago, did you not?" I responded.

He clicked his tongue and walked on. We tracked him as he went ahead, but then he stopped and spoke. "Covenants or Remnants. All defiers of The Light."

"Mind yourself, please," Evie sharply spoke.

Arthus took a step forward, paused, and then went ahead.

Evie released a deep sigh and sat back in the chair. I hadn't even noticed when she stood up.

"That title was from the Hailing Remnants department, wasn't it?" Nilah asked.

"It was about *The Communion*, I believe."

"What's that about?" Evie asked. "It's very out of character for Arthus to study *anything* related to the Dark Schools of Magic."

"It is a little complicated to explain, but said short," I started speaking and leaned my back against the chair. "It's about a ritual which is famous in that country. The ritual performers open a portal into the world of the dead. They can walk into it for whatever they seek to find."

"What?" Evie's jaw dropped. "So they are like spirit mediums?"

Nilah leaned over the table and responded. "No, no. Much different!"

"In what way?"

"Mediums just converse to a spirit or, otherwise said, a dead person, right?"

"Right."

"Well, while performing *The Communion*, they literally step into the realm of the dead physically. They travel it like they were dead, themselves," Nilah spoke, motioning a finger in front of her face.

With a shake of her head, Evie's eyes sparkled with amusement, and a smile naturally spread across my face in response to her delightful reactions. "It's quite deeper than that, though. But yeah, they are a cold and distanced people. That's because they have really high stakes in their daily lives. That's a long story, though," I said.

"I know The Hailing Remnants were just necromancers, and our country had a tough time fighting the armies of the dead. I didn't expect they were actually living in both realms at the same time. Is it alright to call it that, even?" Evie's eyes beamed with interest as she looked at me.

"You could say so."

Evie leaned against the table, propping herself up with her elbows, and tucked her hair behind her ears. We went back to reading, and I found myself enveloped in the wisdom of the book.

"I am scared," Evie broke my concentration.

Both me and Nilah looked at her.

"What do you mean?" I asked. *Hard to word this. Is it because of her beliefs in The Light that she found the origin of our culture scary?*

"I just find it hard to imagine all the time I would need to study your culture, The Hailing Remnants' culture, and all the others," Evie said.

I loosened and released a quick sigh, then let a genuine smile arise on my face. "You don't have to. The fact you're interested in it is more than enough. Believe me."

"But if you had such interest in it, how come you hadn't

read about it until now? You said your country has books on the cultures worshipping our side of sorcery," Nilah said.

"No," Evie shrugged, her face sorrowful. "In Savannah, you can't find any books related to culture from other countries. We have knowledge that would help us in battle, but nothing that would help us *understand*."

Nilah slammed her book shut on the table. Startled, we glimpsed at her cheerful smile. "Alright, you two. It's getting darker and darker here. I heard there's some cool cake conjurer shop in the town. Wanna go check it out?"

Evie didn't respond. She looked at me.

I nodded, "Alright. Honestly, I wouldn't mind some cake. Will you join us, Evie?"

Her thin lips curved a smile and nodded.

The sun was settling down by the time we had our cake treat. Thanks to Mathsmagica's laws, we could enjoy living like the nobles. Despite Brand telling us stories about our parents, we never got to experience the luxury of pronouncing our true family name.

I shoved those thoughts aside with ease, yet they came lingering back on. *Is it okay for us to have a friend?* I wondered as we waved goodbye to Evie and headed to our dorms.

The raw, cheerful emotions burned within our hearts, but we forced ourselves to dampen them. We fought them, as we knew better than to expose ourselves to greater pain.

"Sova, do you think this is real?"

"It is, Nillie. But we have to be smart about it," I said.

"We can be smart and happy at the same time, right?"

Can we?

"One thing is for sure - we can try," I smiled.

The dorm's windows revealed a patchwork of rooms, some aglow with light, while others remained unlit. We went through the entrance and climbed the stairs to the second floor. As by law, each noble should have their private space. Me and Nilah, as twins, had our own bedrooms, each with a personal shower. We shared a small kitchen with a two-person breakfast table.

My back had been bothering me for a significant part of the day. I kept feeling an urge to scratch it. After showering, staying awake seemed a greater challenge.

A pulsing pain stretched from my right shoulder to the waist. The room seemed like it was spinning. I was dead certain it didn't, but my fatigue had grown too strong. A gentle creak sounded the window open as I leaned next to it for a sip of fresh air.

"Hey, Sovie," Nilah knocked and peeked through the door. "Goodnight."

I forced a smile and responded, "Goodnight, Nillie."

The door closed and I couldn't keep straight anymore. I approached the bed and pulled the sheet to the side, yet for some reason, it dropped to the floor. Disregarding it, I crashed my face into the pillow.

Among the Archives

"About Magical affinity. A person is born with the affinities they will posses until death. Whoever has mana in their body can practise all schools of magic, but they will ultimately excel at the one they have an affinity for.

It happens that a mage can have an affinity for more than one school of magic. This, however, happens only to The Shapers. Most of them possess affinity for at least two elements. Elemental magic has conjunctions that are similar to one another, to which is owed the possibility of multiple affinities.

No mage has been born with an affinity to different schools of magic, like Black Magic and Elemental magic, for example."

- Excerpt from "Fundamentals of Magic: For Class 1"

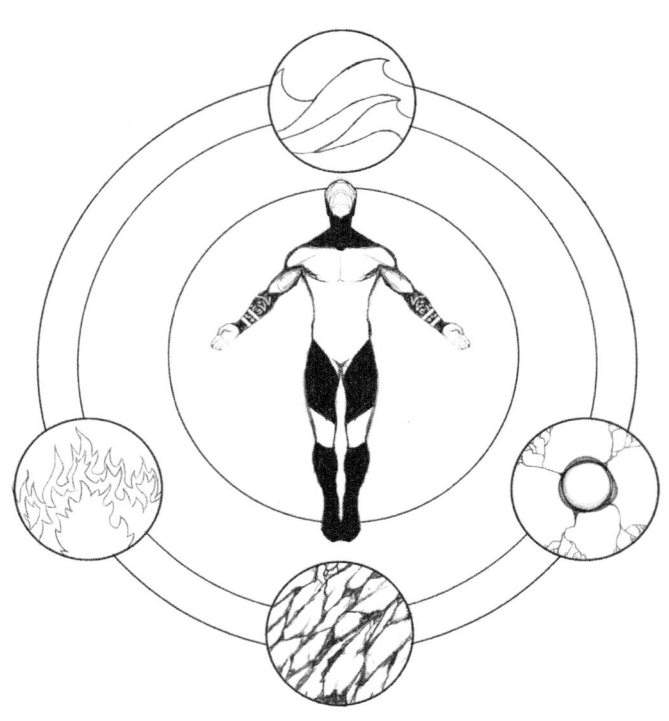

CHAPTER 3
THE KING'S SLUMBER

ENDARIEL'S POINT OF VIEW

The void is sealed.

When I opened my eyes, all I could see was the soft, mystical light emanating from a small arcane bulb. With considerable effort, I raised myself into a seated position. My youthful reflection stared back at me in the mirror. Blond hair and a blue left and violet glowing right eye.

The full moon basked the room in silvery light. *So I must move.*

My feet touched the floor, and a blanket obstructed my very first step. I ignored it and came to the opened window. I closed my eyes, breathed in, and focused on my inner senses. *That presence. I feel her.*

My hand trembled as I raised it to my face, a visible sign that it's still too early to utilise this body. I gazed for a while and attempted to reach the vessel's mana pool. Slowly and gently, I steadied the shaking and once I had the grasp of it; I fuelled the entire body with mana.

I leaped through the window, and to secure a proper landing, a violet mass swirled about me as I levitated steadily to the ground. A backlash across my back immediately punished me for that. I grunted and my whole body shook from the pain. With focus, I recovered the vessel into its normal state.

When I looked up at the sky, the full moon illuminated the surroundings with its radiant glow. Then a wave of magic spread around me and drew an invisible barrier, enveloping me and the silhouette cloaked in the shadows before me.

"My king, I'm afraid it is still too early to use it," she said as she approached me. Red hairs bounced with each step, allowing a peek at her glowing yellow eyes.

"It wasn't exactly intentional. How long has it been?" I asked.

"Two years since we spoke. Have you been in constant slumber?"

"Perhaps. It is different this time. I am encountering memories and dreams of days long past," I spoke honestly.

"Dreams? It's—"

"I don't know if they are dreams. They feel like that, but I see things which haven't happened. Alternate pasts, should I call it? And it's always with *him*. Looking at me... At The Tapestry of Shadows."

"Him? Perhaps it is because of the *Abyssal Eyes?* Do you need anything?" she came closer, allowing me to gaze into her irises.

"How is the vessel doing?"

"I have observed above average control of Black Magic and—"

"What about the others?"

"He hasn't—"

"He is of The Darc family, and you say he hasn't even shown promise in them!?" I yelled, my voice growing deeper than my vessel's.

"It's very dangerous to expose that side of him. Should anyone find out, they will execute him."

"Find a way, Lethalica," I said, my wrathful gaze piercing her. "Don't let this go to waste!"

"Yes, my king," she nodded.

I felt my body shaking out of control.

"It'll be soon. Not as usual, but it'll be *soon*," I said and faced the window I jumped out from.

"Should we schedule meetings more often, then?" Lethalica asked.

"On full moons. Be well, Lethalica. Send Aetherial my regards."

A wind breeze carried me over to the window and I stepped into the room. I tried to make my way to the bed, but it seemed too precarious. I shut my eyes, returning to my slumber.

Among the Archives

"Nobles and commoners.
It is since dawn of time that the Luminari Faith teaches the reason for a gradual distinguishment between the noble-blooded and the common folk.
When Sovah, The Mage of Legends, saved humanity from the forces of darkness, he spread his seed among as many survivors as he could before passing on. And thus, his descendants had exceptional magical prowess compared to anyone else. They had an affinity for magic. Nowadays, they are the ones considered nobles and have, with a right, a much higher standing in society."

- Excerpt from "Laws And Regulations"

CHAPTER 4
SAVING THE LIGHT

SOVA'S POINT OF VIEW

THE WIND BLEW IN THROUGH THE OPEN WINDOW, bringing with it a chilly breeze that ruffled the curtains and sent an icy shiver across my body.

I must have slept too hard to end up on the floor. I got up and stretched, my body rigid and hurting. Nilah knocked on the door and peered in.

"We'll be late, Sovie. What have you been doing?" she pouted, leaning against the door, closed behind her.

Teeth brushed, hair fixed, and face washed, I changed clothes and we went out in a haste.

The day went rather uneventfully. We had classes in history with Master Rodotus. These weren't as interesting as one would expect, as our teacher was a complete bookworm. Unsure if he preferred to spend the time researching his own thing or to just attempt to murder us with boredom.

There were two types of classes. Mutual and separate. As all students had different affinities for magic, some had additional classes separately in their own specialty, while more general disciplines like history and fundamentals of magic we shared.

In all mutual classes, Evie always found her way to our table, and we studied together, gossiped, or suffered the pain of time not working naturally. Of course, it did, but boring classes definitely had some kind of time manipulation ability.

At noon, we studied how to fill mana into magic equations to cast spells. It seemed really odd to me that everyone else was so interested in these classes.

"You pour mana into an apple," Master Hempa spoke as she reached for the apple that shone on her desk. "And then it floats. You could say it is simply *magic*. But when you add the how and why it floats, study the exact quantities required to reach the desired floating effect, you get something else. Does anyone know what?"

I raised my face from the pillow that was my arms.

A student from the front seats raised an arm. "Levitation magic?"

"Nope. Anyone else want to try?"

Multiple voices impatiently delivered false answers.

"Students. What you get..." Master Hempa grabbed the apple and bit a piece. "Is science. That is why the city formed around The Academy is called *Mathsmagica,* after all. The place where magic meets science. All magic is based on math equations. It was such a simple answer. Come on, folks. Wake up!"

The mutual classes passed and Evie went to Illumination Magic classes, while Nilah and I proceeded to Black Magic. Although I was unaware of what others did in their private classes, ours appeared remarkably confined to me. Most of the time, we practiced Level One magic with the pretext that it's dangerous to do anything stronger than that and despite what it appeared; it helped us improve our magic's control.

Evie awaited us at The Academy's exit, leaning against one pillar holding the ceiling. I couldn't help myself from staring for a few seconds as the white robes fitted her well and outlined her body's features. She was just slightly taller than Nilah, reaching just a little over my shoulders, yet somehow she seemed a lot more mature than my sister.

"Evie!" Nilah prolonged and leaped in for an embrace, "Save me from these boring classes!"

"Oh, come on, guys. It can't be that bad, now can it?" she chuckled.

"Oh," I sighed, "you don't want to find out."

"Okay, the best part is, today's classes are done."

"Finally! We're going to that cafe, right? Right, right?!" Nilah jumped.

Evie winked at my sister, and we shared a smile.

A modest mushroom shaped building had small levitating tables shaping small mushrooms with faces atop of them, waving with a hand. *An attractive way to gain clients, indeed.*

We didn't even choose. Nilah leaped at the closest table, which waved at us.

"Look! It is so cute," she petted the fluffy mushroom. "What's your name, little guy? Shroomcho, is it? Or Mushy? Maybe Mushroomy?"

"I am not sure if it has a name, Nillie," I said, taking a seat on the floating cushion.

Evie sat next to me, and Nilah stood straight, towering over the little mushroom-guy.

"Would you like a mushroom soup? A refreshing drink? Or something hot? Choose and say!" the mushroom spoke.

"I'd like a refreshing drink, I suppose," I said, then looked at Evie. "What will you get?"

"I'll get a refreshing drink, too."

"Can I..." Nilah grabbed the little guy, entirely snatching him in her arms. "KEEP HIM, SOVIE!?"

We laughed. "Just make your order, Nilah."

After completing the payment through a magic circle on the middle of the table, our order warped before us. Nilah was over-obsessed with petting the magic mushroom, so Evie and I were the only ones actually conversing.

"So why are you guys so bored in Black Magic classes?"

"It feels a little odd to say this, but it really is for beginners. True, it is important to be an absolute *master* in the basics or you could get yourself and others killed, but despite that, I believe at least half of the students are already above that level," I said.

"Is that so? Would you say that, in Nocturnia, you practiced more advanced magic?" Evie asked, taking a sip from the blue drink in her mug.

"Sad to say, but yes. For sure. It's more like after you hone the basics to some extent, you learn the theory of advanced magic."

From the corner of my eye, I saw Arthus going by. I frowned, scrutinising a stack of at least five equations on his neck.

"Evie, please respond fast. Are there any Illumination spells that you would cast and focus on your neck?"

At my question, Nilah's excitement faded, and she raised her eyesight at me.

"Not any I could think of. Why?" Evie asked, a finger on her chin.

"Let's find out," I said and quickly followed in Arthus' direction.

Among the crowd there were equations from spells other people had cast, but the stack on Arthus' neck was easy to spot.

We followed him from the outskirts of the central district and in no time, we could already see shadows crawling onto the buildings. The living darkness was clearer as the sun had already begun its descent. A smell of wax filled the air and a spell-imbued mist carried itself above the glowing cobblestones.

"The Necropolis," Evie whispered. "What would Arthus do here?"

"Brother, our district is close by, isn't it?" Nilah asked.

"Yeah. The Necropolis and The Umbra quarter share borders."

"This isn't the first time Arthus has come here," Evie said.

"We met close to our dorms. You and Arthus were both there, now that I think about it," I said, hoping my voice didn't come out like an accusation.

"Yes. At that time, I was exploring Mathsmagica's districts and felt a strong magic impulse. That's how I ended up meeting you two," Evie said.

You're smart. Immediately picked up I was doubting you and clarified yourself, removing any tension.

I complimented her with a smile I'm not sure she saw.

"Wait!" I said and extended my hand, putting them to a halt. We leaned on the corner of a wall, Arthus speaking to a figure cloaked in shadows.

"Do you know some kind of hearing enhancement spell, Evie?" Nilah asked.

"Unfortunately, no."

The figure in shadows sank into the floor and Arthus yelled, but I couldn't make out what he said.

His arm extended at the sky. As the Lightforged Sword appeared, its edge illuminated with a luminous divine light. He swung at where his companion used to be.

As the mist dispersed, two portals materialised, distorting the space before Arthus. With each swing, his attacks were effortlessly deflected, the force rebounding and causing him to crash onto the ground. The two portals merged, giving birth to a mesmerising vortex of violet magic, swirling and pulsating with otherworldly power.

Arthus' movements were outright clumsy, as he couldn't get himself off the ground. Out of the portal first emerged a leg covered in drippy, torn black pants. As the figure stepped out of the portal, my eyes opened wide in disbelief. It stood twice as tall as any human I had encountered, casting a shadow over Arthus.

A splash of light next to me took my eyes as Evie summoned her Lightforged Sword and charged towards the revenant threatening Arthus. I followed behind her with a speedy dash.

The undead's pale skin emitted an eerie glow, fuelled by the mana-infused blood flowing through its veins. The revenant's eyes, like smouldering embers, locked onto its prey with a burning red flame.

Evie took a defensive stance before Arthus.

"Get up! What's wrong, Arthus?" Evie asked.

He didn't respond. I stood on her right, and Nilah arrived to her left.

"Arthus?" I asked, looking at him. His eyes were completely red. Around his neck, the equations I had seen now grew like a collar.

"He's paralysed," I said. "Or at least we can consider him to be such."

At that moment, the revenant slung its bony hand, a red

trail of flame behind it. With her left hand, Evie conjured a barrier to ward off the attack, and with her right hand, she unleashed a forceful strike on our enemy. The sword opened a wound, but the undead seemed unbothered by it. Just seconds after, the flaming blood sealed the wound completely.

"Nilah, let's give her support!" I said and directed my hand at the creature. "Level One Black Magic Sorcery: Glimmer!"

A tiny black thunder jumped out of my palm. I cast the spell with lightning speed, unleashing a relentless storm of black thunderbolts that pummelled the creature, while Evie's sword mercilessly clashed against its flesh.

We closed in from every direction, suffocating it with our presence, but it remained steadfast in its position. We couldn't push it back into the portal, but then I thought, *why the hell is that portal still open?*

A dozen equations appeared at the undead's core, and I instinctively dashed back with a yell, "Run!"

Nilah bounced, but Evie was too close. She popped multiple layers of barriers before her. Walls of light made of magic circles glowed in protective divinity.

"Trees of life betrayed by the bright rejuvenating haze," the remnant spoke, its voice low and otherworldly. "Crows pluck away the flesh, deliver it to you."

The undead dropped what seemed to be his defences, opening his arms as if to embrace a loved one. Evie lowered the barriers and used this moment to slash away at it. Each attack splattered its mana-driven blood.

The blood formed crows, and they plucked away at the undead's flesh, forming a smile on his face.

"Evie, step aside!" I yelled and grabbed onto Arthus, an

attempt at dragging him to safety. Nilah joined me, but I screamed, "No! Run!"

"But, brother–"

"RUN!"

"Accept this offering, yet we make acquaintance in fall," the undead voiced and all the crows splashed into a bubble surrounding the spell's caster.

With a swift slash, Evie attempted to pop the bubble, only to have it effortlessly slide off her arm, deflecting her sword. She jumped back and assisted me with carrying Arthus.

"Why's this guy so fucking heavy!?" I cursed.

"It's not logical! He must've been weighed down by magic." Evie said.

Arthus was only pulled three mere metres by our combined strength, while I desperately infused mana into my body to gain the necessary power. As we kept our efforts, the bubble surrounding our enemy emitted a subtle glow, which grew more vibrant with each passing second.

"It's a big cast. This is above Level Four Sorcery!" I spoke my mind.

"Level Four? If that's true, this will wipe the entire area!"

Should we leave him and run?

"Evie?" I glanced at her.

"Yes?"

"Put up your best defence before Arthus and I and run away," I said.

"Sovie, I'll help too!" Nilah spoke from a few metres ahead, her blond hair showing from behind a nearby building. "I'll put up a barrier and reinforce it!"

"Nilah, I told you to run!"

"I can't leave you behind like that!"

"Level Four Necrotic Sorcery - Embers of Fall," the dark voice resonated from within the bubble.

Like a tsunami wave, the explosion of ember-lit blood splashed and spread, illuminating the scene with its fiery glow. The light engulfed us. The only thing I could see was Evie layering barriers, yet my eyes couldn't depict the exact amount. I, myself, only channelled mana before me, sole thought being "defence."

Master Hempa's words resonated within my head at that moment. *Propelling mana into thin air and not settling it into any equation will practically do nothing. A simple relocation. Take a water pot and put a glass of water on top of it. The pot won't heat up the water unless the water is inside, will it?*

My whole body burned. The air I inhaled felt like a razor grinding through my nose and all the way to my chest.

"Ember Harvest," the undead remnant said.

The flames extinguished and got sucked in his palm. He visibly revitalised himself, all the slashes Evie had done across his body recovering.

I looked at Evie and she seemed to be in no better condition than me. She rolled on the ground, trying to extinguish the Ember flames, yet to no avail. The remnant sucked out the flames from her as well, voicing again, "Ember Harvest."

Arthus wasn't conscious anymore. I gazed over to see Nilah was unconscious. Judging by her body's position, she had rushed towards us to set up a barrier in the moment of the explosion.

"Nillie!" I screamed, rage consuming whatever pain I had experienced. "Nillie! Wake up!"

I splashed mana to force my body into movement and treaded to my sister. I attempted to spin her body to face me, but the fear of dealing damage made me retract from that idea.

"Trees of life betrayed by the bright rejuvenating haze," the remnant spoke.

"S-S-Sova," Evie barely voiced.

I looked at the remnant over my shoulder.

My own shadow clung to me, enveloping me from toe to head, at a slow pace, as I stood on my legs and turned to face my enemy.

"Self-exiled into darkness, your wisdom holds true. Moonlit ravens gather your soul," I chanted, black thunder jumping out of my shadow and swirling around my body.

"Crows pluck away the flesh, deliver it to you. Accept this offering, yet we make acquaintance in fall," the remnant spoke, the spell reaching the state of the bubble enveloping him.

"Sova, run if you can!" Evie yelled and pulled up a single wall of light, a barrier meant to protect us. Yet what could that do when the spell earlier blasted through several of those? "I'll hold him off!"

"Bathed in shadows, with your power, we unite. From the palm of my hand, may your rage be true. In the dark I pledge myself to eradicate the light," I spoke, ignoring Evie completely, now my own shadow vanishing as it, along with the black thunder, condensed at the end of my palm. The sphere of darkness expanded with each huge layer of mana I poured into it, then shrunk back.

The bubble of blood was glowing, signalling the remnant's spell was almost ready to release the Ember flames and finish us off.

"Level Four Black Magic Sorcery," I said, the sphere of black magic taking the shape of a crescent with a silver edge, formed by the condensed thunder. "Nocturna's Crescent."

Within a second, the shape propelled from my palm and the sheer force it generated took out bricks from the surrounding buildings. Along the spell's deadly path, the pavement suffered devastation. Upon collision with the bubble, an explosion forced everything in a negative colour scheme, for another second, then a white flash took our sight.

I lowered my hand and took a deep breath. Eyes closed, I gulped before being ready to take in the consequences of my anger.

"Sova... You..." Evie's voice made me reconsider my actions.

I exhaled and opened my eyes.

"Did it."

Black thunders still jumped across the pavements and buildings, but there was no trace of the remnant, nor the portal it came from. Evie, thank god, was just a metre away from where the spell had picked up the pavement on its destructive onslaught.

My eyes could see numbers splattered across the whole area. *Remains of the sorcery?*

I fell to my knees, my legs giving out. A high-pitched white noise scratched at my ears. I couldn't hear anything. My eyes wouldn't move. They were locked into the ground before me. Unable to control my body, I saw my drool dropping onto the floor.

This is it. I misused Black Magic, and it is now claiming me.

My back itched strongly. I clung to that feeling, being the only one I could actually experience. Slowly, I could hear a rejuvenating buzz behind me.

I swallowed and slapped my cheeks, finally being able

to move my arms. A swipe across my mouth to clear the drool made me feel pain in my burned arms. All a good sign so far. I was recovering.

I turned around and saw Nilah, already in a far better shape. The burns weren't glowing. Above, Evie's determined expression helped me study the situation further, her arms directed at my sister's wounds.

"Evie," I spoke.

"Sova? You're conscious?"

I dragged my knees on the pavements. Nilah was on her back and I could see her face. Her relaxed face and soft breathing reassured me she was fine.

"Is she... going to be alright?" I asked, after recalling healing spells couldn't be cast on the dead.

"I wasn't too late. She'll be fine, but her mana source is completely depleted," Evie said, and with a sorrowful expression, looked at me. "And mine is close to that state."

"It is from the Ember flames. They aren't as destructive as regular fire, but they eat away your mana reserves," I explained, then noticed Evie's burns were still glowing. *She hasn't healed herself yet.*

A warping sound came from behind me, and before I could turn around, magic paralysed me.

"By order of The High Arcanist, in relation to a recent use of high level Black Magic Sorcery, you are coming with us," a man's voice came from behind me and the world turned to black.

"That's not the case! Don't take him away, he saved–" Evie spoke, but another mage interrupted her.

"Silence," he said and tightened the blindfold behind my head.

"Just... please... heal... them," I voiced with considerable effort, fighting against the paralysation spell.

AMONG THE ARCHIVES

"Magic Sparkle Dust. It is often spotted after a spell has been broken or an object was hit by a spell with immense power. Said object shatters into dust and glows from the lingering magic in it. Also often seen when illusion spells are destroyed."

- Excerpt from "Fundamentals of Magic: For Class 1"

MATHSMAGICA

CHAPTER 5
PRIVATE MEETING

I OPENED MY EYES TO DARKNESS.

My breath fell still when my memory reminded me of what happened before I collapsed. I was being carried somewhere by someone. But that didn't matter.

"Are they–okay? Did they survive?" I asked, my voice not as loud as I thought it would be.

"They are fine. You needn't worry about them, Black Magician," a manly voice replied to my right. Despite my ability to speak, I was still paralysed and unable to move.

Black Magician, huh? So I'm being carried by racist scum. Why the blindfold, though? Even if this were to be my execution, a blindfold doesn't make sense.

We stopped moving. *Did we arrive?* The smell of burnt wax and old parchment filled the air.

"Release the spell, Dean. There is no need for it," an elderly voice spoke.

"Are you certain? He is dangerous!" my escort announced.

"I appreciate your concern, yet I sincerely hope you don't doubt my ability to fend for myself, should the need arise," the man spoke with a note of humour. "And, Dean, if you please, leave us alone."

Who are these guys?

The paralysis spell faded, and I felt my knees touch the ground.

"As long as the others survive and are healed, I have no regrets. So your accusations—" I spoke, but the elderly voice interrupted me, as my blindfold fell off.

"There are no accusations, I'm afraid."

I raised my head to see a dignified and imposing figure. I couldn't help but feel an aura of wisdom and authority emanating from the man. His age reflected in the white hair on his head. He had well-defined features that engraved a command for respect as soon as I met his piercing eyes in the shade of azure. The black and white attire levitated, pretending gravity was absent in his presence. Claws engraved with runes glowed as they hung on the man's pendant.

Staring in awe, I listened to the man.

"I am Larion Astron. The Director of Mathsmagica's Academy."

Speechless, I observed every move he made as he stepped across his table, full of arcane tomes, multiple quills glowing from the stains of magical ink. He gazed through the small wooden window, beyond which a nexus' flow of light was visible.

"And you, I believe, are Sova Ren," he said and turned to face me again. "Please, rise to your feet."

"It's an honour to meet you, Director Astron. I see you already know who I—" I spoke, as I stepped up.

"Oh, I know, Sova. You and your sister, Nilah, are the only commoners who are attending my school's classes."

I nodded.

"Let me ask you, how do you find your Black Magic classes? Answer honestly, please."

Honestly? This must be some kind of test. I know what nobles are like. He wants to hear how bad I am and how great his academy classes are. Or perhaps–

"Sova, please. I need you to be honest with me. Do you find your Black Magic classes teaching you sufficient knowledge of your effectuated magic?" Director Astron asked, appearing right before me. His height was just slightly above mine.

"Despite the fact that Black Magic is based on–"

"Sova. Don't give me the official and long answer. Short and simple."

This guy. Will he interrupt me one more time?

"Director Astron, I am afraid half the students are above the level the academy is teaching. Rumours are that Black Magic is too dangerous and teachers are purposely not letting us advance," I responded, meeting his judgemental eyes.

Director Astron smiled.

"See? You can be honest," he said and turned his back against me, then strode over to the window and gazed at the nexus again.

After a brief pause, he spoke. "I also believe the lessons aren't going as well as they should be. But that's natural. We all know the cultural differences would create such tension. Even Mathsmagica can't control that. People are, after all, just people."

Unsure of what to say, I waited in silence while we stood there, only hearing a slight buzz from the magic circles operating whatever they were on his table.

"I'm sorry, that was a bit dark, wasn't it?" he asked, smiling at me. "Now, to the reason you were brought here.

Do you know why?"

"I used Black Magic Sorcery Level Four, Nocturna's Crescent," I said, my head surrendered in guilt.

"Do not lower your head, Sova," he said in a demanding tone. "Should a mage from the Light Schools of Magic lower their head when they cast a Level Four spell?"

"I believe not, sir."

"Then why should *you*?"

My mouth went agape, his question lingering in the air.

"I know where you come from, Sova. And I believe any student in the first year who casts a spell of a Level Four or higher should receive a round of applause from The Pillars, The High Arcanists, and all teachers and students."

"Then why don't I?" I whispered, unwillingly.

I put a palm before my mouth, but the words were already out.

"Exactly, Sova," he spoke genuinely. "And even I lack the political strength to reward you for it."

"Um. Thank you, Director Astron," I said, a confused smile shaping across my face.

"Black Magic is the most dangerous. Casting a spell on that level and keeping it under control is a mastery. You can't do that out of simple luck."

I sighed, ceasing whatever he had planned to say, as he now awaited for an explanation.

"I think I lost control of the spell after casting it. My body felt numb and I might have passed out for a while. Evie, a classmate from the Luminari Faith, was there and probably knows more about what I did or not."

"I know who Evie Stratovic is. But that's for later. Let me ask you, Sova, have you seen what happens to one who has *failed* his Black Magic Sorcery?"

I shook my head.

"Their mana pool corrupts, then their skin goes pale, they crack, and finally become ash," he said, his voice hurting. "And now, look at yourself. Do you see any of those symptoms?"

I looked at myself and noticed even my burns were gone. *They healed me on the way here?* At any rate, aside from the burned clothes, there wasn't any trace of me even being in a fight.

"Not really, no."

"Precisely, Sova. That backlash you had came from something else. If you had failed your cast, you would be dead."

"So why exactly am I here, Director? What will become of me now?"

"I see something that the others don't. I will stick my arm out for you. But not just for you. I'll do it for the sake of Mathsmagica. For the sake of humanity itself," he spoke and paused briefly. "You, your sister, Nilah, and the Luminari's Evie Stratovic will answer before me. You will wear clothes that others don't. Call it a symbol. That's what you will be. That's what *I want you to be.* Your clothes will differ as everyone must know who you are. I have already organised everything."

"Symbol of what?"

"A symbol of union. Mathsmagica is all about uniting all of mankind against the threats of The Fog. So what better than show that the biggest enemies history has known - Luminari Faith and Shadow Covenants - can be friends and fight to protect each other's backs?"

"So you're not going to blame me for using Advanced Black Magic? I won't be punished!?"

"Oh, this is your punishment, young man. But only time will show the true scale of it."

"I'm, ugh."

"I know you're confused, but fear not. That confusion will only deepen. But I trust you will handle it. Just know that from this point on, you will have the freedom to cast any sorceries without restrictions. Let the world know that *you* can control Black Magic. Show them they were wrong. Show them you are better."

I stood in awe, unable to believe my ears. Was this some kind of illusion that was brewed for snatching out what I would want to hear? A sort of confession spell?

"And what will I have to do, Director?"

"You will know when the need arises. Now go home and rest. Tomorrow we shall meet again. Inform your sister as well once she wakes up. She should be in proper condition by the morning."

I nodded and turned around, but to my surprise, there was no door there.

"Ah, I almost forgot," Director Astron poked at his desk, then approached me. "Take this teleportation crystal. It is with unlimited uses. As long as you are on The Academy's grounds, it can teleport you to this room, should you need it."

The item, tiny as it was, could easily get lost inside my pocket. I took it into my palm and noticed its smoothed out surface covered with spell equations.

"So many tiny numbers..." I whispered.

"Numbers?" he asked.

"No, nothing. I was just thinking out loud. Thank you, Director," I collected the item. "But will it be okay to just appear without warning?"

"A considerate gentleman, ain't you? And they say The Shadow Covenants are ruthless egoists. Don't worry about my privacy."

"So, I should use this crystal to come here. But can it teleport more than one person at a time?"

"As long as they are in direct touch with you at the moment of teleportation, you will come together," he said with a smile. "While I trust we could converse into mutual benefit, I'm afraid I have something else to attend to."

"Of course, Director. Thank you for this. And for healing me, and—"

"The Light shines and The Dark beckons it," The Director said and paused. "A friend of mine said that a few decades ago. Think about those words. I still do until today. Get Nilah and Evie here first thing in the morning. See you tomorrow, Sova."

The crystal teleported me at The Academy's entrance. My clothes ripped and burned easily made me standout among the other students. There were eyes lingering on me, but I treaded home with a determined urgency. When I entered the dorm, I immediately blasted the door to Nilah's room.

Purple blankets covered her body, and her blond hair glowed with a green hue. My conscience stabbed at me for blasting the door open. There was ample space on the bed for me to take a seat. Nilah breathed softly, her face serene and tranquil. I caressed her hair and fought against the troubles within.

I never expected I would be so close to losing you.

You're all I have left.

I recalled the battle. My fists clenched, and I gritted my teeth.

I wasn't strong enough... "To protect you, Nillie," I whispered.

Savour this gift, Sova. It's but a gift you're not all alone today. Secure it for tomorrow.

I watched her sleep, forgetting my fatigue.

ENDARIEL'S POINT OF VIEW

THE VOID TINGLED.

My neck and back hurt. I opened my eyes to see a blond girl sleeping, my hand resting on her head. Observing my surroundings, I discovered myself awakening in a seated position in damaged clothes. At a glance, the circle-shaped burns hinted at Ember flames to be the culprit.

A green hue glowed under the girl's hair. I leaned to see the cause of it. Numbers. I could see the equations of the spell. I knew this spell. How could I ever forget? In no amount of reincarnations or lifetimes will I ever forget his magic.

"Lingering Blessing," I whispered.

I stood up and looked out the window. *That corner is where I met Lethalica last time.* There was no moon in the sky to show it was time for our meeting. *I awoke without real meaning.*

"Brother," the girl spoke in a sleepy voice behind me.

I turned to face her.

"I must be dreaming. But I'm glad you're okay, even if it's just in my dreams," she said and fell back to sleep.

It is dangerous to remain in this room. Yet, my suspicion proved right. The girl too shares The Darc bloodline.

I opened the door out of the room and closed it silently behind. A small kitchen with a table for two. To my left, another door. I opened it slowly and spotted an empty bed, a mirror opposite of it. *I know this room.*

I sat on the bed and looked at my hands. *Not shaking this*

time. My reflection in the mirror revealed a violet glow in my eyes, concealed by a few locks of blond hair. *His blue colour is lacking this time.* I approached the mirror and pulled my hair back. I smiled, recalling the luck of discovering this vessel.

My back urged scratching. I took my clothes off, revealing a lean figure in the mirror. *So he isn't just mana and magic, that's good.* Then I twisted to the side, revealing a large violet scar ranging from the right shoulder all the way to the left side of the waist. *Hm. It's bigger than it should be.*

Weakness flushed over me, and I surrendered to the necessity of immediate slumber.

Among the Archives

"It is often we see it, yet we don't really pay attention. All spells that conjure items, like Lightforged weaponry, for example. It becomes of Light Dust and upon dismissal, usually returns to Light Dust."

"Some would confuse it with Magic Sparkle Dust, but that is completely different, which you could study in Fundamentals of Magic. Light Dust is pure. It comes from The Light and returns to its glory."

- Excerpt from "Illumination Magic: For Class 1"

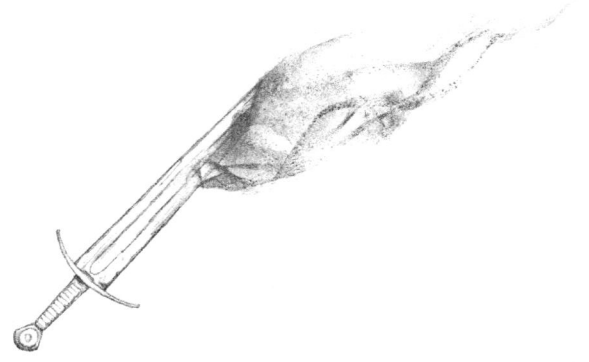

CHAPTER 6
HARMONY ENFORCERS

SOVA'S POINT OF VIEW

A HAUNTING CHILL FORCED MY EYES OPEN.
I couldn't recall anything after being by Nilah's side, so waking up on the floor in my room with barely any clothes on was utterly perplexing.

I suppose I tried to change clothes before going to bed? These days too many things are happening and I can't seem to get a proper rest.

After slapping my cheeks, I splashed refreshing water on my face at the sink, rejuvenating myself. I couldn't help but smile when I heard a gentle knock on my door. There was only one person who did that.

"Sovie, are you okay?" Nilah peered through the door.

I opened my arms wide and enveloped her in a warm embrace, gently patting her head.

"I'm better now. How are you feeling?"

"I'm good. Like new. I slept so much!" Nilah bounced.

"Hey, spin in place," I told her and she did just that,

without hesitation. *Energetic as always. And no spells on you at all. Amazing.*

"Alright, I think you're good. Let's go. We can't be late," I said, closing the door to my room and strolling towards the exit.

"Ah, boring classes first today," Nilah sighed. "I mean, I feel like we should skip the Black Magic lessons. My legs won't move at the thought of it. So tempting."

"Don't worry, we're going to skip a part of them today."

Nilah paused as she put on her shoes.

"Yup," I said, chuckling.

"We can't skip classes, Sovie! We'll get punished!"

"Exactly. We're going to go get punished and then go to class. Forgot about yesterday?"

"Punished? For what? We got saved by some seniors, didn't we? They didn't misunderstand the situation, did they? We were fighting to protect Arthus," Nilah said.

"That..." I paused, wondering if she knew what really happened. "Is not exactly the case."

Maybe she woke up while they healed her and fed her some information?

"Then what happened?"

"Come on, put those shoes on already. I'll tell you everything along the way."

The journey to The Academy was filled with Nilah's infectious smile and enthusiasm as I narrated the story to her. She sounded thrilled about how things turned out. *It might appear quite tempting, but I am not sure if we completely understand the weight of the position Director Astron is putting us at. And using magic freely is more than amazing, but what if the price we need to pay for this is bigger than we can handle?*

"So Sovie got angry," Nilah forced a cute pouting face,

and took a fighting stance as we walked. "Then *beam-beam, boom-boom,* the bad guy goes into oblivion."

"Um. Right. Anyway, do you know how we're going to find Evie?"

"About that," she hummed, diving into her thoughts. "I think she said she's got Illumination Magic classes now!"

"Alright, then we know where to get her."

"Do you think it'll be fine if we snatched her away from classes like that?"

"I don't feel very confident in doing this myself, but something's telling me we should get used to doing out-of-ordinary things."

Each classroom had a unique shape that reflected the type of magic being studied or practiced. With this in mind, we sought the Illumination classroom. It took us several minutes before we arrived before a door above which was a sculpture of an unfolded book with three lines that symbolised The Light flowing into the pages. The voice of the Illumination Master's dictations of Luminari Faith holy texts echoed in a melodious tone.

"Are we really going to barge in on this?" Nilah asked, pressing an ear against the door.

"Nilah, don't do that, you look suspicious," I said and opened the door like there's no tomorrow.

"What is this disturbance!?" a man in his fifties, white Luminari robes on him, yelled at me.

"By the order of Director Astron, I have come to take Evie Stratovic to a most urgent meeting," I said, my voice resonating within the walls of the classroom.

"How dare–" the man started yelling, but trailed off when I revealed the teleportation crystal in my hand. "In the name of The Light, it's true. But why wasn't there an official summoning? Whatever."

Eyes narrowed, I carefully examined each table, determined to find Evie among the displeased students' faces. The classroom was elevated at twelve steps of height and I saw her coming from all the way in the back.

"Evie Stratovic, I am afraid this... student is stating the truth."

Evie threw a disturbed gaze at me, but I smiled to melt away that insecurity.

"Thank you, Master," she said. "Light be with you."

"Light be with you too, child," the teacher said.

"Happy studies, everyone," I said and walked out.

As the door closed behind us, the corridor filled with the echoing sound of our footsteps.

"Sova! Nillie! What is this?" Evie asked, her cheeks flushing pink.

"I wish I had time to tell you more about it so you can prepare, but that's not the case," I said and looked around to make sure there were no people watching. "Put your hand in mine. Both of you."

I had the teleportation crystal in my palm and first Nilah placed her hand in mine, and then Evie on top of my sister's.

"What is this crystal?" Evie asked, frowning.

I put my left hand on Evie's, her silk skin as gentle as the softest flower petal.

Alright. Focus.

With closed eyes, I conjured up an image of Director Astron's office, feeling the vibrant energy of the student halls fade away, giving way to a faint but distinct aura of mystical energy.

"Where in The Light's name are we?" Evie asked.

Sounds like the correct reaction.

As I inhaled, the unmistakable aroma of wax mingled

with the musty scent of old parchment. I opened my eyes to see the shelves of arcane tomes, scrolls, artefacts of unknown origin, and the familiar desk, behind which stood the commanding figure of Larion Astron.

"First, dear students," Director Astron's wise voice captivated our attention. "I would like to apologise for interrupting your classes."

He rose from his chair and walked around the desk. The sound of quills scratching on parchment filled the room, continuing to write in his absence. "I am Larion Astron. Director of Mathsmagica's Academy."

Evie lowered her head and hit a knee on the ground. "It is an honour to be in your presence!"

Nilah followed in her steps. I stared at them. *Should I do the same? I didn't do this yesterday.*

"Please, raise yourselves. I have little time so we have to rush this, no matter how disapproving I am of that idea," he said, and we were in a vast hall.

We teleported as seamlessly as that? Holy smokes.

Lined up in front of us were boxes, carefully labelled with each person's name, waiting to be opened.

"Please, from this moment on, you will wear only this when you're on Mathsmagica grounds. These clothes have self-recovery magic imbued in them, so you can always clean them in a second. It is mandatory that everyone knows you are a Harmony Enforcer."

"Harmony Enforcer?" I asked, opening the box.

"That's the name for what you represent," he said and looked at me. "You remember what I told you yesterday, I believe. Be that change everyone needs to see. My time is limited, so I will leave the rest to you, Sova Ren."

"Okay, but what do we do now? You said we'll find out—"

"And you will. For now, what you must do is wear these uniforms. I hope next time we see each other, I'll see how they fit you," he said and looked at the girls. "I believe this choice was correct. Until, well, later."

Director Astron disappeared into thin air, leaving us behind.

"Can someone explain what in The Light's name is going on?" Evie shook her head.

"Um. I apologise. I thought this would go differently. It seems the Director was in a real rush, huh," I said.

"He talked to you the most, so I suppose you're supposed to explain the details," Nilah poked me.

"Well... I guess."

A bald man in black robes interrupted us. "I'm sorry. The dressing rooms are this way," he said, pointing with his hand.

We went into separate rooms. There was a mirror in mine, so I thought likewise of the other two. I took off the black coat and the white shirt, a small M for the school's logo on it. Opening the box, I couldn't help but notice how smooth the fabric of the new uniform felt against my skin as I dressed. Slipping into my clothes, I couldn't help but notice how they seemed to have a mind of their own, gently adjusting themselves to fit me perfectly. *Now is this punishment, or literal babysitting?* I smirked.

When I was done, the mirror revealed a most splendid image. The black pants had dimensional rings attached to the belts, providing a clever solution to carry additional items without sacrificing space. The outfit comprised a blue shirt adorned with black fishnet, which covered the collarbone. Over it, a black coat featured a striking red arrow extending from the shoulder to the area where the solar plexus would be. Inside, the same royal red colour graced the material, adding to its pleasant appeal.

For the first time, I admire my own image in the mirror. Who would know having blond hair and blue eyes would fit royal clothing so much? Well, technically, I am royal blooded, after all.

With my old uniform cradled in my hands, I exited the room. The bald man shook a finger before me. "No, no. Please, leave the clothes here. We'll take care of them."

"Oh, okay." I said, my shoulder slumping slightly. "Where are the girls?"

"This way, please," he treaded, and I followed.

The man pointed to a door at the end of the hall and waved his hand at it. A way to conclude his instructive purpose, perhaps. As soon as I stepped outside, Evie's captivating beauty mesmerised me. She looked as if she was born to wear that uniform, outshining anyone else in the world. *And I thought I looked good.*

"I think they are better than the original uniforms," Nilah said. "At least they are more comfortable, for sure."

"Hey, look at that. Sova looks outstanding!" Evie said, pointing at me.

"Oh, you look three times better than I do, please."

Their uniforms matched mine, but their blue shirts extended to their collarbones, while the black fishnet fabric began there and extended up to their necks.

"Alright, I think I have a lot to say, but I'll fill you in later. We should return to classes now. We're about to have a lot of—"

A bell rang throughout the halls, and sentences took shape, floating in the air before each person.

The Light shines, and The Dark beckons it.

The necessity for harmony and union is neigh. For defiers of law have emerged and order must find a means of being restored. For that, I have formed the Harmony Enforcers. Handpicked students with extraordinary potential. Follow in their footsteps, chase The Light, but accept The Darkness that comes with it.

To all dear masters, lesser teachers, and fellow students, be aware! The committee I have formed is completely legal and is in active force from this point on.

Its current members are: Sova Ren, Nilah Ren, and Evie Stratovic.

Consider that they may bypass all magic restricting laws for the sake of the duties they must perform.

I hereby sign this in the name of Mathsmagica Academy's Director Larion Astron.

"...trouble," I finished my sentence.

The texts disappeared as we read them. I looked at the girls and gulped, a nervous smirk on my face. "Well, now you know."

"I blame Arthus for this one..." Evie said, facepalming.

Among the Archives

"... Before even countries dared to put names to their community, Savannah we declared to be first. Little doubt it was because Sovah The Legendary Mage was born here. We, and not just us, but all countries, should be grateful to his being. He pushed nature into obedience. He aligned the structures. And he aligned the world. The books say he was a God, but he still died. Yet speaking his name to this day is exactly what makes him a God. He bestowed The Light and allowed us to transcend into nobility. I still wonder, why did humanity fall so low as to put a shell on itself? Perhaps because of the fog that surrounded us after his passing? Or maybe he cast it as a punishment for our own lack of worth..."

-Excerpt from "Notes of a Savannah Historian"

CHAPTER 7
MASTER LETHALICA'S CLASSES

The creaking of the clock mechanisms filled the air as the arcane hourglass shifted.

It was late to join the independent classes. Rather than going there, we made a beeline for Master Lethalica's classroom. The seats were devoid of other students, so we settled at our customary place in the back, away from any distractions.

Classmates burst through the door, their gazes scrutinising us as they entered. Innocent curiosity, vigorous envy, or blatant religious discrimination. All of those stares were easily recognisable, drifting in the air like an uncomfortable silence.

"Something tells me Director Astron's plan might have backfired," Evie leaned towards me and whispered.

"It is natural that this happens. I suppose this is what the punishment is about," I shrugged.

"Okay, so why exactly are we all punished?"

"I used Level Four Black Magic, Nillie."

"Yes, but you did. We didn't," Evie said.

I glared at her.

"No, I didn't mean it like that! I'm sorry." Evie said, with a note of remorse.

"Maybe next time we should just die." I forced a smile.

"Sova... I didn't mean it like that."

"Hey, she didn't–" Nilah poked at me, but I poked her right back.

"I know," I chuckled. "Look at how serious you two are. Loosen up."

I let out a hearty laugh, and Evie responded with an adorable sigh and a pout, instantly relieving the tension.

"Alright, listen up. The main idea for the Harmony Enforcers is to display union. The Director found it fascinating that followers of The Shadow Covenant fought against Hailing Remnants in order to protect people from the Luminari Faith. And furthermore, it seems the fact you were healing Nilah made a big impact as well." *At least to me.*

"So that's why harmony. It's about union," Evie spoke.

"Yeah. A big part of this is just the way I understand the situation. Note that these are not Director Astron's exact words," I said, leaning my back against the chair.

"So does that make you the leader of the Harmony Enforcers?" Nilah asked, poking me.

"There is no such thing as a leader, Nillie," I frowned.

"But look at this. We're both looking up at you, aren't we, Sova? I agree that you're the leader," Evie said, chuckling.

"Ugh... If you say so. Hey, why's everyone forcing things on me all of a sudden?" I raised my hands.

The girls laughed at me and suddenly I noticed the silence in the classroom, many gazes malevolently peering at us. Master Lethalica arrived at the table before the blackboard.

"Now, students, may I have your attention?" her seductive voice snatched the eyes away from us. "Master Rodotus isn't able to come today, so I'll also be replacing his history classes. On that point, would you want to start with that and then continue with Elemental Magic?"

The class wholeheartedly preferred to take history first. Not because of great interest. Everyone just wanted to get rid of that class faster.

"The lands beyond The Fog still await our rediscovery. The books tell us about lands just beyond a sea distance of travel," Master Lethalica spoke. Everyone listened in on the lecture. Was it because she looked the way she did? Or just she had a way with words. "What exactly is 'The Fog' we don't know. But whoever travels beyond it never comes back. The creatures that emerge from it are of different races we have tried to identify. Some match definitions from books of age, yet we don't know exactly why we're being attacked by them."

She wore azure robes, delicate embroidery adorning its edges, depicting elemental motifs. The rings on her fingers caught the light, casting shimmering reflections of silver and sapphire crystals, as her sleeves hung, defying gravity. Her red chest-long hair floated to the side, revealing cat-like pupils surrounded by a saturated yellow colour.

I narrowed my eyes at her every time I saw her. Be it in classes, or in The Academy's halls. A number pattern always floated about her and I couldn't make sense of it. The pattern shifted at all times so I couldn't remember the equation of the spells. *She is a Master Mage, after all. Perhaps I just can't comprehend it. Yet.*

"Well, students, in today's program there should be also an introduction to The First War, but I can see you need a break," Master Lethalica said.

"Master, forgive me for asking this question," a

student from the front rolls raised his hand. "What's the point of studying history when we're just soldiers in training? We're not in a normal university and we all know that."

"Yes, and we should just practice how to exercise our magic and win fights against the creatures of The Fog," another said.

I leaned forward, as if it would help me hear better.

"Dear students," she said with a sigh. "The purpose of history can serve you in battle, as well."

"But Master Rodotus has obviously never waged a battle! He's just a bookworm. That's why he's got this job as a history teacher and nothing related to practical lessons."

"That's right," Arthus said from the other side of the classroom's first rows. "We are here to *make* history. Not *study* it!"

"Oh, Arthus is here? And he seems healthy. I didn't notice," I said.

"And didn't you see him when you snatched me from my Illumination classes?" Evie asked.

"Eh. I was looking for you, not him," I shrugged.

"Oh, Sovie, you were just dazed by Evie's beauty. Don't lie," Nilah said.

I looked at my sister with the most threatening gaze I could throw. "Say what, Nillie...?"

The classroom transformed into a chaotic exchange of words until a resonance deafened the voices.

Numbers. I can see numbers across the whole room!

All students glared at each other in confusion as they spoke, yet their voices were unheard.

Air magic. Master Lethalica just now manipulated the air so voices wouldn't vibrate through it. I smiled at that realisation.

"Silence, students," she said as she raised her hand.

"We make history every day. But what is the point of that, if nobody will remember it?"

Everyone fell in thought. I grinned as I wrote my first sentence for this entire class.

"Here's what. I'll let you have a quick break and we can continue with Elemental Magic classes."

With Master Lethalica's uplifting words, their spirits soared and they burst out the door, as if breaking free from years of captivity.

Determination burned brightly in Nilah's eyes.

"Careful what you say, sis," I raised an eyebrow at her.

"Guys, haven't you thought about our history? All five countries fighting over each other just because they have some differences. Did we really need The Fog to unite?"

"Unite? Come on, sis. You're better than this. Which part of Arthus attacking us screams union?" I frowned.

"Hey," Evie leaned before me, a sweet perfume reminding me of lilac filling my nostrils. "Which part of saving Arthus by casting forbidden Level Four Sorcery screams union?"

"Alright, I'm guilty," I raised my hands, confessing.

"I mean, ugh... Yes, but we also have Mathsmagica, right?"

"For some years, yes," I said with a sigh. "But people don't change just like that. The fact we're in these roles proves it," I said, pointing at my Enforcer uniform.

"I think we should all just have faith," Nilah sighed.

"And those are the wisest words, despite being too confusing on their own," Master Lethalica said as she stood next to me.

I looked at her, closing my notebook. *Crap. I hope she didn't see I've hardly written anything.*

"My apologies. I didn't mean to eavesdrop on your

conversation. You three are the only ones who didn't go out, so I wanted to make sure you knew about the quick break," she said.

Our eyes met, and being so close to her, I felt this strange sensation again. A certain aura, similar to Arthus' father. Also close to what I felt from the people escorting me to Director Astron yesterday. Her beauty, though, was unrivalled, even with these predatory eyes. Or maybe they were just an addition to it.

"Yes, Master. We kind of... prefer to stay here and talk," Evie said.

Master Lethalica smiled and nodded, then went down the stairs. I noticed some numbers faintly traversing from her to us. I took my notebook, flipped it to the back side and wrote the numbers under the other equations. *It's clear enough so I can perfectly copy it.*

I stared at Master Lethalica, scrutinising if more equations would become clearer, while Nilah spoke to me, but I ignored her. Black hair and a sweet perfume obstructed my vision. I raised my gaze to meet Evie's brown eyes and a cute pout.

"I know she's pretty, but you're more than obvious, Sova," Evie said.

I facepalmed, trying to fight the shame. *That's what I get for seeing things others don't.*

"And what are you writing here? Spells?" Evie asked, looking at my notebook.

I slapped it closed. "Um, nothing too serious. I'm just practicing my memory."

"Oh, are you now?" Evie teased.

"Hey, so what happened with Arthus, exactly?" Nilah asked.

Thank you, sister. You really are a foxy one. Put me in trouble, but also save me from trouble.

"Well, he got petrified and burned, but he received treatment from the Luminari experts in healing, so he was more than recovered by the morning," Evie said.

"That's great to hear," Nilah nodded.

"Well, in all honesty, it's almost as great as Sova drooling at Master Lethalica," Evie joked, leaning on her elbow.

"Hey. I'm not," I said, poking Evie, like I would Nilah.

Wops. I did that by habit.

I expected a punch, a holy light falling upon me like a paladin's graceful ultimate attack, yet none of that happened. Evie's eyes opened wide, and she blinked a few times, then chuckled.

"Oh, come on, you were," she said.

While we gossiped the classroom buzzed with people who came back from the break.

"Alright. For the sake of this class' efficiency, I will need to see which of you belongs to The Shapers religion. Please raise your hands," Master Lethalica said.

"Why is she asking a religious question? Shouldn't that be banned?" Nilah asked.

I stretched my arms back and said, "It's just for convenience. To join The Shapers, you need to have an affinity to at least one of the elements."

"You in the back? Excuse me, what is your name?" Master Lethalica asked. I looked around and realised everyone was looking at me.

"Sova?" I spoke in a confused tone.

"Which element do you have an affinity to?"

At that moment, I realised my hands were in the air from my stretching. "Oh no, I am sorry. I was... stretching."

"And that's the guy from the director's announcement? Really?" some muffled voices reached my ears.

Chuckles filled the classroom. Evie poked me and I blushed, lowering my head.

"Nice one. And there I thought you were even more special," Evie whispered, chuckling.

"Way to go, bro." Nilah patted me on the back.

"Students," Master Lethalica said, a sphere of water forming and following her hand as she motioned with grace. "Among the elements, which one do you believe is the strongest?" Her hand made another circle and an orb of flame manifested. With each next circle, the next element took shape. "Water, fire, earth, air, or ice?"

One Shaper raised a hand to speak, but the teacher dismissed him.

"Fire," Evie said.

"Any other thoughts?"

"Water," Nilah said.

I studied that. It's Earth. Not because of its power, though. This is just censorship.

A majority of voices picked out fire to be the strongest.

Master Lethalica waved her hands and the flame sphere expanded.

"It is in human nature to believe that fire would burn everything. It is the brightest and scariest of them all. Yet for it to burn, it needs air, doesn't it?"

"Okay, but shouldn't it be the strongest, anyway?" a student asked.

The sphere of rock expanded, turned to dust, and surrounded the fire as she spoke. "Yes, it might seem to be. But throw dirt on a fire, and it perishes." The dust gathered together, extinguishing the fire entirely. "And the same goes for water."

The sphere of water burst all over the room like a tsunami to drown us all, but in a second's moment, the dust turned into a rock and changed shape, collecting the water like a small basin.

Strong wind blew towards us, my notebook attempting to fly off, like some other students' pencils and papers. A wall of rock took shape between us and Master Lethalica, ceasing the air current.

"And like that, earth defeats fire, water, and air. As for ice?" Master Lethalica disposed of all the elemental leftovers, leaving the classroom in what it was before her spells. "Does it even need an example?"

An ice prism took shape to her side, and it dropped to the ground, shattering to pieces.

Everyone besides The Shapers stood in awe as she gestured at the one who had tried to speak up earlier. "You may speak now."

"Yes, Master. We owe you our thanks for granting us with the most simple explanation of the earth element's superiority," the student bowed, and then explained. "It is the fundamentals of what we learn in our religion. As Elemental Magic is the most used *secondary* spell asset, my advice is that everyone should pay greater attention to the earth element. It is, after all, *not manmade*."

Master Lethalica smiled and extended her hand forward, palm facing up. With the teacher's subtle downward movement, I felt the ground beneath me shift.

"We're descending!" Nilah said.

Evie stood up, and we followed her example.

We were all at the level of the first steps of the classroom. Master Lethalica walked in our direction, her robes defying gravity.

"Now, students. It is time to *break the ice* with some exercise."

Why are you coming towards us, though?

"Behind this door, we'll find a portal. It's time for some field training. Make up groups of three before you enter. I will wait on the other side," she turned around and her voice seductively resounded. "And please, don't make me wait too much."

Oh, in Nocturna's name! I panicked for a second.

She went through the door behind us, and the students' faces all beamed up with excitement.

Evie looked at me with a mischievous smile. "Wanna team up, you two?"

Among the Archives

"... What a fearsome delight. The power to devour not just the physical, but ethereal realms as well. That is Black Magic. For its potency, I fear, the toll on one's mana pool could be grim. Many fail and die to their own spell casting, but not because of bad control. That's just a false rumour. It is because a single Black Magic spell costs a couple of times more the mana than the other schools' spells..."

- "Perceptions of Darkness" by *Brand Ren, A Librarian*

CHAPTER 8
PRIVATE LESSONS

T HE DARKNESS BEYOND THE DOOR ENVELOPED ME.
Icy crystals created a mirror-like effect, reflecting my image in every corner of the room. The smell of ozone lingered in the air. In the centre, Master Lethalica stood resolute and tranquil, as she always did. Startled by the warping sound, I turned around to find Nilah and Evie entering, one right after the other. I enjoyed the smell of lilac as Evie came next to me.

Nilah's face lit up with delight as she marvelled at the walls of ice, reflecting her own image almost perfectly. Evie quickly scanned each corner with a single glance before playfully winking at me.

So you're used to seeing this, is that it?

I smiled in response. We formed a line beside each other, all of us earning a nod of recognition from Master Lethalica.

"Alright, students. Just so I'm not mistaken, can you tell me what each of your affinity is?"

"Illumination magic," Evie said first.

"Black magic," Nilah said next.

After a slight pause, I nodded. "Black magic."

"What an interesting combination. I don't find it surprising that the newly found Harmony Enforcers would form a team among each other. Perhaps you really are the finest example of what Mathsmagica should be."

"Thank you, Master," Nilah bowed.

I exchanged a grin with Evie.

Calling us pioneers doesn't sound like the worst type of outcome. Black Magic and Illumination Magic mages always hated each other. Nice irony.

"So, none of you have an affinity for the elements. That's good for this exercise. In the world, you might find yourself facing enemies that would require use of magic which differs from your affinity." A circle-shaped board of ice emerged from the ground. "Place your hands here. When you jump in, you must use only elemental magic. Don't forget there are three of you. Help each other."

We nodded and placed our hands atop one another over the board.

"Let's do this," Nilah beamed.

"As a team," Evie added.

"As Enforcers," I said.

"Keep in mind you can take as much time as necessary. Don't be harsh. And *be careful*," Master Lethalica said, looking at each of us, counting on a confirming nod.

After a moment of closing my eyes, I was suddenly transported to a majestic mountain landscape. Dark clouds dominated the sky, rendering any hope of seeing the sun futile. As we trod into the snow, a satisfying crunch echoed with each step we took.

"Teleportation? Again?"

The wind blew in at us, carrying a bone-chilling howl. The frigid air was like tiny blades against my throat, making each breath a struggle. I covered my face, protecting it from the snowflakes the wind carried.

"Remember what Master Lethalica said. Let us try to manipulate the ground to build a wall to protect us from the wind," Evie said, and she bashed her hands against the snowy surface. A rock as tall as my waist took shape before us. "Come on, guys. Let's take shelter."

I gazed at the source of the wind. A big mess of numbers and equations slowly approached.

"No," I said, interrupting Nilah, who was just about to raise the wall higher.

"No?" they both asked.

"Look ahead."

The ground shook. A blue figure five times my height approached.

"An ice golem," Evie said.

"Should we try to melt it?" Nilah asked.

"The Earth element is supposed to blow it into pieces..." Evie said. "According to what Master Lethalica revealed to us in the lesson."

"Perhaps if we were Shapers, yes," I said and the ice golem leaped, landing in front of us. The swirling snowflakes filled the air, making it increasingly difficult to see anything.

"I think we should make a strong wall to trap it," Nilah proposed.

"Or a meteorite to crash it!" Evie yelled, fighting the noise of our coats rustling.

"Yeah, good luck with that," I laughed. "We could try to focus on making a boulder and pushing it off a ledge on top of the golem."

"That actually sounds achievable," Evie nodded.

The golem lunged towards me, swinging its massive arms down with a thunderous crash.

"Sova, are you okay!?" they both yelled, as I landed a few metres back.

"I'm fine. Watch out! We should spread so we can kite him!" I said.

Didn't expect he'd actually attack. Is this safe? Yet, what the hell in magic is safe in the first place?

"Kite him?" Evie yelled as she ran around the golem.

"It's just baiting him to attack us, but making sure we avoid the attacks," Nilah responded.

With a thunderous swing, the golem tried to strike Nilah, but she quickly jumped to the side, narrowly avoiding its attack.

"Alright, Evie, now you get close to him," I said. The golem moved around and blasted in Evie's direction as she successfully evaded the attack.

"And then it's my turn," I said, dashing towards the golem. Its torso spun the upper part of his body, making an all-round scale attack. In a synchronised motion, we crouched down to dodge the incoming danger.

"Alright, we've got the attack patterns memorised. I suggest we conjure that boulder now, or we'll just get worn off with time," I said.

"Okay, let's focus on the proper spot. Where do we conjure it?" Evie asked.

"Why not try above its head, after all?" Nilah asked.

"What? No," I laughed. "There! You see above that cave? We can bait it by going in there when the boulder is ready." I pointed with my hand. *It's not a grandiose plan, but it appears to be feasible.*

"Alright. I'll start first," Evie said and directed her hand at the ledge above the cave. "Okay, let's do it."

Just as Nilah pointed her arm out, the golem launched into a full-scale attack, its massive fists swinging around. *Okay, we just dodge by crouching or sliding.*

As the attack soared overhead, I glanced upwards and caught sight of Evie effortlessly levitating in mid-air. *Curses! She jumped!*

The golem, using its spinning momentum, propelled an icy arm up. I swiftly caught Evie in my hands, the thunderous crash of the Golem's attack echoing just inches behind me.

"By The Light!" Evie said, as I landed and let her step on her feet.

"Keep moving!" I said and looked at Nilah, who was just about to get hit as well. "Nilah, dodge!"

She leaped to the side and rolled back several times before she recovered. The boulder that was being conjured fell in the shape of small rocks on the ground.

"Alright, let's try something else. You girls keep it distracted, and I will focus entirely on conjuring that big boulder, alright? It will take me some time, but as Master Lethalica said, that's not a problem," I suggested.

Both of them nodded in response. I leaped over to the cave and extended my hand up. The ice golem stopped moving and suddenly fixated whatever icy bulk served it for a head at me. *He's aiming at me.*

"Damn, so being away also won't work," I cursed. "Argh, this is making me angry."

Nilah kept running when I saw her reaching for the pocket rings on her uniform. She took out a vial with blue liquid. *You're running low on mana, Nilah? Not good.* I scrutinised her, noticing she was enforcing her body with mana constantly. *Doing those athletic moves takes a toll, but there's no other choice for now.*

I looked at Evie, but she appeared fine to me. Perhaps her mana pool was greater than my sister's.

At this rate, my sister won't be in any good shape. Screw this exercise. It's harder on her than it should be.

"Perhaps it's because we aren't shapers that we shouldn't use earth magic?" Evie suggested. "Maybe we should use something more practical."

I brought my run to a halt, standing firm and facing the enormous giant before me. My cloak rustled with the wind as the golem spotted me as an easy victim.

Then what's more practical against ice if not fire?

"I think this should slow it down," I said, pointing my finger at the golem. "Level Three Fire Elemental Sorcery, Spark of Flame."

I pictured the spell's equations just as Master Lethalica had written it on the board a few weeks ago and then poured a huge chunk of mana into it. Then, to make sure I gave it my best, I left the last bit of the equation to an open entity. I sank another chunk of mana into it and yelled, "Overcharge!"

Flame erupted.

For three seconds, a wave of scorching fire, a few times bigger than the golem, swallowed it whole, melting everything in its path.

The wind ceased, and steam took away my sight.

"Sova!" Evie yelled from the side. "Are you okay?!"

She came next to me and took a moment to assess the situation, as Nilah joined to my right.

Okay, I think I overdid it.

"Sova, that flame...?" Evie asked.

"Um..." Nilah facepalmed. "Sovie, I think you, um..."

I still stood with my finger extended forward.

We got teleported back to Master Lethalica. I didn't

move. *What will be the consequences of this? Fuck. I overdid it so bad. Even if we may cast all kinds of spells now, being able to cast an elemental spell at this magnitude shouldn't work the way it did unless you're with an affinity for Elemental Magic! God damn! How did this even happen, really? Brand had always told me about the risk of this happening. I wasn't careful enough. Curses!*

The room suffocated me. I didn't dare look Master Lethalica in the eyes. Sweat poured down my forehead and back.

"Lucky," she finally said, her predatory eyes studying me.

Correct. The best way to approach this situation!

"Right? I must've been so lucky to cast such a strong fire spell!" I said, laughing.

"I think–" Evie started, but Master Lethalica dismissed her with a hand gesture.

"Lucky because I'm the only one who could see what happened there," Master Lethalica said.

I swallowed and expected what next she would say.

But she was silent. She walked around us. I could feel her unshifting gaze on me.

"So you have an affinity for Black Magic. You are with The Shadow Covenant, right?" Master Lethalica asked.

"Yes, Master," Nilah and I said in unison.

"Show me your runes."

Nilah curled up her coat's left sleeve and revealed her wrist. An arcane rune engraved onto her skin, marking her as a member of The Shadow Covenant and allowing her to take part in the rituals. I curled my sleeve and revealed my rune, too. I guess it was the first time Evie saw those from up close as she gazed with interest.

"Do you know you could've dealt with the golem in a

more simplistic way? Like, for example, making a boulder big enough to seal the cave's exit would make the golem crush itself even trying to reach you," Master Lethalica sighed.

"I am sorry, I was—"

"No need," she interrupted me. "What you did has earned you something else, young ones. Perhaps it would be an interesting gamble. But you are Harmony Enforcers, after all."

"We don't even know what that exactly means, Master Lethalica," Evie spoke up.

"Why, that's only natural. It is because you are the ones that give meaning to it. You are the taboo breakers," she spoke, her voice turning dark towards the last sentence. "You are the taboo enforcers."

"Sovie..." Nilah grabbed my sleeve and held closer to me. *I know what you're thinking, Nilah. We're probably screwed.*

"And exactly because you are that, I have an offer for the three of you."

We exchanged glares. *She has an offer? Not a demand?*

"I will give you three private lessons. Mark you as the exceptional students that you are. Especially you, Sova. Your prowess in magic control is beyond Nocturna's realm. The last person who roamed with such a gift fell to his own death twenty years ago," she spoke, walking around us. "Do you know who that is?"

"Lumiel Darc. Despite the conspiracies, the Luminari Faith often mentions that name. The Holy Order of The Light executed a law for his termination, yet officially he turned to ash," Evie spoke.

"Oh, someone's been loyal to their studies," Master

Lethalica said. "And what about his children? Do you know?"

"They perished, along with Lumiel and his wife, Erica. Misuse of Black Magic, the books say," Evie replied.

I looked at her, unable to hide my shock.

"Yes. And that is why even The Hailing Remnants ceased to believe in The Shadow Covenants. The entire world closed their doors for them. The danger of Black Magic being too great. Stories say some roamed the realms of the dead in search of The Darc family, but they weren't to be found there. For, after all, Black Magic devours not just the physical, but the ethereal, as well. No Communion was successful at it," Master Lethalica spoke.

"But why would they even want to do that?" I asked.

"Who wouldn't? Imagine bringing an undead mage with such potential. It is the ultimate tool," she responded. "Ah, at long last. Another team has succeeded in the task. Would you three kindly meet me tomorrow after classes? We could start the private lessons."

We agreed and silently walked out of The Academy. Me and Nilah worried that whatever we said might make us public enemy number one. While on the other side, I did not know what was inside Evie's head.

I gulped as my eyes met hers. We hadn't spoken about what we would do after this and somehow an unease grew between us.

"I am kind of tired, so I plan to head back home. I will see you two tomorrow, right?" Evie asked.

"Evie," I started, but found myself unsure of what I wanted to say.

"Sure, Evie. We'll see you tomorrow," Nilah said.

"Okay, Light be with you." Evie said and went on her way.

Without even discussing it, we headed towards our dorm. I tried speaking to Nilah, but she didn't seem up to it. We went home and after a shower; I sat on my bed, looking through the window.

Lumiel's children perished because of a misused spell, huh?

I walked before the mirror and forced my voice to sound like what I imagined my father's excited tone would be. "Well, Sova. How were your classes today? Oh, you did that!? Show them you're a D–"

"Sovie?" Nilah opened the door.

"Come in, sis."

With her blond hair cascading over her face, she sat on the bed, her gaze fixed downwards. I went over to her and rested my hand gently on her shoulder.

"You think we should go back?" I asked.

"And leave Mathsmagica behind?"

We stared at the floor together.

"No. I mean to just talk with him," I said.

"You mean Brand?"

"Yeah, and tell him about all that's been happening. He warned it would be dangerous to reveal other affinities."

"We can just send him a letter for that. And besides, you know what he would say..." Nilah stood up and curled her arms before her chest. "You two! I told you not to deal with that school! They're all impostors! Oh, damn it, why'd I even bother with Lumiel...?"

"Yeah, but he would then sulk for a few minutes and say," then in unison, we spoke. "But what would I do without you two blessings cranking my nerves up?"

We laughed for a while and then Nilah went in front of the mirror. As she gazed at her reflection, she marvelled at her radiant face and lustrous hair, delicately tracing her slender jawline with her hand. "I sometimes wonder if I look like mom. What do you think, Sovie?"

"Well, according to Brand, we're a big curse because we look so much like them. Well, unlike me, dad had black hair, I think. So I guess you look like mom," I shrugged.

I leaped across the bed and looked out the window again.

"I think we should do it. Perhaps it will actually work," I said after a few minutes of silence.

"Do what?"

"For the first time ever, just be ourselves."

Nilah's eyes went wide open, and she rushed next to me, almost pushing me through the window. "Are you crazy, SOVA!?"

"What?"

"We can't risk letting anyone know," she said in a whisper.

"No, I don't mean the family name. I mean, you know what Brand always told us about our parents. How they had multiple affinities and changed people's lives through that. Perhaps we can discover just how much of that gene we have in us," I spoke, but saw she was still quite unconvinced.

"You mean... try all sorts of magic?"

"Let's start with Elemental Magic first. It's like the opportunity came to us, anyway. And nobody will call us, you know what name, if we had just two affinities, right? Brand didn't ever tell how many affinities dad had, but he always paused and said they were a lot."

"It's crazy..." she said, but a smile widened across her face. "But I like it!"

I extended my hand to her and told her to do the same.

With her hand in mine, I whispered, "You remember the equation for Spark of Flame, right?"

She retracted her hand and put it on her mouth. "No, you're mad. I'm not setting the dorm on fire!"

"Trust me, you won't. Give your hand here."

Following my instructions, she visualised the spell's equation, forming a spherical shape in her palm. I could see the numbers take shape.

"No, a little less mana than that," I said.

The numbers shrunk, and I told her, "Alright. Now activate it."

A small spark lit up in her palm.

"Now don't get too excited or you'll blow us up," I chuckled.

She cancelled the spell and bounced across the room, jumping over the bed and running out to the kitchen and back. I couldn't help but let a hearty laugh out.

"Alright, Sovie. We're doing it! I can't wait for tomorrow's classes!"

Using the Harmony Enforcers as a disguise, we could actually pull this off. We can be ourselves. Or at least, closer to what we are supposed to be. We are the taboo and the director himself is behind us.

Among the Archives

"These Shapers end up being nothing more than a joke. They have the potency of wielding the elements themselves, storm cataclysm upon a peaceful world, even! And they don't dare send their own people to aid us on the frontline. I'll never forgive those bastards. Should we clear The Fog, we should immediately charge into their lands and crush them. "

- *"Letter to King Belarion Creston," Unknown Sender*

CHAPTER 9
FIRST ENFORCERS TASK

A spark rippled the air.

"Now, the equation is incomplete, and that is why you had only but a spark," Master Lethalica spoke, her sharp outlined eyes piercing me. "Though it did seem powerful, when you add the second part of the formula, you will give it a shape for the spark to follow. Think of it as a cage. Try it now."

I opened my palm and observed Nilah and Evie doing the same. While reproducing the equation, I visualised the precise trajectory I desired the spark to mimic. As I closed my eyes, the formula materialised in my mind, and I envisioned it taking the form of a majestic crown. I poured the mana in and looked at the results. Above my palm, a spark rippled through the air, following the shape of a crown. I kept burning mana at a gentle, steady pace so the spark would be a constant beam.

"Sova, that's not the most practical shape. I confess, though, an eye-catching one at this state of the spell."

I followed Master Lethalica's attention to Nilah. Hers

was in the shape of a... mushroom? I could see our teacher's confused expression.

"Very good. Your ability to control your flow of mana is remarkable. So is your fire affinity," Master Lethalica spoke.

Then we reverted our attention to Evie. Sweat on her forehead, and dedicated concentration aimed at her palm. Sparks rippled in all directions at a chaotic pace. I tilted my head to the side, straining to envision what shape her sparks were meant to take, but my efforts were in vain.

"Perhaps," Master Lethalica put a hand under Evie's. "You should try with a simple shape. Picture a circle, and then run a spark along its edge."

Evie nodded her head and did as told. The spark had a slight chaotic movement, but the circle was distinguishable.

"Alright. Now try to make a second spark immediately after the first one," our teacher instructed, and right as Evie succeeded, she spoke. "Now, continue adding a new spark constantly until you can make it look like a single radiating beam."

A desire to proceed beyond felt inappropriate. My sister and I had this much under control with ease. As descendants of the Darc Family, we had yet to discover how far our affinity for magic would expand. Though, asking for more guidance at this point made me feel bad for Evie.

"For you, twins. Step three of this spell is the most dangerous one. You lose control over the flow of mana and you explode in flames," Master Lethalica spoke and turned her back against us. "Cancel the spells and watch. All three of you."

From the far distance of the training room, square walls of ice, each ten metres tall, erupted from the ground. A barricade many would consider would take a team of

Shaper mages to build. *And she did it in five seconds, just like that.*

Master Lethalica extended her right hand, delicate fingers gracefully stretching out. The rippling sparks took the shape of a sword. It glowed strongly as she spoke, "When you enter the third step, it will emit light stronger the more mana you pour in it."

My jaw dropped as she grabbed the fiery spell, her hand bursting in flames which for whatever reason didn't seem to damage her or her gravity defying sleeves, and threw it forward.

"Level Three Fire Elemental Magic, Sinner's Devastation," she said, the fiery blade bursting the ice barricades on its touch, vaporising them from existence. As the last one fell, Master Lethalica blinked twice, her eyes jolting left to right. In an instant, small cubes of ice emerged across the room, including some floating in the air.

We rendered the display finished, but then Master Lethalica said, "Stage two, Annihilation."

On the other side of the room, the fiery blade split into numerous small spheres of vibrant, blazing light. They all shot out at their targets, striking down each of the miniature cubes. In a matter of moments, wisps of steam filled the room, billowing up towards the ceiling as the ice cubes dissolved into nothingness. Finally, the dancing fires dwindled, and Master Lethalica shifted her attention towards us. I expected her to be flexing her astonishing ability, but her face remained unfazed as ever. *Was this really a piece of cake for you?*

"That is the full potential of the spell. As Harmony Enforcers, you may cast it, but I don't recommend you do unless you are completely confident in controlling the third step."

"But, but... You said it's a Level Three spell," Evie said, her eyes wide.

"And it is, Evie."

"But aren't spells of this scale supposed to be Level Four and above?"

"Not necessarily. What makes a spell Level Four Sorcery isn't so much its scale, rather than it is a mixture of attributes or complexity. For example, casting a spell as big as this one, but enhanced with a Black Magic's Glimmer, would make it level four," our teacher said and smirked at me. "Now, I don't want to give you any dangerous ideas here. First master this level to perfection and then you could think of adding Glimmer to it."

"Does this mean that I can combine Elemental Magic with Black Magic at will?" I asked.

"In the future, yes. Now, no, unless you want to get yourself killed."

Nilah put a finger on her chin and asked, "Then does that mean that we would be creating new spells?"

"Indeed," Master Lethalica said.

"By Nocturna's darkness, that's so exciting!" Nilah bounced.

"Look at her go," Evie chuckled. "But Nilah, please, don't risk your life over that. Making new spells really doesn't mean much if you don't get to cast them again."

"Evie is correct. This is the philosophy of a Master of Magic, but as my private students, I can tell you this," Master Lethalica said, forcing our breaths to a halt. "Magic is magic. It flows. Spells are the formulas used to cast them as ideal replicas of the original spell, but that doesn't mean they have to be the same as it. A Master sees all spells as one and all magic as one."

The door to the training room opened, and a man in

white Luminari Faith attires came to us. "I was told to deliver this to The Harmony Enforcers."

"And how did you know we were here?" Master Lethalica asked the bald man.

Oh, it is the guy from the dressing rooms!

"Director Astron said I would find you here, Master Lethalica."

The man took out a small letter from his pocket and gave it to me.

"Now, if you'd excuse me," he bowed his head in respect and walked out.

"Dear Harmony Enforcers. It would appear the time for your first task has come. On the outskirts of Erleen has been an outrage of beasts attacking villagers. Our information is scarce, but I can judge that you are eligible for the task. You are to go to Erleen and seek the source of the danger. Even if it proves to be challenging, I trust in your power to extinguish it. You are to depart as soon as possible. May Magic guide you on this journey."

Underneath, I could see the director's signature and stamp.

"Wait, what? We're going to fight beasts!?" Nilah pulled her hair.

"You expected humans? The hell, Nillie?" I laughed at her.

"Extinguish the source of danger? This sounds like a task for graduates! We're only first years," Evie said, glancing at me and Master Lethalica. My smirk faded as I acknowledged the weight of her words.

"Students," Master Lethalica called out to us in a wise tone. "It might seem frightening at first, but if Director Astron has put so much faith in you, I trust his judgement.

All three of you are incredibly strong. All you have to do is to be calm, assess the situation."

The girls nodded, yet they kept their heads low. Our teacher's gaze pierced me and I felt my heart rush.

I get it. I accept this role.

I put my hands on Evie's and Nilah's shoulders. "Alright, Enforcers. This is our first task. We shall deem it done and rid of those who disapprove of our power."

This wouldn't usually be what Evie needs to hear, but I could see her Luminari colleagues looking down on her when she walks with us. She's in the same place we are. Director Astron is giving us a chance to prove ourselves, so we should do it. Be the prime example of what Mathsmagica is all about.

The sun had set long ago. Evie and Nilah bought mana potions and other accessories they found would be good to have for the journey. They both glanced at me with displeasure. Nilah, I knew, she was just envious of my mana pool. But Evie, I had no clue. Perhaps she thought I was flexing in front of her.

We arranged a meeting hour in the morning and wished Evie a sound rest. Before I knew it, we were already at our dorm. I expected us to have a very exciting conversation about the private lessons, but we were so totally drained that we ate and hit our bedrooms.

Damn. I don't feel my mana pool exhausted at all. Like I've used hardly one percent of it, yet why do I feel so tired?

I cuddled into my blanket and gazed out the window. *Soon it'll be a full moon, it seems.* Thoughts of the potential we could harness excited me, and I falsely foresaw that would keep me awake all night. I blinked my eyes open and the vibrant blue sky, in the company of gentle warmth of the sun's rays streaming through my window, greeted me.

"Alright, time to go," I said to myself and prepared to head out.

The meeting point was in front of The Academy's entrance. From there, we would walk our way to Erleen. A day of walking away, but as Evie arrived, we could see Master Lethalica next to her and behind them, three dakes followed.

"Hey, guys!" Evie waved, her smile throwing a ray of light into my heart. "Look what I brought!"

"No way! Evie! You brought dakes with you!?" Nilah leaped for a tight embrace.

"Are those for us?" I asked, trying to dismiss Evie's gorgeous face from my mind.

"Yes. This is Ognena." Master Lethalica pointed at the red-furred creature. "Then this handsome black furred one is Sablezarb," she said, petting the thick fur of the blue-eyed creature. "And this is Snejlica. Despite her creamy white fur, she's one to enjoy basking in the mud the most."

I had seen dakes before, but never so well-cared for like these. They licked Master Lethalica's cheeks, and she petted them back. For the first time, our teacher seemed thrilled. *I guess she loves them.*

"We get to actually ride dakes?" Nilah looked at Snejlica. The beast approached her, its head like that of an enormous wolf. It studied her with its cat-like irises and then allowed her to pet it.

"Yes, and I think Snejlica already picked you," Master Lethalica said.

The black beast's blue irises gazed at me, its hostile appearance leaving me in wonder if it hated me at first glance. Stepping closer to Evie, it affectionately poked her arm with its nose, which had a dog-like warmth to it.

"Your name's Sablezarb, right? I guess you'll be my

trusty companion on this journey," Evie said, petting its thick fur, the beast closing its eyes, nourishing the sensation.

Did I just wish I was a dake for a moment?

"That leaves me with you, doesn't it?" I approached the red-furred beast. Its blue eyes gazed at mine for a moment, then it looked to the side. "Really? You hate me at first sight, too?"

"Remember to feed them and give them water. You know what they eat, right?"

I exchanged shrugs with the others, but Evie actually responded. "Never meat. Just grass. Right?"

"Yes and no," Master Lethalica said, her hand scratching my beast's chin. "Stick to grass, but if something arises and you need to, give them meat. They'll get extreme strength, but after a while will have terrible tummy aches."

We nodded and the girls' beasts lowered their heads to the ground, making it easier for them to jump on their backs. I approached mine and with a sense of unease; I put my hand on its back.

"Your name's Ognena, right? Will you let me mount you?" I asked.

The beast unleashed a low guttural sound, its menacing growl reverberating through the air. But as Master Lethalica approached and gently petted it, the beast's aggression subsided, and it obediently lowered itself.

Despite being on all four feet, its height was at my chest. I didn't want to risk jumping on its back like some maniac.

"You listen to Sova, okay Ognena, darling?" Master Lethalica kept petting it and the dake twisted its head so one of its eyes met mine.

From her attires, Master Lethalica pulled out three small gems. I could see spell formulas imbued in them.

"Students, take these. Should the danger prove too much and the situation is out of control, pour a fraction of mana into those, and their magic will teleport you back here."

I grabbed mine and studied it for a while. *I see a similarity in the formula to the one that Director Astron had given me. Maybe it differs because of the coordinates?*

"Thank you so much, Master Lethalica! You might seem coldhearted and a little evil at times, but you are really kind at the core!" Nilah spoke with a beaming smile.

"Oh my," Evie facepalmed and then, with a chuckle, bowed her head towards our teacher. "We appreciate your masterful guidance and support, Master Lethalica."

"Stay safe," she said.

"Alright, Harmony Enforcers. It is time," I yelled. Their dakes departed at that moment, but Ognena didn't move. "Oh, come on, girl. Ognena, let's go."

The beast twisted its head to look at Master Lethalica and she waved her hand goodbye. Ognena then looked at the others and, in a gallop, chased after them.

AMONG THE ARCHIVES

"They built Mathsmagica purely for the sake of training mages and sending them to war. I can't tap into these students' minds yet, but I can tell many of them really love my Mushroom Cafe. Who would expect business to blossom like this? Perhaps all of them just find some kind of solace in seeing something cute. If that's how it is, then perhaps I too am a soldier in this war. Though I don't have to battle with beasts. I carry a different function."

- *"Letter to Director Astron," Hiccup Cupcup, Mushroom Cafe Owner*

MATHSMAGICA

CHAPTER 10
SAVING ERLEEN

The books whispered tales of rivers cascading down majestic mountain peaks, while the lush forests extended their emerald embrace. Meanwhile, the vibrant flowers basked in the warm rain of sunbeams.

And they were true. Loria, the country of the Celestial Weavers, stood west of Mathsmagica. Our first task as Harmony Enforcers wasn't far from the borderline. A small village called Erleen. That is the fact which brought unease to me. Why would dangerous beasts appear so close to the safest place in the entire world right now?

We rode next to each other, our dakes - Ognena, Sablezarb, and Snejlica - tirelessly advancing pace, cutting down the distance to Erleen.

"So, do we have an actual plan to follow?" Nilah asked.

"Nilah is right. We should, indeed, think of a plan," Evie said.

They were both looking at me. *Alright, being a guy with a plan sounds good, but I'm pretty uncertain of what lies ahead.*

"Well, the Tracer spell which Master Lethalica cast on

us should be pointing straight to the location we need, right? We can go around it, scout, investigate, and then decide on our next course of action," I said.

"It was so funny that Master Lethalica forgot to cast that spell because of the dakes. First time I have seen her distracted like that," Nilah said.

"She really was out of character," Evie chuckled. "The way she used air magic to propel herself to us and ice so she can slide on it was yet another remarkable deed, though."

"Yes, right! She was so cool! A little threatening, too! By the way, this *Tracer* spell I didn't hear when she cast it. What kind of spell is it?" Nilah asked, as her dake, Snejlica, bounced over a fallen branch.

"Concentrate on the *idea* of where you need to go and you will feel like a compass guiding you to our location," Evie explained.

"I think she meant what school of magic, Evie," I said, smiling.

"Ah, sorry. It's Illumination Magic, actually."

"What? So Master Lethalica isn't just a Master of all elements, but she's also able to cast other sorceries?" Nilah shrugged.

"Ah, no, no. She is indeed a splendid Master, but the Tracer spell is a simple Level One spell," Evie said.

"Does that mean you can do it, too?" I asked.

"Of course."

There was a lake nearby, and the dakes went over to drink water without even asking us. They lowered their heads, letting us trode around while they chewed on the green grass. It amazed me to think that these creatures could sustain themselves on nothing more than a few blades of grass. Why weren't we humans so energy efficient?

Nilah laid on her back amidst a field of flowers, petals in rainbow colours surrounding her. I smiled as I enjoyed the sight of what came at the back of my head as "she looks happier than ever."

Evie petted Sablezarb as he chewed on the grass, his threatening blue gaze landing on me each time my eyes lingered on Evie for a while. I couldn't help but think how the new uniform fit her so much. With her pale skin contrasting against the colourful backdrop, she appeared like a celestial being amidst a garden of paradise.

"Sova?"

Walking with poise, she traversed the soft grassy field and found a comfortable spot to sit, her eyes captivated by the tranquil lake stretching out before us and the striking blue mountain looming in the distance. A soft breeze wafted the delightful fragrance of the colourful flowers, blending with her perfume, transporting me to a mesmerising oasis of beauty.

"Lomia sure is beautiful, isn't it?" Evie asked, as I sat in the grass next to her. "Do you have something like this in Nocturnia?"

"I only wish we had. There are some really amazing buildings, gardens, and monuments, but nature is definitely different from here," I said, looking straight. "What's it like in Savannah?"

"We have beautiful nature, too. Not like this one, it's just different," she responded, drawing a lock of hair behind her ear. "The Light has influenced a big part of the land."

I could imagine The Light transforming the flowers into big, shiny petals, creating trees that stood tall and provided an impressive shelter from the scorching sun on hot days. However, no matter what it offered, I yearned to see something even more captivating here. Right in front of me.

"Sova? Do I have something on my face?" Evie asked me, her eyes opening wider into confusion.

"No, sorry. I just... thought you look really beautiful," I said, unable to believe the words coming out of my mouth, but I didn't mind it. It was what I thought.

Evie's usual pale cheeks turned to pink, but she kept eye contact. Her soft fingers made their way to reach mine. Time slipped away, and suddenly our hands linked, creating an unexpected and intimate bond. Evie's delicate hand resting atop of mine flushed my cheeks, but I accepted and enjoyed it.

"Thank you, Sova. You are very cute yourself," she said and looked at the mountains across the lake, avoiding eye contact.

My dake, Ognena, nuzzled her wet nose against my neck, causing a sudden chill to run through me.

"Hey, you two, let's go. Our dakes are ready," Nilah said, already mounted on Snejlica's back.

"Alright, let's go," Evie said, and let go of my hand. Her warmth leaving my palm sent a painful crack within my heart. "Coming, Sova?"

"Of course," I said and mounted on Ognena's back.

After about an hour of travel, the village came into view, nestled amidst lush farm fields and dense forests. The sound of a nearby waterfall surrounded the village, its river serving as a lifeline, nourishing the community. As we strode down the slope, we passed a bridge in the forest which lead us to a sign, "Erleen."

"The Tracer spell points to the side of the village, though," Evie said.

"Master Lethalica probably pointed us directly to where

she suspects the beasts to be coming from. Perhaps we don't need to enter the village, after all. What do you think?" I asked.

A horse with thick white fur galloped past us, its body splattered with blood, and neighed with each stride.

"I think we should check out the village," Nilah said.

"Quickly. They might be under attack!" Evie said and pulled her dake into a dash.

We rode as fast as we could. Past the forests, we could hear bone-chilling howling and the villagers' screams of terror.

"I recognise that howl!" Evie said.

"Werstripers," I said. Nilah nodding in agreement.

Several villagers lay across the fields, blood decorating the fruitful plantings. We advanced across the curves of the streets, broken windows and blasted down doors on all houses. After the next turn, I saw a man, numbers spreading from his palm across his body.

"No, don't do it!" I screamed, and the man engulfed himself in flame. A two metre beast with thick long fur with glowing white stripes on it clawed at his body.

He was a commoner and tried to cast a noble class spell. Damn it.

Sablezarb catapulted Evie forward, her Lightforged Sword taking shape. As she landed, with a quick dash, she sliced through the werstriper's thick fur and it bled in sunrays. Disoriented, the beast threw its claws at Evie, yet with her free hand she erupted a beam of light - a barrier of a sort - repelling her opponent's force back at it. Left wide open, the beast's chest burned in The Light's punishing glow as Evie sliced through it. Defeated, the beast fell to the ground.

"They are weak. Let's split and meet here when it's over," Evie yelled, as she turned left.

"Stay safe!" I yelled back and faced Nilah. "Keep close and don't waste your mana. I'll handle this."

We took the right turn and didn't find any other creatures to battle. The road led us to the biggest building in the village - The Village Hall.

I sought to open the door, but it didn't move at all. *Perhaps it's* barred.

"We are here to help, open up," I said.

"Like hell I would! And let you in along with the werstripers!"

"We are the Harmony Enforcers of Mathsmagica Academy. We've come to deal with your problem," I said.

To my left, Evie approached, seemingly unharmed. *Was there only one beast or what?*

"If what you say is true, then do your job," the voice yelled from behind the door.

"That's what we're here for. And it's done. I have slain the beast!"

"There were dozens! We have resources to last us here for days! Find them and tell us when you killed them all!"

I shrugged at Evie and Nilah.

"Let me scout from atop," Evie said. Light pulsed under her feet and she launched into the air, hands gripping onto the roof of the two-floor building. After a minute, she came back and answered all our unasked questions with a single shrug.

"Let's roam the village. Houses included. They won't trust us now, anyway. But let's stay together. If there's a group of those beasts in a house, it could be dangerous if we encounter them alone," I said.

We carefully explored all houses. Some had basements, so we checked there as well. The only thing that made an impression were the gore scenes left behind the werstripers' victims. The people here seemed to live simple day-to-day life with just a few of them having some basic magic scrolls. Spells to help with cleaning the dishes or other common work. I believed there wasn't even one person of noble blood in Erleen.

The sun had set, and we approached The Village Hall.

"It is safe," I announced after delivering several knocks on the door. "You can come out."

"Are you certain?" the voice asked.

"Yes, we are," I sighed.

A couple of screeching sounds later, the doors opened and a man in grey farmer's clothes came out. He studied us carefully and nodded his head. People emerged from the building, their steps filled with fear, and quietly assembled in a solemn gathering.

They lost people; they lost crops, and Nocturna knows what else. No wonder they gathered in silence. Where should they even start?

"I am the... new village mayor now," the man with the farmer's clothes spoke. "Lohn is my name."

"We have an idea where the beasts are coming from, but perhaps some local insights might prove us well. Lohn, could you tell us what's happened here?" I asked.

"Does it need telling? It's obvious. We work our crops, they come out of the forests, they kill, they go away."

"Mister Lohn," Evie nodded her head in respect. "Were there no Celestials among you to help fend off the beasts?"

"The City had given us one Celestial. The Flow was with him at all times, yet before a group of those beasts, his limbs only proved to be insufficient," Lohn sighed. "He was a promising youngster, just like you three."

"Sorry to hear that," Nilah said. "So he fell to a pack of werstripers?"

"Indeed. Mathsmagica is closer than the closest city in Loria, so our late mayor thought it would be faster to call for help from there."

"Lohn, what do we do now?" a woman's shaking voice emerged from the crowd.

"Yeah, what first?"

"The crops?"

A chaotic flurry of questions erupted from the crowd.

Lohn raised his hands in the air and waited for the silence to settle in.

"I am just like you. Nothing but a simple villager. My father was the man of wisdom, not me. But he taught me well. First, people, we bury the dead. Then we mourn them. Tomorrow morning, *all of us,* back to work!" Lohn spoke, his voice loud and almost commanding.

As the people, unified under his short yet sufficient speech, dispersed, I yelled. "All of you wait!"

"What is the meaning of this, Enforcer?" Lohn asked.

"The forests," I replied in a low tone. "They're glowing."

Howls pierced the skies, and heavy footsteps shook the earth.

"The pack has gathered," Evie said.

I stepped forward; the people rushing behind me. With each step, a magic circle appeared underneath my feet.

"I will handle this."

The air around my body distorted as the magic circles enveloped me and disappeared once they reached the top of my head.

"Level Three Black Magic Sorcery, Rancour Edge."

I dashed to one side and counted on Evie to handle the other side. With a jump, I propelled myself a few metres into the air, arms expanded to the side. From my fingertips, I cast multiple more Rancour Edge spells and then closed my hands together. The air rippled with black magic, thunderous edges crashing into the incoming pack of werstripers.

The beasts did as expected and focused on me. Claws leaping at me, their murderous white eyes glowing with the magic residing in them. Each hit that landed on me ended up in a bloody mess for my attacker. Despite the huge toll of mana it cost me, I covered my body with Rancour Edges as a shield. *Best defence is a good offense.*

I spun and struck each beast I saw. Their glowing stripes faded shortly after colliding with me. It wasn't long before I leaped above the fallen beasts in the chase of those who attempted to run away.

With a fierce battle cry, I dashed and pierced the towering werstriper in the back and delivered the ultimate strike. Panting, I brushed the sweat off my forehead, the Rancour Edge spells colliding with each other into ripping black sparks.

I looked back and sought to find Evie and Nilah. They were still fighting. I dashed from rooftop to rooftop until I reached the fray. Adrenaline rushed through my veins, fuelling me with more power. Yet, before I leaped into the fight, a few deep breaths served me well so I wouldn't lose control of my spells. Flashes of Illumination Magic contrasted with the black thunders originating from my attacks. Nilah preserved her mana by standing guard before The Village Hall, Lohn the sole villager next to her.

The final beast went down as The Light burned its flesh straight to ash. I dismissed my magic and Evie's Light-forged Sword dissipated.

"It's over now. They're all dead," I said, sweat going down my forehead, as the wind rustled in our coats.

"You two are a real flashing duo when you fight together, you know?" Nilah chuckled.

Evie looked at me and smiled, and I responded likewise.

"Lohn, you can let everyone come out. We'll go take care of the source of the problem, but we hunted down each one of the werstripers in this group," I said.

Lohn seemed unconvinced, yet he opened the door. People came out, and we greeted them with a smile. "We've taken down every last one of them. We shall proceed to–"

"Go away!" A woman screamed at me.

What?

"You monster!" Another screamed, then picked up a rock from the ground and tossed it at me. The impact of catching the rock in my hand sent a jolt of pain rippling through my palm.

"Lowlife Covenants! Get off the village!"

"You'll only curse us further!"

"What are you saying? We just saved you," I spoke, my eyes staring blankly.

"Dear villagers, we used our powers to serve a good purpose. Why are you saying this?" Evie asked, her voice hurting.

"You witch! Traitor to your own kind! Kill them off! Kill them!"

"Yes, how could a Luminari side with Covenant Scum?! You betrayed your own!"

"We are past those times, madam! This is why Mathsmagica–" Evie tried to explain, but the villagers threw stone after stone, screaming at us.

A wall of light separated us from the villagers. Evie's barrier crackled with energy, providing us with a sense of security as she persistently argued her case, a futile attempt at conviction.

I looked at my blood soaked into the stone in my palm. Nilah pulled my hand and looked at me with mourning blue eyes.

"Let's go Evie," I said, dropping the bloodied rock on the ground. "We've secured their safety. We've done our job."

"But, Sova, they just—"

"They called you a witch too, didn't they? Those types of people hear only what they want. They can't be convinced with reason."

"But... This isn't right," she turned to face me. "This isn't justice."

"That's right. It isn't."

We walked to the bridge where we entered the village, our dakes chewing on grass as they wait. Incredibly smart creatures. More impressive than I initially thought.

We jumped on their backs and rode to where Master Lethalica's Tracer spell pointed us to.

"It doesn't really feel right anymore..." Evie said.

"Don't go down that road," I said. She lifted her head to face me. "It leads to darkness."

"But we saved these people! Why did they throw stones at us!?"

"Evie," I paused. Recalling Brand's advice to never expose our Black Magic to non-covenants, I thought of the proper words to say to her. For she, after all, had never been discriminated for her own birthright. "Good isn't met with good. The balance would break. If we seek a reward from the people, then we would be wrong. We should seek the reward in us, for it is already there."

"But—"

"And that sucks," Nilah said. "But it is in Nocturna's teachings that this way we preserve balance."

My dake bounced over a boulder and I almost fell off.

"Talk about balance," I said, shrugging. The girls laughed and the depressing atmosphere faded into a lighter one.

Nail-sized bugs glowed in a breathing pace of blue. Thanks to that, the forest at night was bathed in a gentle luminescence, casting ethereal silhouettes on the trees. The tracer spell buzzed within, hinting the place we needed to go to was closer, yet no matter how we looked at it, it seemed to be behind a waterfall. We disapproved of the thought of getting the dakes' thick fur wet in the night and left them behind.

I climbed up the rocky surface and just a few metres higher it curved in, revealing a cave. Bugs illuminated its walls, and small transparent mushrooms glowed in sapphire and velvet, creating a picturesque sight as soon as I stepped in. The cave opened into a monumental space. Flowing water reflected a tapestry of illuminating flora that created a surreal atmosphere. The girls followed in my steps and shared my awe. Nilah clumsily tripped into a velvet mushroom, the scent of roses filling the cave.

"Oh, Sovie, they are so cute, and they also smell nice!" Nilah bounced, as she picked herself off the ground; her mushroom assailant lay defeated in front of her face.

"Let's just hope it's not poisonous," I laughed.

Among the Archives

"...I have been looking after this gifted child for half of my life now. I fear what might happen to one who would draw his deepest anger. May the wisdom of darkness guide him, for should he be manipulated into a tool, then it would solely depend which side of the coin he stepped on. Should the worse happen, well... Nocturna, watch over us.."

- "Perceptions of Darkness" by Brand Ren, A Librarian

MATHSMAGICA

CHAPTER 11
THE ANUBI AWAKENS

THE TRACER SPELL POINTED BELOW US. The thought of taking a swim into the flowing river close to the entrance of the cave crossed my mind, but the water would be bone-chillingly cold. We basked in the lovely lights and sought for over an hour where our location would be.

Numbers? I thought as I saw equations flowing opposite of the water's current. The water was incredibly shallow, and after several turns across the green humus illuminated by a stack of sapphire mushrooms, it took a slope down.

"Girls, here," I said and pointed at a hole enveloped by mushrooms, sloping deeper into the cave. "I'll hop in first."

I leaped down, and after the curve, I hung in the air for a few seconds until my feet landed on a slippery surface, almost resulting in a certain knockout. Despite the unchanged scenery, I noticed numbers floating in a specific direction. *There's more of them. We're closer to the source.*

"Okay, girls. One by one, jump down and I'll help you land," I said.

Following the grinding sound, a figure suddenly

dropped into view within seconds. With a mana reinforced leg, I caught it in my arms. *So light.* It was Evie. I held her in my arms and it felt surreal. We stared into each other, my heart rising its pace. A drift towards her face pulled me in, but the sound of my sister leaping out of the hole brought me back to reality. Evie's eyes popped wide, and she extended her hands up to protect herself. Nilah landed in her arms, and the impact of our fall jolted me. Whatever happened with my mana control was no longer within my understanding, leaving us crashing to the ground.

"Ugh, Nilah, why are you so heavy?" I grunted as she got off.

Nilah gave a hand, raising Evie to her feet, and when I extended mine, she put hers in a tight lock before her chest.

"What? None for me?" I asked and picked myself up.

"Stupid Sovie, you're so unreliable at times," Nilah clicked her tongue, and they both laughed.

"Oh, is that the game you're playing now, sis?" I laughed back.

"Which way from here?" Evie asked, her eyes reflecting the countless glowing lights of the magical plants covering the cave's walls.

"That way," I said, pointing at the incoming flow of numbers like mist that hovered centimetres above the ground.

"Tracer spell doesn't seem to be quite useful at the moment. Something caught your attention there?"

I looked at the numbers again and nodded. "Yeah."

Nilah acknowledged with a nod and followed along. I looked at Evie, who hesitated for a moment. It wasn't distrust I recognised in that one second of uncertainty. It was pure curiosity.

Maybe one day, Evie, you too will learn that I see magic differently from others.

The route I led them to ended up being a dead end. A wall that curved along the ceiling of the cave. To them, for sure, it seemed so, but I could see a huge stack of numbers, quite resembling a curtain before me.

"It's a dead end?" Evie asked.

"I'm not sure," I responded. "Step back."

I opened my palm and concentrated my mana on it.

"Level Three Fire Elemental Sorcery, Spark of Flame," I said, a blaze erupting from my fingertips, the wall before us cracking like glass before the heat.

The air grew heavier as the flame extinguished and the wall shattered into glowing magic sparkle dust, floating slowly towards the ground.

"Are you ever going to use that spell properly?" Evie joked.

"Like what? Start a campfire?" I asked, laughing along.

"Look, guys! It's so sparkly!" Nilah beamed.

In Fundamental Magic classes, we learned about this. The glowing light within the particles is from the residing magic, and they are incredibly light, hence they appear to be floating rather than falling. Master Hempa informed us about this event that occurs when a spell gets broken.

Once the glowing curtain fell down, before us were two gold coloured columns in the shape of humanoids with their heads reminiscing that of a dog. Their hands, mighty and strong, held onto the ceiling, adorned with intricate curves. Between the mighty humanoid columns was a gate, its hinge shaped in an arc, sapphire glowing runes into them.

Evie touched the left statue's leg, and then Nilah did the same to the right one. They sought to find a key that would open the door. The numbers on the runes somehow made sense to me the more I stared at them. An itchy feeling across my back forced me to shrug. Eyes locked onto the runes, I tried to scratch my back.

"Evie, do you think maybe we have to reach the snouts? They are sticking out, so maybe we need to pet them so the door opens?" Nilah suggested, jumping to reach the statue's head.

"Should we climb up to them, though? What if we break the sculptures?"

"Sovie just blasted the statues with fire. I think they'll last our weight."

"Anubi, rest in Eterna," I said, and the runes spun, the door sliding open.

"What? How did you do that?" Evie asked, and Nilah's confused glare stated the same question.

"I'm not really sure," I responded honestly. *I didn't see it at first, but it's the first time the numbers shape letters.*

We stepped through the doors and there was no longer a sign of any humus, mushrooms, or whatever plantlife. Beyond the entrance, magic flame torches lit ablaze in a violet fire. The golden bricks, gleaming with a flawless polish, shimmered in the light, forming towering walls that reached a height of around ten metres.

"What in the world is this place?" Evie asked, feeling the polished brick with her hands. "It reminds me of the old temples in Savannah."

"So, you are familiar with this place?" I asked her.

"Not exactly. I just see resemblances."

"So you have glorious temples like this in Savannah?" Nilah asked, dreamy visions of exciting journeys visible in her eyes. I couldn't help but smile at her innocent excitement.

"Sort of," Evie said, smiling.

Columns separated the vast rooms, and we followed along the velvet lit torches, as they showed us the way. Between each room stood a pair of two metre tall statues of humanoids resembling the columns at the temple's entrance. These creatures wore golden armour and held perfectly sharp, shining spears.

"They're not looking at us, are they?" Nilah asked, as we passed by another pair of guards.

We paused our advance and looked at them closely. Shadows hid their eyes.

"Hard to tell. I hope not," I said and stepped further.

After passing the next pair of guards, the room was more expanse than the rest and instead of flat pavements; the room had bright pink crystal stairs leading down to an enormous gate at least eight metres tall and wide.

"Can you feel it?" Evie asked.

"Yeah. It's here," Nilah said.

"I feel it, too. If you're low on mana, better drink up now," I said, looking at Nilah.

Ready as we were, I pronounced the words again, "Anubi, rest in Eterna."

The hundreds of carved images of dog-headed humanoids interacting with each other swirled in an odd shape, reminiscent of a story-telling device. They shaped a circle in the middle, which glowed in its outline. With a final diametre of about three metres, the mechanism split the door in half, and each side retracted within the side walls.

A vast expanse stretched out before us, its floor resembling a starry night sky, embellished with shimmering golden circles. The ceiling was out of eye-reach, golden columns spiralling ever higher. But my eyes couldn't waste a moment more on that. They held onto the object that stood directly across from me, perched precariously on the edge, right next to the wall. Stairs lead to a hovering violet crystal, electrical bolts dancing across its surface. It wasn't just beautiful. It pulled me in with an ethereal allure that was impossible to resist.

I strode towards it, eyes forever sunk into its beauty.

"Sova, wait! Don't go there," Evie said.

"Sovie, it could be a trap. Let's look around!"

With each step, I could feel the irresistible force drawing me further into the depths of the unknown, my heart pounding in sync. It was finally within my grasp. As I touched the crystal, I marvelled at its size, just big enough for my fingers to encircle.

With a loud thud, I was sent flying across the room, landing at the entrance. A constant throb in my back sent painful shivers through my entire body. I opened my eyes to a comforting sensation easing the pain.

"Level Three Illumination Magic, Light's Embrace," Evie said three times in a row.

I hopped back to my feet, numbers emanating out of me. *It's her healing magic.*

A sheer pulse of power blew around Nilah, pushing her blond hair out of her face. The arcane rune on her wrist glowed underneath the black uniform, her hand extending forward as a black bow took shape. With precise fingers, she pulled a thunderous arrow all the way behind her shoulder and said, "Level Three Black Magic Sorcery, Black Arrow."

The thunder cracked through the air, echoing with a compelling boom as it struck its target. A pitch-black shadow cloaked in darkness. Magical rings on its fingers and bracelets adorned with runes were the only way to depict its humanoid features.

This isn't a doglike humanoid, this is something else!

The arrow, upon collision, dispersed around it, following down a phase barrier which was, until now, unseen. Evie summoned forth her weapon and took a battle stance next to me. I cast the same spell as my sister and dashed to the side, securing a safe distance to avoid friendly fire.

"Nilah, don't cancel out the spell. If you need to take a mana potion, do it. Let's give it oppression from all sides," I said. "Make an opening for Evie!"

Black thunder cracked through the air, crashing into our enemy's barrier. Whereas Evie's glowing slashes, the creature moved to avoid.

"Alright, we can keep this until it gives in! It's three against one," I yelled, setting off another arrow.

From the other side of our enemy, a piercing scream resounded, and a moment later, something slammed me into the wall.

Evie's spell kept healing me, so I didn't break too much, but to see my sister bashed into the other wall sent a shiver down my spine. A three-metre tall doglike statue stood with its spear raised to deliver the decisive strike.

"Nilah!" I screamed out. Evie dashed lightning fast to parry the statue's attack. Light walls erupted from her sword and she pushed the creature back. I rolled to the side, avoiding an earth-shattering attack from another doglike statue.

"You disrupt the Anubi's rest," the statue spoke in a deep, resonating voice. "Now you pay with your life."

Among the Archives

"Only in darkness can a couple seal their souls into a permanent bond. When the shadows consume the newlyweds, the wisdom of love flows through them, invoking Nocturna's blessing. No couple could find true love without it. The choir will lead the chant of a spell of fortitude. All the attendants and witnesses would charge an ash pyramid with power. The celebration's main event is to imbue the pyramid with enough magic to help the couple start on their new journey together."

- "Ancient Scroll: Cultures and Rituals," by unknown.

CHAPTER 12
THE VOID CRYSTAL

I SPRINTED TOWARDS THE STATUE, the thunderous crash of its spear striking the ground beside me. My heart pounded as a sweeping attack aimed for my legs, but I managed to leap just in time, narrowly avoiding it. I tapped into my mana reserves, feeling the energy surge through me, and pointed my hand at the creature.

"Level Three Fire Elemental Sorcery, Spark of Flame," I said, a wave of flame engulfing the creature away from my vision. I couldn't see anyway, so I turned around to check on how Evie and Nilah were doing. Before I saw anything, I crouched as a swing towards my head almost finished me.

"Formidable indeed, yet as Anubi, we remain unphased," the doglike creature said.

"The Anubi? To hell with you!" I yelled.

A light flashed as Evie's Lightforged Sword went across The Anubi's chest, followed by a swing from the other Anubi that was thrusting at her, but thanks to her calculated manoeuvring, it crashed its spear in the chest of its brother.

"Curse the humans," the attacking Anubi said, while the other one shattered.

"Sova, I'll take the statue from here. I can't damage that spectre!" Evie said and pointed at the hovering creature, holding the violet crystal in its shadow-massed palm, as it chased Nilah. "Help Nillie!"

"Brother, I..." Nilah spoke as she readied a black arrow, blood streaming down her shoulder. "I'll take it down."

The arrow reflected off the spectre's barrier, crackling around it. I extended my hand and took a shooting stance, forming a black bow and arrow as well. Our combined attacks against the spectre only seemed to confuse it which one of us it should chase first. Was it sentient at all?

At one point, it vanished, our arrows colliding into each other and sending a resonating crackle throughout the room.

I cancelled the spell and dashed to see her. "Nillie, how bad is it?"

She looked at her shoulder, face contorting with pain. "It'll be ok. We'll deal with it later."

A sound much similar to a detonation took my attention, as the spectre materialised once more.

"Wait, I thought we beat it?" I asked, drawing on my Black Arrow spell.

"It just phased out," Nilah recognised and sipped another mana potion. She shivered as she extended her arm, but the black bow appeared and dispersed. "It's not working!"

"What do you mean, Nilah? Focus!"

"Mana isn't reaching the equation! I can't cast the spell!"

"Try again!" I said, pushing her to the side, avoiding a sweep of the spectre's claw-like rings. *At least it's slow.*

I looked at Nilah's palm and noticed the equation for the spell was there, but mana wasn't reaching it.

What's going on? I noticed the faint equations emanating from the spectre. *I see it! And the whole area! It's been leaking equations all this time! Whatever it really does, it seems that it's impacting spell casting.*

We dodged three more claw sweeps, and I concluded Nilah would cast nothing anymore. Was it because of panic, due to depleted mana, or just fatigue? It was too dangerous to perform Black Magic when one cannot cast it even once.

"Nilah, just stay safe. Don't push yourself to attack," I said. "Don't use Black Magic!"

I shot a few arrows at the spectre and ran, pulling its attention to me. It willingly chased, which pulled a smirk out of me. "Evie, I'm coming to you. I'll need you to cover for me!"

Evie grabbed the point of her blade and slammed her sword's handle on the ground, multiple barriers appearing one after another above her.

"Level Three Illumination Magic, Pillars of Truth," she announced, and two columns of light emerged behind her Anubi opponent. It raised its spear high above its head and swung at her. Bright chains of light emerged from the pillars, forcefully pulling its limbs apart. It struggled, trying to pull free, and as it did, Evie screamed, pouring all her strength to enhance the spell. "Overcharge!"

I couldn't decipher them, but dozens of equations flew across the air, chains following them and gripping onto the Anubi's body. The barriers above Evie's head dispersed, and she turned to face me, sweat pouring down her forehead. She panted, her breath visible to me.

"Can you cover me?"

Evie responded with a nod, her eyes scouting around.

Nilah walked close to the room's wall, successfully remaining un-targeted.

My shadow folded towards my body, creeping from my feet up. "Self-exiled into darkness, your wisdom holds true. Moonlit ravens gather your soul. Bathed in shadows, with your power, we unite."

Evie swung her sword at the spectre, and the flashes of light went through it, like it wasn't even there. Despite that, it relentlessly targeted her with its attacks, but witnessing her nimble movements, I couldn't help but feel a sense of security. She was so athletic. Her fighting style was not only effective and deadly but also exuded a mesmerising beauty. Her coat swished and rustled with each swift movement as she rolled, dashed, jumped, back flipped, and slashed with the power of The Light.

"From the palm of my hand, may your rage be true. In the dark I pledge myself to eradicate the light," I finished the chant and gazed upon the crescent menacingly spinning before my palm. It's devastating power distorted the surrounding air. The Anubi shook the ground, an otherworldly scream raging our eardrums, as it broke the chains. It dashed towards me, forcing me to redirect my spell to it. "Rend the ethereal! Level Four Black Magic Sorcery, Nocturna's Crescent!"

With the spell unleashed, my eyes flew open in disbelief, and a deep sense of dread consumed me. In a split second, Evie's dodge brought her right between me and the Anubi, right as the spell left my hand.

Light.

There was only light. I couldn't see anything.

I slapped my ears, but couldn't hear. As the light faded, my surroundings became dimmer, and I could finally see again, with Evie's voice breaking the silence. "Level Five Illumination Magic, Pillar of Light!"

I stood in awe as her black hair floated with an electrifying energy, while she remained in the midst of a radiant pillar of light, reaching her hand towards the sky. The light moved like a fierce flame, propelling itself heavenly upwards. Neither the spectre nor the Anubi could move.

The light contorted as black lightning struck around it. My jaw dropped. *Nocturna's Crescent is inside!*

As if the pillar was lightweight as a toy sword, Evie swung down, the ray of Illumination and Black Magic crashing on our enemies. Silence followed as darkness and light devoured our foes in an ultimate explosion of magic.

Evie remained motionless, her Lightforged Sword transforming into a shimmering cloud of Light Dust. In a subtle gesture, she shifted to the side, casting a quick glance in my direction, her smile warm and inviting.

I rushed to her as she fell on one knee.

"Evie, are you okay!? Did you get hit!?"

"I'm just a little tired. Mana's almost gone," she spoke in a tired voice, yet her smile didn't fade. I grabbed her in my hands and she relaxed her head against my chest.

Nilah kneeled next to us. "Evie, take this."

A mana potion was definitely a solution, but why didn't Evie drink one herself? Evie accepted it with a nod and drank.

"Did I hear that right, Evie? That was a Level Five!?" I shook my head, my voice in awe.

"Can't let you be the only one with surprises, can I?" Evie chuckled, and then sipped from the mana potion. "It's not just the mana. I might need to have some rest after this one."

Evie gently let go of me and sat on the ground. Nilah

went around her so she could provide a soft support to Evie's back.

My eyes fell victim to a floating object in the air where the spectre used to be. The violet crystal shook as if it was about to burst. It glowed stronger than before and it called upon me. Captivated beyond reason, without a will to deny, I obeyed its summoning. Evie rested on Nilah's chest and I took confident steps towards the mysterious crystal.

"Sova?" the girls asked, but I couldn't bother with answering.

I grabbed the crystal as it fit accurately into my palm. The smooth surface of it seemed to vibrate with an electric energy, leaving me with an unfamiliar yet strangely nostalgic feeling. I immersed myself in the bliss of encountering its ethereal power emanating from the periwinkle walls. A moment later, it crumbled into the tiniest particles, yet none of them fell out of my reach. Each particle sunk deep inside my skin. The scar across my back itched, yet the violet energy coursing through my body seemed to tame that hindrance.

The mesmerising violet captivation held onto me, its fragrance enveloping my senses until it finally released its grip. I turned to see the girls. Nilah cradled Evie as her blond hair mixed with Evie's black. My sister's closed eyes and unnaturally pale skin filled me with a sense of dread. Blood had stained her uniform's sleeve and seeped into her torso, leaving a gruesome mark. My heart throbbed, and I swallowed with effort. *What have I been doing with this happening right next to me!?*

"Evie, are you awake?" I shook her arm softly, kneeling next to them. "We need to heal Nilah! I think she's lost too much blood!"

Evie raised her head to meet my eyes. "Use the teleportation crystal from Master Lethalica."

"There's no time for that, Evie!"

"I can't cast any spells..." she said, her voice weak. "That Level Five took the best of me."

I shook my head, the teleportation crystal already in my hand. *It's too risky. Teleportation without a person willingly committing to it is dangerous... and she's not even conscious!*

"Can you please try? Don't execute the spell, just start it up. Please!" I begged Evie, holding her hands.

"Please."

She nodded softly, and I moved Nilah to lie on her back. Evie kneeled on her left arm's side, and I was on her right. I gazed at Evie, studying every single movement she made. And there it was. The equation which formed the healing spell appeared with a faint glow as Evie tried to cast the spell.

I copied her arms' movement and looked at the equation, trying to replicate it. Then I saw the opening brackets into which I figured were where the volume of mana was supposed to go.

"To cast it, you just conclude the equation after the volume, right?" I asked.

"Yes. This is Level Three Illumination Magic, Light's Embrace," Evie said and her equation dispersed, the magic cancelling itself out.

I suppose that's the backlash of the Level Five she cast. Evie really can't cast a spell right now. But... I can.

"Level Three Illumination Magic, Light's Embrace." I said and forced as much mana as I could as long as I felt the spell was stable. Nilah's body glowed in a faint light as the spell's divine healing engulfed her. Unaware if there were any other wounds besides her shoulder, I slammed a wave of healing across each part of her body.

"Sova...?" Evie observed, awestruck, as the light shined, outlining her feminine lines.

My eyes met hers and I knew I had no answer to the question she had.

Without a sign of how much time had passed, the fatigue in my posture meant I kept the spell going for a long time. Evie advised me to take a break, but I couldn't. Not until my sister opened her blue eyes and smiled at me.

At last, she did.

"Sovie? Thanks," Nilah said, as she raised herself into a sitting position. "I feel like I've basked in the sun."

"And in a way, you have. Perhaps something better even," Evie said.

Nilah opened her arms and hugged Evie. "I'm happy you're okay."

"Now we can finally go," I said and picked up the teleportation stone in my hand. "Place a hand on me, girls."

They did, and I thought of Mathsmagica Academy and Master Lethalica playfully petting the dakes. I closed my eyes and in a moment; I inhaled warmer air and the ambience of the city resounded in the distance.

"We made it!"

"And where... are the dakes?" Master Lethalica's voice reached my ears.

Among the Archives

"Whatever I could transcribe would speak of a great conflict that struck the danger of dividing people. The so called 'Dragon Hunters' rebelled against Sovah's decisions. What exactly they rebelled against, I couldn't tell. Yet, I find why conspiracies easily tap into this to fuel their arguments. Sovah's assassination probably was their doing. Unlike the official statements. To speak of it, the grand burial of Sovah The Legendary Mage was perhaps with an empty coffin. Or was it a doppelgänger?"

- "World's Conspiracies" by Henk Bink.

CHAPTER 13
TAPESTRY

Master Lethalica locked eyes into mine, a cold, unforgiving glare.

"Forget the dakes! Evie needs help!" I pointed at Evie. She stood with a weakened posture. You could easily see that she had given everything she had to walk.

"We left the dakes at a safe place, but we couldn't go back to them," Nilah said.

As Master Lethalica looked at the sky, I could have sworn I saw numbers shooting out of her eyes at lightning speed. *She cast some kind of spell to see the dakes or what?* She sighed and walked over to Evie's side. With a condescending look at her, she asked, "Nilah, can you aid Evie to the healer's quarter?"

With a nod, my sister agreed to it, and as I was about to speak, Master Lethalica glanced at me with her yellow cat-like pupils.

"Come with me, Sova." She commanded and then, in a soft tone, added. "You need to report."

I followed her as we walked through the academy's

floors. The columns supporting the ceiling were adorned with enchanting runes that emitted a vibrant hum. The halls were filled with the faint reverberation of lectors' voices, teaching the secrets of magic.

Are we going to the director's office? It wouldn't surprise me if she knew where it was, as apparently only a handful of people do. Perhaps I should let her know that I'm not among them and I use a teleportation crystal to get there?

"Master Lethalica, excuse me," I said, stopping in place. She turned around and looked at me. Her height almost matched mine, but something about her person made me feel a lot smaller. "I usually teleport to Director Astron's office."

"He didn't show you the way?"

"No," I picked the teleportation stone from my pocket. "He said I should always use this."

"That's alright. It would have taken us a bit of time to reach it, but if you have that, then you can use it."

"Should I do it now?"

"Go ahead, I'll follow."

I gripped onto the stone and imagined the Director's office. His full of magical items desk self-employing themselves to use, and the mana nexus seen from outside the window.

"I think he's busy. It won't let me teleport," I said, taking a look around.

"There is a meeting with The Pillars today. Perhaps it already started," Master Lethalica strode past me, waving a hand in a follow me motion. "Let's go to my classroom and you can report in detail."

"About the dakes," I started as we walked. "We left them next to a waterfall to which–"

"Not in the halls, Sova. And don't worry about the dakes."

In silence, we entered the room I felt all so familiar with now. The faint smell of ozone filled the air, and my mindset recalled the memories of elemental magic blooming within these walls. After one of the private lessons, Master Lethalica had told me she designed the classroom herself, which is why it was so flexible in changing its shape. Her elemental magic was on such a high level that in seconds she could make it look like a completely empty flat hall with four walls, and in another few, make it look like a typical classroom you'd sit and take notes in.

"Okay, Sova," she sat at a table on the first roll. "Tell me what happened."

"Well," I sat on the chair next to her and spoke. "We started by saving the village."

After going through the story, Master Lethalica didn't seem surprised by any part of the story. But, I suppose, that was to be expected. *A Master Mage of her ability probably has experienced these kinds of things tenfold, if not a hundred.* I saved out the information that Evie cast a Level Five spell. It would have explained why she was in a poor condition, but I had an intuitive call out that Evie wanted to hide how capable she really was.

"So you touched the crystal, and it sank into your skin?" Master Lethalica asked, standing up and grabbing my right hand. "Do you feel anything different?"

The itching in my back's scar came to mind, but I found it shameful to mention.

"I was like a prisoner in that moment. Like... as if I had no will of my own. Like I was a spectator. Condemned to holding onto that crystal."

Her long red nails reached my chin, and she pulled my

head up. The yellow pupils contrasted with her red hair as she leaned closer to me.

"Master Lethalica?" I asked as at a slow pace she kept leaning towards me, her eyes not even blinking as she gazed into mine.

"Tell me, Sova," she softly spoke. "Do you feel something different in your mana reserves?"

Almost certain I had sweat burst down my back as her seductive presence was as intense as the situation was confusing and weird.

"What—"

"Sova, close your eyes," she said.

God damn it. Controlling my breathing seems to be the hardest thing to do in this world. Why should I close my eyes? Why is she so close?

In a moment, everything felt calm and a chilly breeze whooshed over me. Her voice resonated otherworldly, "Now focus. Look around you. What do you see?"

My eyes closed, I pictured myself in a black hall of emptiness where only her voice still resonated.

"Nothing. It's just me in an empty dark hall."

"No, Sova. Look, but not with the eyes."

I'm already with closed eyes, aren't I?

"Let mana flow out of your skin's pores," she instructed. "Disperse it around you. Paint the hall with it."

I imagined my mana going out of my pores in the colour of blue, taking mana potions for reference. Slowly, I could see numbers turning into tiny strings. They changed their colour from blue to purple as they shaped an undiscernable shape before me.

"What do you see now?"

"I am unsure what it is. But it looks incomplete. I can feel it like a tiny fraction of what it's supposed to be."

"Keep painting. Just *let it be*," she said. Reason told me this made no sense, but somehow, I knew exactly what to do.

A mist of blue colour dispersed from me, and it traversed the surrounding space, glowing in all colours. As the colourful mist sank into the darkness, it left me mesmerised. My jaw dropped. A large chandelier hovered above, blue flames dancing atop candles. The huge bricks in the walls made place for the astonishing sculptures of knights holding swords, edges broken in the middle of their length. The longer I looked at my surroundings, the more I could see, but my vision blurred. Only what manifested before me had a clear outline and intricate detail.

"What do you see, Sova?" Master Lethalica's voice resonated.

After a slight pause, I found words to speak it. "A... tapestry."

"Can you describe it?"

"The more I look at it, the more it changes," I said as the tapestry shifted. "I don't know how I can tell it's a tapestry, but somehow I do. Yet what I see defies that."

"Keep going. Tell me more."

"There seems to be an image. No, perhaps, more than one image. But I can't tell it, as there are flames burning it, then a water vortex swirling through it, and then other things that move and shiver. I can't really find words to describe it well enough. It's like a book that keeps turning its pages, and each page is either fire, or water, or an earthquake? And... other things... I guess?"

"Good, Sova. Now focus on this task. Tell me the colours that you recognise, even faintly."

"Black. The outlines are shifting in a black colour, and it's also adding shadows and depth."

"It is the most defined colour?"

"I think so, yes."

"Okay, continue."

"I see red. Yellow, white, blue. There are others, but it's hard to recognise exactly. After the black outlines go through the tapestry, I see it flash in a violet colour."

"Violet? Can you associate the colour with something?"

"Yes. I think it's the same colour as that crystal I told you about."

"Look around you again, Sova. Do you see something else?"

I did as asked, but everything was blurry. It made me feel sick.

"There used to be a knight with a broken sword, but everything aside from the tapestry is too blurry for me to discern."

Suddenly, I opened my eyes and shivered. Master Lethalica's yellow pupils gazing at me from a little over a breath away. I swallowed hard as she let my chin go and slowly leaned back, drawing a distance between us.

"What was that?" I asked, panting, her chilly breath lingering on my nose and mouth.

"In this world, there are three fundamental truths. Life, Death, and Magic to rule them all."

I looked at my hands, feeling the mana that had poured out of my pores in the air.

"What you saw is something only a certain few others remain capable of witnessing."

"But what did I see, really?"

Master Lethalica didn't respond to my question. She paused for a while and smiled. "Life is to bring progress. Death is to complete it. While Magic is to see the truth."

I shook my head in confusion.

"See not with the eyes, but with magic, Sova. In that Tapestry, you will find all truths."

With a nod, I tried to let this knowledge and wisdom sink in. Mesmerised by all the events, I stood in silence.

"I think you should go have some rest. Director Astron will know of your successful mission today. Surely he will announce the astonishing ability of the Harmony Enforcers tomorrow. Prepare yourself for that," she said, striding towards the door.

I followed her and went out first.

"You have done well, Sova," she said in a soft voice, a smile forming on her youthful, yet somehow mature, face.

I smiled back and bowed my head. "Thank you, Master Lethalica."

AMONG THE ARCHIVES

"Shall you let magic be one with you, it will flow. Listen to me, humans. Your life perishes faster than the trees reach true maturity, yet within that short span, your potential for growth is exponential. At one point, you will feel 'the click'. It will let you tap into your inner self and reach The Tapestry of Shadows. Once you reach it, your potential shall truly unfold."

- "Ancient scroll: Heraciel's Teachings," by Just a Mage.

MATHSMAGICA

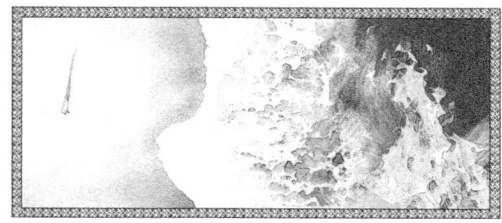

CHAPTER 14
RAID

"Dive deeper into the essence of magic. Why is it Mathsmagica if we can't put the maths down to the magic? A real mage should always spiral endlessly into the depths of the equations to reach–" The professor spoke, but bells rang, interrupting. After the chiming melody ended, we stood silently in wait for the announcement.

"By order of Director Astron, The Harmony Enforcers will join today's raid. Sova Ren, Nilah Ren, and Evie Stratovic are to respond to their summoning immediately."

Raid? What is this?

The message repeated twice. I looked at Nilah and nodded towards the door. My chair scrubbed against the ground as I stood up.

"Curses. Lectures are becoming more and more chaotic since they formed this group. You're free to go, Enforcers." The professor said with a sigh.

"Thank you, and we apologise, professor," I said, walking between the rows of desks.

"A raid? These guys? For real?"

"Aren't raids for graduates?"

"At least we'll be seeing them no more."

The students exchanged whispers as we went past them. The door shut behind me and Nilah followed on our way down the stairs to the Summoning Hall. On our very first day at the academy, we were told where you should go in case you get summoned. Another floor down. We saw Evie rushing across the hall. Exchanging a quick wave we continued together.

Amidst a few other rooms around, we saw the one with sculptures of knights standing guard. *That's the Summoning Hall!* The door itself was big enough for all three of us to pass through. I grabbed the handle, and it opened automatically, splitting in the middle and retracting itself within the walls. The familiar face of Director Astron stood in wait next to a large desk fitted on the wall. Countless scrolls lay on it in an arranged order. To the side, shelves packed with an assortment of magical items.

"Sova, Nilah, Evie. I'm glad you came so fast," Director Astron said.

We walked onto the inviting red carpet, which led into the centre of the room, as the door behind us sealed itself shut. Evie walked next to me, and a smile naturally formed on my lips. The delightful aroma of her perfume filled my senses as I inhaled.

"As usual, my time is rather scarce, but I hold you three in high praise, hence a personal interaction seemed most appropriate."

"Nice to see you, Director Astron," Evie said, bowing her head in respect. We followed her example, doing the same.

"The Pillars seemed most pleased with the result of your last assignment. They asked me if I'm willing to let you fill in missing members on raids. I didn't expect this to be as soon as today," Director Astron spoke and his tone suddenly went grim. "But two of our raiders have gone missing. They were best suited for this kind of case as well, but it's indeed unfortunate."

"What happened to them?" I asked.

After a brief pause, his eyes met mine and, with noticeable grief in his voice, he said, "Nobody knows. They were a couple. But just last night, they both disappeared."

"Director Astron, I'm sorry if it's confidential, but can I know the names of the missing raiders?"

"It's Velarian and Roselia."

"Do you know them?" I asked Evie as she put her hand before her mouth. With a subtle nod, she confirmed.

"They are from the few necrotic mages who reached Knight Rank. At any rate. From these shelves you can get all the items you'd need. If something is missing, you have a short while before the other two come for the general briefing of the raid."

"It's going to be just five of us? I imagined raids would be of many people," I said, looking at Nilah and Evie, as if they would know.

"Sova," Evie chuckled. I frowned at her, yet her sweet laugh forced a smile out of me.

"What?"

"We're mages, not footmen!" Evie said.

"Well, Evie is correct about that. The raid shouldn't need fifty people. Based on the magical energy, The High Arcanists measured the three of you and the other two should be enough." Director Astron laughed.

"For being the genius brother you are, Sovie, I thought you'd figure that out." Nilah laughed.

"You too, Nillie? Seriously?"

The door behind us opened again.

"Bureaus! Henrith! You're here just in time."

"Director Astron!" The taller one startled, bowing his head. "The Flow goes through you!"

The other one bowed his bald head and greeted.

"Today your team will comprise five, instead of typical four. As you know, Velarian and Roselia are missing. But despite all three of them being first-years, I assure you, they will not hold you back."

"I am Bureaus Hickey. I have an affinity for fire and water. Nice to meet you, Enforcers," the bald young man said. Dressed in a black robe, left sleeve blue, right sleeve red. His neatly trimmed beard was a notable feature, but what truly caught attention were his green left eye and blue right eye. That. And he was as short as Evie.

"I'm Henrith of the Moor family. My affinity is, as you probably guessed by now, Flow Magic. Let's watch our backs," he said, smiling. Matching my height, Henrith wore a sapphire martial arts robe. He had shaved his hair on the sides and tied the rest in a ponytail at the back of his head.

They shook hands with the girls first, of course. We spoke our names, but only Evie said her affinity.

"While it is essential that raid members all know each other's affinities, I will say that Sova and Nilah's are Black Magic... and something else," Director Astron spoke.

The guys frowned at him. "Something else?" Henrith asked.

"Well, now, let's just say you'll see when you do."

"This feels a little dodgy, Henrith," Bureaus said.

"Do not doubt Master Director Astron. His wisdom is unparalleled. If he states we are to see them as our comrades, we should," Henrith spoke, yet I noticed him gazing at us with caution. "Enforcers, let us perform this raid and come back home safely."

We nodded in agreement.

"So where is The Briefer? Is he late again?" Bureaus asked.

"Today, that would be me, Bureaus," Director Astron said. Bureaus immediately apologised.

"There is an outbreak of undead in Domainia. Across The Plainlands, a village got entirely shifted into undead. We believe it is a minor cult of *necrotics* that went out of control."

"Hailing Revenants, huh? Would've been really nice to have Velarian and Roselia with us on this one..." Bureaus sighed.

"Indeed," Director Astron confirmed. "The portal gate will lead you straight to the mage tower at the hill out of the village. The High Arcanist on the case reported the undead are alive only at night, and that no magic energy was active during the day."

"Yeah, Hailing Revenants for sure. Damn." Henrith cursed, gritting his teeth.

"Do not be that worried, Henrith. The Harmony Enforcers already have defeated Hailing Revenants before," Director Astron smirked.

"They have?" Bureaus' mouth went agape as he stared at us. "The Light must be strong with you, Evie."

"It wasn't me, though." Evie chuckled.

"What?! Then who?"

"It was me," I said, raising a hand.

Henrith and Bureaus both froze, their eyes on me.

"Well, that's a little more reassuring. It seems the rumours about you guys might be false, after all," Henrith smiled.

I would like to hear more about that, for sure.

"Alright, refill your dimensional rings—" Director Astron

trailed off, looking at the two guys who had simple pouches on their belts. "I mean your inventories. Refresh your inventories and be on your way! This room is packed with most items you could need for a raid, so go for it."

The door we came through swung open, revealing a mesmerising blue portal instead of the familiar academy hall. Bureaus and Henrith handpicked mana potions and an assortment of scrolls, while we opted for a few potions and the teleportation stones, to be used in dire situations.

Director Astron waved a hand in our direction. Evie, Nilah, and I quickly converged around him. He put a palm on my shoulder and spoke, "My dear Harmony Enforcers, execute this raid with no holding back. What you do today will make history for all of Mathsmagica to learn. Let them know. Show them who you are. Carve your name in history. Carve by magic."

"Director Astron, I appreciate your faith in us, but I heard only graduates go to raids. We are just first years," Nilah whispered.

"And you are better than all the rest. They just don't believe it yet. But I do. I believe in you," he said with a deep, fatherly voice. "Now go. Free the people of their non-permanent death!"

Henrith and Bureaus stood beside me, their expressions determined, as we exchanged a knowing nod before stepping into the swirling blue portal.

Rays of light pierced the clouds, shedding light upon the ghost village. With plenty of time before nightfall, we thoroughly explored the mage tower, ensuring it would provide a secure sanctuary. My eyes traced through each brick in the tower, yet no lingering spells or traps were evident, aside from whatever medium helped the arcanist connect to it at the top. The more I explored through it, the more I noticed the rough texture of the stone bricks, adding to the impression of a normally built tower. Along the staircase and small rooms of the building, there was an absence of both corpses and living beings. Henrith and Bureaus shared their experience, explaining why securing the mage tower was important for each raid. Apparently, some raids could take days, and the barriers each mage tower can put up could keep the raiders safe against the majority of threats.

For hours, Henrith meditated, floating on the tower's balcony, while Bureaus read a book regarding Domainia's history. Only then did it come to mind, Bureaus' birthplace was this country. And we would practically cleanse a village he might have been to before. Perhaps even people he knew? I didn't dare ask.

I had the pleasure of speaking with Evie and Nilah, exchanging jokes and just gossiping, while sitting atop the tower's roof. Evie's perfume wafted towards me on a gentle breeze, making the wait even more enjoyable.

Bureaus climbed to join us as the sun had almost hid beneath the horizon. "It is time, Enforcers. Within minutes, the undead will come to life."

We slid into the tower, and Henrith levitated back to the ground. I could see numbers shifting across his body, which I guessed to the others appeared as an aura around him. I felt it, though. Power.

With Bureaus in the front, we descended the hill and into the village. Dark clouds marched into the sky, casting an ominous shadow that hastened the arrival of night. A mist covered our feet and a rotten smell lingered in the air. The buildings' bricks were covered in a slimy, green mucus, and it emitted a visible miasma seen from a distance. Glancing over my shoulder, I saw that the mist had completely shrouded the landscape behind us. No sign of the mage tower or the hill.

"For this to work, I will just use brute physical force. I am unable to permanently put them down, but I will protect you from close-ranged harm if you're casting any spells," Henrith said.

"Something similar here. I can conjure flames strong enough to melt the bones, but that would take a little too much out of me and we don't even know how many and what we're going to end up facing." Bureaus looked at us over his shoulder.

"So that means we extinguish them by The Light, or by annihilating their souls with Black Magic," I said.

"In imbalance of nature, I bend thee to my will. Protect the crop for life begins. May you hear this plea, for I shall preserve by annihilation! Level Four Elemental Fire Magic, Flame Tsunami!" Bureaus flicked his finger, a spark emitting from it and in the next moment, it exploded forward into a fierce flame, sweeping through the village's streets. The flames passed through all the windows and doors, like a controlled tsunami of fire. "Alright, better to lure them out rather than get ambushed."

Growls and screams of the dead pierced the air just as the flame's wrath vanished. Out of each house, several zombies, their flesh burning, jumped out and rushed at us.

"Bureaus, can you keep a wall of flame before us to protect us?" I asked and looked at Nilah. "Let's use range for start!"

I extended my hand forward and spoke, "Level Three Black Magic Sorcery, Black Arrow!"

Black Thunder jumped into my palm, shaping a bow, and I launched arrow after arrow, each vanquishing several zombies at once. Nilah did the same.

"We can push in. Let's advance forward! Keep the wall up, in case any try to get through," I said, and Bureaus did as asked.

The air crackled as our arrows fell our opponents. I shook my palm, dispersing the bow, as I saw no more undead coming at us.

"So that's that. Easier than I expected, honestly." Bureaus laughed.

"I didn't even get to punch anything. So much for the preparation," Henrith shrugged.

Evie and Nilah looked at me as I gazed at the one building to the side. I could see numbers and equations flowing out of it.

"We're not done yet, guys. I can sense something from that building." I pointed at an ordinary house. *Saying I sense something would be more understandable than telling them I can see numbers and magical equations, right?*

"Are you sure?" Henrith asked, shaking his head.

Bureaus shuffled toward the house. As he reached for the door handle, Henrith approached him and placed a hand over his chest. "Bureaus, in close quarter, it's better if I go in first."

They exchanged nods, and Henrith opened the door. "That's strange. Why is this door intact?" Bureaus wondered. "It's supposedly made of wood. Why didn't my flames burn it down?"

"Keep your guard up," Evie said as her Lightforged Sword emerged out of Light Dust. "There must have been a magic barrier protecting it."

The living room, which appeared deceptively small from the outside, now stretched out before us in an impressively large space. The wooden table, in the middle of the room, stretched for at least a couple of metres in length and was half as wide. On each long side, a glass of crimson red liquid caught the light. Heart-shaped candlesticks, each with its own unique design, lined up from left to right, creating an unconventional gothic romantic ambiance. The candles flickered in an ash-coloured flame, and an aroma of cinnamon filled the room. The two chairs had vibrant red pillows with a fluffy texture, attached to their intricately carved wooden frames.

"What is this? Did we ruin someone's romantic dinner?" I laughed.

Bureaus and Henrith exchanged worried gazes. "I don't like the look of this."

I walked forward, circling around the table. I picked up one glass, and the ground shook. Startled by a deep rumbling, I pivoted and watched as a wall descended into the ground.

"Let's say you planned that," Bureaus smirked at me.

Stepping into the room, we were met with an eerie silence and a distinct lack of furniture or decoration. When I reached the middle of the area, the floor felt unstable beneath my feet, and I noticed my right foot sink a few centimetres into the surface. Runes illuminated the room, casting a blue hue on the brick walls. We stood back-to-back, suspecting an attack. The equations formed around us seemed familiar to me. *Evie's prepared protective barriers, I guess.*

The floor moved down, serving us like an elevator. Surrounded by darkness, we couldn't see anything besides the blue hue of the runes powering the lift.

"I just hope it'll take us back up later," Henrith said.

"What, you can't jump that high? Come on," Bureaus joked.

"Never tried jumping a hundred metres, to be honest,

but maybe if you put your robes above your head, and light a small flame, you'd become an air balloon, you moron," Henrith said.

We all laughed. But the lift slowed down, landing us before an open gate before us. We stepped forward, Henrith taking the lead. He came to a halt, briefly exploring the gate's material with his fingertips.

"What's wrong?" Nilah asked.

"I'm sorry, it's just..." Henrith said and pushed the gate open.

We all went out and lined up next to each other. The rocky walls of whatever cave we ended up in went all the way into complete darkness above. But what was at eye-level was more than daunting. The path ahead was paved, but its once smooth surface was now marred by patches of mould. It guided our gaze at buildings that boasted the most stunning and detailed designs, reminiscent of the illustrations I had only encountered in books about Algama.

"Bastards," Bureaus raged. "They dare replicate their country's wicked architecture in my homeland! I'll burn it all!"

"Bureaus, wait!" Henrith jumped before the short Shaper. "We don't know what you'll force out of hiding like that."

"But this is heresy!"

"Henrith is right," I said, walking forward, the girls following me. "I don't think we'll find mere zombies here."

"You're just a Shadow Covenant, aren't you!? What would you know, huh!?" Bureaus lit a fireball in his hand.

"Bureaus, don't do this!" Henrith stood in front of his friend, but got pushed aside.

I looked at the mathematical equation of the fireball in

his hand and copied it. Extending my hand slightly to the side, I opened my palm and poured mana, closing the bracket, a fireball rippling the air as it appeared in my hand.

"What would you know?" I asked him back.

Both Bureaus and Henrith stood like incapacitated, the fireball in his hand extinguishing. "But you... How can you make a fireball spell?"

"If you plan to turn your back on us, better let me know now. I'd rather get this over with before anyone's life is at risk to an enemy we don't even know yet," I said, cancelling the fireball spell.

Nilah shook her head in disappointment and walked on. Evie followed her, and shortly after, I joined them.

Among the Archives

"It is not mandatory to speak the spell's name. Yet, it is just another way for the caster to keep his mind focused on it. After all, control is the most important thing when it comes to magic."

> *- Excerpt from "Fundamentals of Magic: For Class 1"*

MATHSMAGICA

CHAPTER 15
RITUAL OF LOVE

THE BLOODY RIVER TWISTED AS ITS BED TRACED CLOSE TO THE PAVEMENT WE STEPPED ON.

Few metre long trees had their glowing leaves floating closely to their branches, and now and then some would fall, gently striding atop the river current. Columns with intricately detailed figures of faces carved into them held onto the massive building before us. As we crossed the wooden bridge, we caught glimpses of the river through the gaps between the logs that formed its structure. Once we went across, stairs curved gently to the right, leading us to a grand gate.

"Sovie," Nilah gently pulled my sleeve. I looked at her and recognised what she meant.

"It'll be alright. Don't worry," I said, patting her head. *I know you're worried about the Shaper Bureaus, but in case something happens, it's three of us and just two of them should Henrith decide to protect his friend. Which, honestly, would be stupid.*

I looked at Evie and smiled. *And we have her ability to*

instant cast that Level Five spell. My eyes lingered on her for too long, I guessed, as she smiled back, tilting her head to the side in question. I deepened my smile and pushed the gate, feeling the resistance as it refused to open.

"Henrith, can you?" I asked as I pushed the gate of stone once more.

"Of course," he said, and with our strength combined, the gate slid open.

The reverberating rumble of stone grinding against the floor filled the air. As each wing of the gate opened wide, to my surprise, I stepped over not pebbles, not cobblestone, not pavement. Shiny, reflective tiles with masterful paintings on them. My gaze extended further, revealing that the pictures were composed of anywhere from four to eight tiles, forming a striking, expansive image.

"Wow. Have you seen something like this, guys?" Evie asked.

Everyone said no, and I shared nods with Nilah. "I've read this in books. The illustrations were similar to this, but I don't recognise any of the paintings, specifically," I said.

"Well, it's not like we've really studied thoroughly the whole Hailing Revenants thing." Nilah shrugged.

"But you have an idea what this might be, right?" Henrith said in a soft voice.

"Weren't your other two members of the raiding group from the Hailing Revenants? How come you don't know?" Evie asked.

Not a word escaped the lips of the two raiders as they kept their heads lowered in shame.

"Can you try to guess? It's on my tongue, but unlike them, I would dare to speak it," I said and walked further in. *Discriminative bastards.*

"It's not like that, you know?" Bureaus said in a treble voice, as he followed. "They were distant from us. They hated us. So we just hated them back, but focused on finishing the job, whatsoever."

I turned to face him, but then my mouth went agape.

"They were really self-absorbed and—"

"Where's the gate?" I asked, interrupting Bureaus.

Thankfully, everyone had passed through, so we weren't separated, but that didn't change the fact that I could see no way out. I saw no numbers or equations on the stone wall, which meant there was no magic to conceal the gate.

"By The Flow, it's gone!" Henrith touched the stone wall. "Should I try to blast it open with my hands?"

"You mean the wall?" Nilah asked, frowning.

"No, wait. Let's not rush this," I said and looked around. At each corner, there was a knight holding onto something. One held a spear, the other a harp, and on the left side of the hall, they had a drum and a mug. "Perhaps it's a riddle which we need to solve to get out."

"Curse this. We don't need to solve it when we can just push our way out," Bureaus said, jumping into the air, water pushing his legs further above. "Level Three Elemental Water Magic, Forcing Jet!"

His hands, resembling cannons, unleashed a torrent of water, as powerful as a raging storm at sea. The water decimated as magic circles appeared all over the wall and sealed away Bureaus' spell. Landing gracefully next to us, he cast an inquisitive gaze in our direction.

"Well, I guess it's time for the puzzle," he shrugged.

The tile under his left leg glowed. We looked at it for a while and when he noticed; he jumped off with a shriek.

A smell of rot reached my nostrils as a half-decomposed

arm reached out from the tile. From the corner, the knight blew the horn so loud, we instinctively covered our ears. We hastily got to the middle of the room, drawing our distance from the rising zombie. Each tile we stepped on glowed. *It's a trap. These tiles are imbued with summoning spells! I couldn't see the equations because of the reflections. Damn it!*

"Try to not move! Each tile has a summoning spell imbued into it!" I yelled.

Bureaus opened his arms, fireballs shaping in each one. "Level Three Elemental Fire Magic, Fireball!"

He threw flames at each zombie, but without overcharging them, I could tell they hadn't the power to burn bones into ash.

"Nilah, I'll do it. You watch my back, okay?" I turned to my sister with a smile. She nodded, returning the gesture.

Black thunder shaped a bow into my palm and I stepped to the side, so my arrows wouldn't do any friendly fire. As I pulled my first arrow and it cracked through the air, demolishing zombies' souls, I heard Henrith grunt.

"No! The tiles!" Evie said, her Lightforged Sword glowing in her palm. *Oh, right! I told them, yet I made the mistake of moving! Damn.*

Three zombie hands arose from the tiles I had stepped on. Evie slashed at them, but even with lost limbs, they kept rising.

"They need to complete the summoning, or their soul is still in both realms, rendering them invulnerable to damage!" Nilah said.

That being said, it only made things worse. As Evie moved in to strike, she stepped on four other tiles. Henrith moved swift and precise, striking down the limbs of the emerging zombies, returning to the tiles he departed from.

"It seems if you move between four tiles and always return to the starting two, those two won't activate!" Henrith yelled.

My arrows struck the last of the initial zombies and I dismissed the bow, turning to the newly summoned in our midst. The spear knight from the corner of the room struck the tiles, forcing a snare to resonate between the stone walls. Evie slashed at the zombies, The Light cleansing their souls into ash.

I looked above us, as the resonance of the knight's strike jumped into the cupola above us. Only then did I notice it was even there. The walls were so high that I hadn't paid attention to the paintings above us.

"A woman with her four knights, is it?" Bureaus asked, gazing at the masterful art.

"If I were to decipher this, I'd say they are celebrating something," Nilah pointed out.

A glowing light from the spear knight's corner took my attention. A good chunk of tiles glowed.

"He activated the tiles!" Henrith said.

"It's okay! We are far enough. I can take them down from here." I said, readying the black thunder in my palm. "Just step aside and take care of the zombies you'll summon."

They did as asked, and I released my Black Magic, blasting through the rising zombies.

"Sova, the mug knight. Look," Evie said, and then Nilah added, "It's glowing."

I released my spell and looked at it. The mug was no longer made of stone, but rather of glass. Now transparent, I could see purple liquid inside it. There was some kind of magic happening there, but the equations were swinging. Even as I scrutinised, it was hard for me to decipher it.

The spear knight hit the ground once more, but after that, the drum knight struck, as well. They formed a beat. The harp knight played a gentle melody.

"Woah, woah, woah! They are serenading us!" Bureaus laughed.

Henrith's eyes jumped from corner to corner.

"Behold, a carnival of souls!" A female voice came from the cupola above. All tiles glowed with light, zombies emerging from them.

"By The Light!" Evie whispered and kicked the arms on the ground, shuffling closer to me and Nilah.

"In The Shaper's name," Bureaus said as his hands glowed from the balls of flame he conjured.

The melody kept ongoing, and once the zombies were out of the floor, they charged at us.

"Nobody get close to me!" I yelled. "Level Three Black Magic Sorcery, Rancour Edge! Times ten!"

I enforced my legs with magic and jumped amidst the zombies. I spun and struck each one, the Rancour Edges covering my body, transforming it into a soul-devouring weapon in touch.

I moved along, zombies focusing on me, as I became the closest prey for them. I welcomed each one with a bare-handed slash through their body, carving through them like a knife through butter. A low grunt of an assailant from my back forced me to turn around. It's palm gone, black magic burning away at where used to be a wrist.

"Out of your misery," I said, slicing through its head.

Flashes of light and black thunder raged from the others' location. I looked with the corner of my eyes to see the knight's glass was filling up with purple liquid.

I wrapped up the zombies on my end, and I had to wait

for the new ones to spawn, so I dashed back to help the others.

"Sova, you secured that angle! Let's go there and I'll make a large-scale flame to put them all down!" Bureaus said and his arms glowed as if they transformed into lava.

"No! We'll suffocate!" Evie yelled. *She's got a point.*

"What?" Bureaus frowned. "Fuck! I'll just add water later!"

"Don't risk it. We've got it under control as it is now," I said.

"Argh! Fuck!" Henrith yelled, as a zombie bit his arm. With a whoosh, he spun, his right leg landing into the zombie's head, propelling it through the crowd of undead.

Evie pointed her arm, and The Light began healing his wound. "It won't heal fast, and it'll hurt a lot. Bare with it," she said.

"Should I say thanks?" Henrith asked in a sarcastic tone.

"You should," Nilah frowned.

Bureaus tripped into a rising zombie's arm as he walked backwards. He fell to the ground, screaming in horror, as all the nearby rising zombies grabbed onto him. A sight that easily would induce nightmares. Fire exploded from his back, setting his assailants ablaze. They continued to grasp onto him, his robes igniting from his own fire. He shifted as water bursted chaotically around him. A near miss of Bureaus' water jet interrupted Henrith's leap to kick the zombies, preventing him from getting close.

"And you call yourselves raiders!?" Evie frowned, and in a flash of light, cut through all arms on one side of Bureaus and then with another flash of light, the other side.

With unconcealed annoyance, I approached Bureaus at a rapid pace and pulled him off the ground. *Pitiful idiot. Is this what Mathsmagica graduates offer?* As he stood on his legs, his sleeves partially burned, I noticed his hands shaking and eyes jumping corners in horror.

The beat of the music quickened up, and the zombies' speed increased accordingly. Henrith jumped before us, striking multiple lethal hits with his fluid martial arts abilities, empowered by mana. He grunted as his wound was still healing, but he proved to be tougher than Bureaus. *I suppose that's from The Celestial Weavers' discipline training.*

Evie slashed, her sword leaving trails of light. She covered Nilah, who launched black thunders into the zombie horde. Bureaus conjured fireballs and overcharged them to deliver sufficient damage.

The music, at last, stopped. Ashy remains of the zombies covered the tiles. The knight raised the glass as if for a toast. Then, in the middle of the room, the tiles rounded up one above the other, forming a staircase going up. The cupola split in four, and retracted outwards, creating an opening for the stairs to continue expanding higher.

"Drink your mana potions if you've depleted some. We should follow these stairs," I said.

They all took a sip from their potions.

"What about you?" Henrith asked. "Why don't you drink a mana potion?"

We locked eyes for a few seconds. "I don't need to. Let's go."

I went ahead first. The steps were really narrow, and it was easy to fall off. They spiralled into a circle of pink-hued light at the top. *Huh. This oddly reminds me of Nocturna's Eclipse.*

"Be careful and stick close to the stone pillar holding the stairs, okay?" I turned back to warn the girls. The other two nodded as well.

I looked down for a moment and my head spun. Pressing my back to the pillar, I focused my eyes on the stairs ahead until I recovered.

"Sova, are you okay?" Evie asked. She was closest to me, followed by Nilah. I gazed into her eyes for a few seconds and I pushed myself to recover my balance.

"I'm okay. I just needed a second."

My vestibular recovered, and I strode up. The cupola's opening narrowed down, allowing only the stairs to pass and a slight opening for the pink guiding light.

I walked into the brightness. When I glanced to my left, I saw a graceful crimson waterfall cascading with a soft rumble. Everywhere I looked, there were trees adorned with glowing pink leaves. The rest of the raid members paused, awe-struck as I was.

The path descended solely in one direction. We pressed on until we arrived at an altar embellished with glistening leaves, wine-filled glasses, and flickering candles.

"What in the world is this?" Evie asked.

There, before the altar, a man in black leather pants and a leather jacket knelt, his bare chest gleaming under the dim light. With his head bowed, his face remained concealed beneath a cascade of brown hair that fell past his shoulders. His thighs were stained with drops of blood that kept dripping from the hole in his chest. The man's arm reached upward, as if he was presenting a sacrificial gift - his own pulsating heart gripped tightly in his palm.

Above him, she floated gracefully in mid-air, her long black hair cascading around her, adding to her unmatched naked beauty. As I blinked twice, I figured she didn't float. It was not magic. A silver device trussed her neck and legs, forcing her body to remain at a forty-five degree angle.

"This is impossible," Henrith said.

Bureaus made a few steps back and landed on his butt.

With a gradual movement, the kneeling man turned his gaze towards us, his eyes meeting ours in silence. I couldn't help but shudder at the sight of his completely black pupils, with only a tiny white dot in their midst instead of irises.

"My love," he said, shifting his head into its original position. "It appears our ritual has been tainted."

He looked at us again with a studying sight.

"No matter. It shalt keep abaft, afore else."

As soon as the man opened his right palm, a fearsome white spear appeared. Its design mimicked the shape of a spine, with a black orb near the top that expanded its width. Above the orb, the bone contorted and transformed into a formidable spearhead, gleaming with sharpness.

He rammed the spear through his heart and straight into the maiden's chest. She gulped and spat blood on his face. The device which held onto her released its grip and the man pulled the spear closer, along with the maiden. He caught his heart and squeezed it into the maiden's. As a popping sound resounded, he pulled the maiden by holding their mended hearts into his own chest. He fell to his knees once more, and the maiden cradled him as he collapsed.

Silence hung in the air with anticipation.

The candles extinguished, and the leaves ceased their glow. The maiden crawled into the man's back, unifying their bodies, and after the blood stopped spilling, he raised himself back to his knees.

"That's Velarian and Roselia..." Henrith said in a soft voice.

Roselia hung from Velarian's back with her long hairs floating as if gravity were absent. Her face seemed calm, her eyes closed in slumber. Velarian's chest wound no longer bled. He struck the ground with his spear, helping himself up, and faced us.

"My beloved Ritual of Love... Has failed! All because of you," Velarian murderously gazed, tears floating out of his eyes into the air, lacking the need for gravity.

AMONG THE ARCHIVES

"The Light shall bless those who traverse the realm of sin by basking in the holy fountain waters together. The newlyweds strip before an authorised holy figure and holding their hands, should splash each other with water. After claiming the blessing of The Light, the couple can proceed to celebrate their souls' binding. When the sun fades into the horizon and a full moon arises, the newlyweds must commit the act of love or the blessing would become a curse."

- "Luminari Faith Rituals," by unknown.

CHAPTER 16
DESPAIR

Orbs vibrating with magic appeared as Velarian traced an arc above his head.

"Watch out! Don't let those hit you!" I yelled, as the orbs shot out at us with incredible speed.

We spread within a second. The orbs detonated, unleashing brilliant flashes of light that illuminated the area, while debris from the pavements and dirt floated weightlessly in the air before dropping back down.

Bureaus threw a ball of flame at Velarian. I stared with anticipation, curious to see if a spell of that calibre would even touch him. Roselia, eyes still closed, extended an arm to meet the attack and blue hexagons appeared, shaping a barrier to negate the spell.

"Nilah, Black Arrow!" I yelled, and jumped in the air, drawing out a thunderous arrow from my Black Magic spell. "Now!"

Soul-rending arrows propelled and crackled in the air, yet they both got negated by Roselia's barrier. Evie readied her stance and, together with Henrith, dashed towards Velarian. Just as they approached him, he and Roselia simultaneously pushed forward, a shockwave shoving all assailants back. With a grunt, he held his weapon to the side and walked in Evie's direction.

"My time is now," Velarian spoke, rotating the spear-headed staff in his hand. "Begone!"

He slammed the ground with the tip of the staff, the orb on it sparkling. Numbers seemed to come alive before me, swirling across the ground like a vivid shade. Everything, including the dirt on the ground, exploded in an ash-coloured eruption. The debris floated mid-air for a few seconds before they tumbled back to the ground.

Nilah shot arrows at him, but Roselia's barriers negated them. Ocean-like waves resonated, as I saw Bureaus propelling himself into the air, water jets blowing out of his legs.

"Oh he, the Shaper of origin, punish thy fool who dared taint your land. Rich be the shape of your judgement upon my enemies," Bureaus' voice resonated unnaturally as chunks of debris from the ground flew out towards him.

"He's making a large scale spell! Run to the side!" Henrith yelled, backflip turning into a rushed jog.

"Nilah, we are far enough away. Let's make an opening!" I said and showered Velarian with black arrows.

Some of my projectiles crashed through the rising pavements, others splashed in the dirt, but most struck into the hexagonal barrier. I ran across the perimetre, positioning myself so Nilah's arrows came from Velarian's left, and mine came from his right side.

Velarian pulled his weapon out of the ground and in a slow motion drew an arc-line before him.

"Evie! Barriers!" I yelled, as she had just gone far enough to be out of danger.

"You're too far!" she said, charging at me.

"Protect Nilah! I'll be fine!" Evie flash-stepped and appeared next to Nilah, shaping a wall of light before them.

The arc before Velarian resonated in a screeching sound as it launched, slashing through the air. I cancelled my spell and mimicked Evie's barrier equation. After I poured mana, no light wall appeared before me.

I failed.

Henrith's feet smashed into the ground as his back obstructed my line of sight.

"Henrith!" I yelled out. A blue magic circle appeared before him, expanding metres wide. The sound of chiming bells rang as it absorbed the slashing arc attack.

"But how?" *I thought Henrith was a Celestial Weaver. They're all about empowering their bodies. How did he cast a barrier?*

As the magic arc disappeared, Henrith faced me and dropped a scroll on the ground. *Oh! The scrolls from the Summoning Hall! I never thought they could be so useful.*

"Come on!" He said and pushed me to run. "This will hit large."

Black smokes filled the air above us, Bureaus' water streams not visible. I scouted the area to assimilate the situation. The debris no longer floated up, but... *where are they?* Evie and Nilah stood behind the wall of light, keeping watch on Velarian.

"Level Four Elemental Fire Magic," Bureaus' voice resonated from the smoke clouds above. "Apocalypse Tempest!"

Velarian looked up leisurely. After silence, followed by a smoking burning ball of flame. It flared so vigorously, one would think it was the sun. Velarian rotated his spine-shaped staff within the palm of his hand and met the meteorite head-on. Two more meteorites followed right behind, each exploding into hellfire. The flames were so hot, my forehead sweat despite being about a hundred metres away. With each breath, my lungs burned from the hot air.

I underestimated Bureaus' ability. Raiders pack some intense fire-power.

An explosion resonated yet again, as another meteorite crashed into the ground. *I'd expect the fire to spread across to us, but Bureaus seems to be controlling it. I can't imagine what we'd do if he lost control of the spell, though.*

"Have you seen this spell before?" I asked Henrith, trying to depict anything besides metres tall flames, obstructing vision of anything else.

"Yes, I have. It'll be over soon."

"Is there a chance he could lose control of it?"

"You really underestimate us, don't you?" Henrith sighed with annoyance. "No surprise. We weren't seen in the best light, especially with what happened earlier."

I nodded without taking eyes off the flames. The last meteorite fell and Bureaus descended slowly to the ground, only a hand–away from the menacing fire.

"This will finish Velarian and Roselia, for sure. It's a pity we had to lose them," Henrith said. "Here comes the last part of the spell."

Bureaus expanded his arms wide into the air and, with a clapping sound, he united them together. In complete sync with his arms' movement, the flames gathered together in a single pillar of fire. I guessed Velarian was amidst it. I squeezed my eyes shut, the brightness of it feeling like staring directly at the sun.

As it dissipated, the pillar transformed into a swirling vortex, stretching upward into the sky. Hexagonal barriers faded, and Velarian spoke. "Ah, I recognise this sorcery. Bureaus..."

"Velarian? Have you come to your senses?" Bureaus asked, taking a step back. *He's scared. Bureaus is fucking shaking.*

But then again, who wouldn't be? *A Level Four fire spell and Velarian walks out unscathed...*

My gaze fell to Evie, thinking about her Level Five spell. *Maybe that's one of our best bets. I'll carry her in my arms out of here if she's unable to move, but it might be the only way for us to survive.*

That... or...

"I have never lost senses," Velarian slowly advanced towards the fire mage. "Why have you come to interrupt my ritual?"

Bureaus startled, falling to his butt as Velarian towered above him. Yes, Bureaus was about a hundred–sixty–five centimetres tall, but Velarian's height seemed inhuman. I dashed alongside Henrith, and a few seconds later, Evie also joined us.

"Velarian, your twisted ritual turned an entire village's people into undead. Do you realise that?" I asked, meeting his menacing black pupils.

"It would have all went back to normal once the ritual was done," he said. "But thanks to your interference, we lost control of it."

He smashed the bottom part of his staff against the ground. A resonating thud prepared equations for protective barriers.

"But now we've become this abomination. And all is lost." He looked at Roselia's face over his shoulder. "She's still so beautiful."

His hands shook as he slowly grabbed his face and pulled his hair back. "Madness is taking over. For I, Velarian, am no longer."

"What do you mean, Velarian? You're still conscious, aren't you?!" Henrith said. "Excuse your form. I'm still talking to you. The person is here!"

"...for I am." Velarian's voice turned gritty. "The host of souls!"

He swiped his staff in an arc, unleashing an almost point-blank attack. We leaped in the air to avoid it. As we did, Velarian jumped, the ground beneath him cracking. His free hand grabbed Henrith by the face and threw him at me. With a bone-shaking crash, we collided into the ground, the sound of Velarian's malicious laughter ringing in our ears. Henrith rolled out to the side and dashed at Velarian. I jumped up and cast Rancour Edge. Seeing Henrith's equations floating around his legs, I copied them, poured mana, and closed the bracket. I felt light as a feather, powered by the same spell he used, whatever its name was.

Henrith threw several kicks toward Velarian's face, but the hexagonal barriers appeared right in the moment of contact. The menacing laughter resumed as Velarian reached to grab Henrith again, forcing a smile out of me. *Very greedy to try the same thing twice on a Celestial Weaver!* Henrith spun, kicking Velarian's hand to the ground, and with the same rotative movement of his body, he landed an attack on his face, shaking him off-balance.

Roselia opened her eyes and frowned. She extended her arms at Henrith, and in front of her pale-skinned arms, emerged hexagonal barriers. Each one pushing the Celestial harder into the ground.

A black arrow crackled through the air as Nilah shot from the distance. Alarmed, Roselia released half of the barriers and directed an arm to protect Velarian from the ranged attack.

I was right behind Velarian, and Roselia's arm extended

above me. I jumped, Rancour Edge making my hand nothing less than a dimensional soul cutter. Half of her arm turned to ash, Velarian smashing his staff's spearhead into me, as they both screamed in agonising pain.

Evie dashed from Velarian's right side and unleashed her Lightforged Sword in a combo of slashes. Henrith was freed from the barriers, as Roselia used her remaining arm to shield Velarian from Evie's onslaught.

I picked myself up from the ground, casting Level Three Illumination Magic, Light's Embrace. The pain in my stomach faded immensely, as I poured a huge chunk of mana into healing it. Evie's blade lit up in a flurry of slashes, her movements a mesmerising spectacle of athletic combat. Nilah ran across the perimetre providing ranged support. Henrith recovered and unleashed rapid, bare-handed attacks on Velarian's left side.

Velarian actively began wielding his staff in combat, compensating for Roselia's missing arm.

"A worthy sacrifice," Velarian said in a menacing voice, his staff meeting Evie's sword in resonating clashes.

He leaped into the air. Henrith prepared to jump after, but from Roselia's hair, hundreds of orbs propelled downwards, burning through Henrith's skin. I shot a black arrow, but Roselia cast a barrier at the moment before impact.

"Bureaus, get the fuck up!" I screamed and rushed to Henrith's aid, who shook, standing in a battle stance. *This must be some meditative way of recovering.*

My feet bouncing off the rubble of pavements, I shot arrows, getting closer to Henrith. His bite wound was still healing, and with all his skin pierced by those orbs, I couldn't think of him being able to keep fighting. Evie released a battle cry, unleashing a combo on Velarian, pushing him away.

"Henrith! I'll help–" I trailed off as I saw his eyes were blank. *Fuck.* "Oh, Nocturna, damn it. Fuck!"

I extended my hands at Henrith and spoke, "Level Three Illumination Magic, Light's Embrace!"

Within seconds, his shaking ceased, but he remained unconscious, standing on his feet in a battle stance.

"And just when I thought we were winning," I whispered through gritted teeth.

"Burea–" I yelled, but shut my mouth. The majestic robes burned, and all colours tainted by blood. *Those orbs hit him too...*

Something clicked in me. Perhaps because of the years of training my mind into self-control, I could tell. For the first time, I experienced despair.

Underneath my feet appeared four magic circles, each one bigger than the other, twirling in a mesmerising cadence. Before both my eyes, eight magic circles, each bigger than the other, expanded ever-forward. I extended my right arm, my Shadow Covenant rune glowing brightly through my Enforcer uniform. A magic circle appeared across my palm, which I gently closed.

"O Nocturna, I disrupt thy sleep, for my desire is our secrets to keep." I chanted, as I kept track of Velarian attacking Evie and pushing her down, despite Nilah's ranged support. "Hear my voice, I plead, your whispers I heed. Eyes aglow, runes alight, I call upon thee, in this darkest night."

"In disgrace of The Light, this spell I weave. In thy name, let darkness cleave," I finished the chant, my sight losing sense of colour, presenting me a monochromic image of Velarian thrusting his spear in a certain to-hit attack. "Level Five Black Magic Sorcery, Eyes of Death."

My finger snapped. A black sphere ruptured space-time

where Velarian's hand was thrusting, breaking it in two. He screamed in pain, facing me. I focused on his left leg and snapped my finger. In an imploding blow, the second sphere took away his leg, disintegrating it into magic dust. He fell down, making it look like Roselia was standing tall in his stead. She pointed her remaining arm at me and I saw an immense pile of numbers gathering in her palm, but then I snapped my finger. A sphere took away her remaining arm, disintegrating it as well.

My vision returned to normal. A flash of light, accompanied by the ringing of holy metal, went through Roselia's neck. Her head fell before Velarian.

"Fear not. We shall make love... in death," he said and Evie sliced through his neck, then jumped off, graciously landing with a thud before him.

I fell to one knee, sudden fatigue taking me over. My back itched like never before. I shook, trying to resist. Pain accompanied the itch, further enhancing my torture. My hands sought their way to remove the upper part of my uniform and I tried to scratch the scar on my back, but as my hand made contact, it burned my fingers. Violet sparkles lingered on it.

"What's wrong Sova? Are you okay?" Evie dashed to my aid, Nilah joining her.

"Sovie? It's your scar!" Nilah yelled, pointing with a finger.

"What in the world is this?" Evie asked, her voice a whisper.

"Evie, can you heal it? I don't know what's happening!" I mumbled through teeth.

"I can try, okay!" Evie said and cast a spell on my back. I didn't feel any difference. "The spell is cancelling itself out! There's nothing to heal!"

"What do we do? Sovie, how can we help you!?" Nilah kneeled next to me, tears in her eyes.

Wish I knew. I hit the ground with my fist. A familiar sensation came to my mind, along with Master Lethalica's words. *See not with the eyes, but with magic.*

I tried to focus and, easier than before, I was before that tapestry again. A violet light engulfed it, rendering all other colours faded in comparison. I stepped closer to it, and I could discern a gigantic eye of a creature I had never seen. It had big scales instead of skin. I reached my hand out and touched the tapestry. The eye closed, and the tapestry went back to normal, adding contrast to all other colours. The tapestry resumed its constant shifting, maintaining its right to left motion, but this time I noticed a vibrant yellow image sparkling even more intensely than before. Somehow, I felt it. I felt The Light in it.

"Sovie?" Nilah asked to my left, and Evie touched my cheek from my right.

"I think he's better now. Whatever happened, he's calm, but... his eyes?" Evie spoke.

My gaze hadn't shifted from looking forward until now. My hand touched Evie's on my cheek, and then I looked at her. She pulled back, alarmed.

"Sova, why are your eyes... violet?"

"Are you better, Sovie?" Nilah asked me. "Your back isn't sparkling anymore."

"My eyes?" I asked, blinking rapidly and shaking my head. "I don't know."

I put my uniform back on and shook my head again. "I'm fine now. Thank you both."

Among the Archives

"They all said about a golden gaze coming from his eyes. Everyone believed he was a god. Not because of anything else, but because he could bend the world to his will. There was no force in the world that could match him.
Research says he died shortly after the celebration of his twentieth years. Though his death many believed to be staged. Why would one fake his own death when he is at the peak of the world? The answer has always been simple. How could we give an answer to a question related to a god?"

- *"Research of Gods and Men," by Hindergrith Beren*

CHAPTER 17
DELAYED AWAKENING

ENDARIEL'S POINT OF VIEW

THE VOID IS BRIGHTER.

I awoke to the same ceiling as usual. My skin breathed void. The dormant energetic flow roused from its sleep, gradually building in intensity. After a deep breath, not as heavy as before, I used magic, lifting myself for my feet to touch the floor. I faced the mirror to meet the void stronger in my eyes. *Good. I am becoming.*

I gazed at the window and opened it. Closed eyes, I reached out to Lethalica. She sensed me, I could feel. Avoiding the risk of being noticed, I preserved my strength by looking at the clouds, illuminated by the city's magical glow, as well as the spires striking into the sky.

It didn't take long before she awaited in the shadows. I leaped through the window and landed on the ground, soft as a feather, the violet essence of the void supporting my weight.

"It worked, I see. But I still haven't felt it happen,"

Lethalica said, her red hair and yellow eyes meeting mine, as she stepped out of the shadows.

"Because it hasn't yet," I responded, studying the consistency of my magic within the vessel. "Yet the void is more... accustomed."

"I started feeding the vessel with void crystals. So far, only one, but I will keep doing so should the circumstances allow it," Lethalica said, smiling.

"Only one? Are you certain?"

"Yes," she frowned. "Why wouldn't it be? Is it too weak?"

"No. It's the opposite," I said, lifting my right palm to eye level, observing the consistency of void sparks in it. "Compared to the previous vessels, with only one crystal, I notice huge accommodation to the void."

"Hm," Lethalica smirked. "Perhaps it is because of Sova's affinity."

"So you delved deeper into it, as I demanded?"

"Have I ever failed your orders, My King?" she asked, bowing her head.

"Of course not." I dismissed that opportunity, flapping my hand to the side. "What of it? Tell me, now."

"I gifted him the knowledge of it." Lethalica raised her head to meet my eyes. "The Tapestry of Shadows."

"He could tap into it already?" I asked, frowning. "Formidable."

"He saw the colours of Illumination Magic, all Elemental Magic, Black Magic, Flow Magic, and most importantly, Void Magic."

"Did he have it before being in contact with the void crystal?"

"I am not aware, for I hadn't even attempted to find out. Singularity Magic belongs to the one and only person who possesses it. As the dragons who gave these humans the knowledge and power of magic, I can easily claim that rule has not yet broken."

"Choosing the child of Lumiel proved to be the best decision I might have taken in this life that I so spasmodically live," I said, my voice low. "What have The Wings brought of Aetherial Wrathblaze?"

"He has been gathering our followers. The leaders have been preparing their pawns for The Awakening Ritual," Lethalica spoke, and after a brief pause, she sighed. "They have been ready for half a year now."

I looked at the clouds just as they opened up a little space for the moon to shed its light. I reconciled in thought.

"Endariel?" Lethalica's eyes widened.

"Yes, I am still here." I said, releasing a breath I didn't know I was holding. "We should act now. I realise what has been keeping me dormant for so long."

"The students' last report mentioned Sova's scar had brought him to his knees after his latest battle. Is it related to that?"

"Indeed. When he was still a baby, I heard The Tapestry of Shadows call out to me from within his fragile body. Then I saw it. And so did you."

"The reason for his mana capacity. The Shadow Veil?" Lethalica asked, narrowing her eyes.

I looked at her in wait, but she wouldn't continue. "Did you not see anything else?"

"I... I didn't," Lethalica frowned. "Was there else?"

"There was. And is. Yet I still have very limited access to it. Only faintly did I see it occur."

"Forgive my lack of perception... What is it?"

"The Abyssal Eyes," I said, a smirk uncontrollably widening my grin.

"That's..." Lethalica shook. "It is the same set as *His*!"

"Indeed. What irony, isn't it?" I snickered silently. "To have Sovah The Legendary Mage's birth given powers. In my very own possession. He would contort in terror."

"The Abyssal Eyes... The main reason Sovah became what he was. The ability to see the very structure of the world and copy every single magic he sees. Why did The Tapestry of Shadows even conjure this law-bending abomination?"

"Once I awake, for sure, I could access it willingly."

"This is outrageous," Lethalica whispered, hands shaking as she grabbed her forehead. "It must be a coincidence, right?"

I studied the way she reacted, yet I couldn't help but frown. "A reason to shiver is lacking. This is good news, Lethalica."

"You know the vessel's name, Endariel, don't you?" She asked, startled.

"I have heard the sibling call him Sovie. What of it?"

"His name is Sova. The same as The Legendary Mage, but without an 'h'!"

A coincidence? Or an occurrence? I had to bow my head to Sovah in the past and experience ultimate betrayal by his followers. The human stain. He was the only human worthy of respect, but in the end, he was just that. A human. His greed claimed his life. It is impossible for him to plan something so far ahead. Or... is it?

"It sends a shiver down my spine. Yet human life couldn't possibly plan thousands of years ahead. A hundred, or even a few hundred, I accept. No more," I muttered.

"But Sovah wasn't *just* a human."

"Oh, but he was," I said, placing my hand on Lethalica's shoulder. "He *was*."

"I know many people name their kids Sovah, Sova, Sovaren, or other derivatives, but I think there are too many things tied together here." Lethalica caught my hand and held it in hers. "Affinity to all magic, The Shadow Veil, but even The Abyssal Eyes? And your awakening is also slowed down. Aetherial told me some leaders believe you might not even awaken anymore! That you're dead!"

I smiled.

My grip tightened around her arm and I pulled her, the void gently propelling me towards the sky. From the dorm's roof, we had an unobstructed view of The Academy's impressive pillars, with occasional tantalising glimpses of the moon whenever the clouds parted.

"Endariel?" Lethalica looked at me with confused eyes.

"Sometimes we find wisdom not in spoken words, but in silence."

We remained reticent, taking in the view of what the humans had created. *Thanks to our knowledge. Thanks to our magic.*

"We shall not disappoint the leaders. It is time to prove to them they didn't believe in a false king," I spoke, staring into the horizon. "We shall hasten the awakening. The more we let Sovah's shadow loom over us, the more mistakes we could make."

"But how will we do it? The vessel could break if he takes too many void crystals..."

"There might not be a need for it. After that last battle Sova had, he had depleted more of his mana pool than he ever did before. That and the void crystal let the void get mixed into it."

I faced Lethalica, stood up firmly, and spoke in a

commanding tone. "Prepare the trial. We shall commence The Ritual of Awakening," then in a low menacing tone I said. "But warn them to send the strongest."

"So be it, my King." Lethalica bowed her head. "I will pull the strings."

A soft violet light contoured around my body and I floated mid-air in a slow descent towards the window I had come out of. "Prepare him well, Lethalica. Make him a master. He needs to deplete this Shadow Veil. Then, The Wings will spread."

Among the Archives

"... And as such, our promising students Velarian and Roselia, we conclude to have fallen victim to the Ethereal Phantom 'The Host of Souls.' A pity that such talent had been lost to the dark schools of magic.
The Hailing Revenants' tendency of channelling energy from dangerous ethereal beings proves to be a case we might have to put under control.
Contrary to that, the abilities of The Harmony Enforcers seem to have proven top notch once more. The pure control over their sorceries seems to push their value to be above that of some of the graduates. They are yet to shine; I am certain.
I conclude the raid was successful."

- "Report for raid 934" - Director Larion Astron

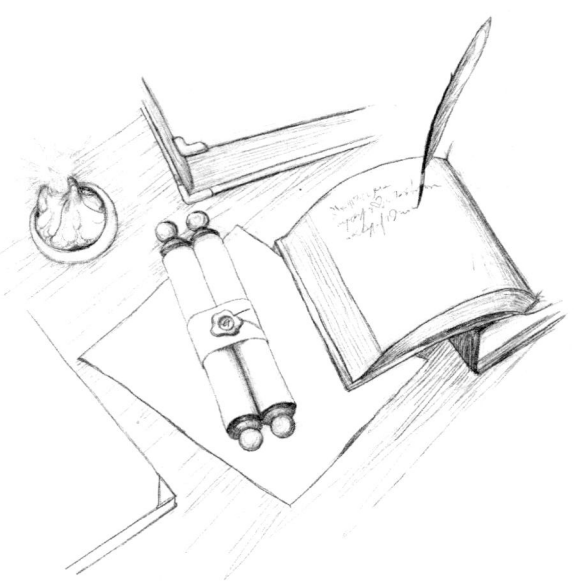

CHAPTER 18
THE WILL OF THE PILLARS

STUDENTS PASSED BY AND THEIR LINGERING GAZE WAS HARD TO MISS.

A couple of days had passed since our first raid. I noticed Director Astron's genuine interest as I shared my report, but the spark in his eyes made me second-guess myself. *God knows what he'll send us for next time! Sometimes I wonder if he's not trying to get us killed.*

I didn't mention the scar on my back, and even if I could see Evie preferred to report about it, she didn't. The other two, Bureaus and Henrith, reported separately from us, so I had no clue what they said. *I wonder if they asked how come I could conjure a fireball in my palm despite having an affinity for Black Magic?*

By the might of coincidence, while we were sitting at our favourite mushroom cafe, Henrith joined us. Initially, I was more distanced to him than to Bureaus as he meditated for the major part of the day, but he proved to be more reliable when we got to combat.

He had been silent for at least five minutes, just

listening to our gossip about Elemental Magic theory. "Thank you for allowing me to be in your company." Henrith bowed his head.

"Are you leaving?" I asked in a natural tone.

"I wasn't planning to. But I trust it good manners to be grateful," he said and sipped the cold drink from his mushroom shaped cup.

"You're being too respectful," I laughed. "We should be thanking you. You're a graduate, aren't you?"

"I am. But ranks like that are rather disregarded once you walk into battle, right?" Henrith smiled. "I appreciate you exalting me, nonetheless."

Well, I'm not so sure about exalting you too much. I'm just being polite.

"You managed to pull through all the lectures at The Academy and actually got a score to pass! That's admirable!" Nilah said in a cheery tone, as she squeezed the magical mushroom into her embrace.

"Your combat prowess is formidable, Henrith. You were unlucky to fight the undead. That's all," Evie said.

He paused for a moment and let out a deep sigh. "It is a pity. Velarian and Roselia were astonishing mages."

"They were, but they played with a force too wicked," I said, sighing. "The Dark Schools of Magic are the most dangerous, and really underestimated by society. The hatred revolving about that is rather misdirected and misunderstood."

"I agree, Sova. But this only makes me ask you more questions." Henrith's gaze locked onto me.

"Pardon?" I frowned.

"How can a first year like yourself be a master of Black Magic? Are you hiding your true age?"

Evie and Nilah chuckled at the accusation.

"I wish, Henrith." I chuckled. "It is all hard work, practice, and spending sleepless nights and days tapping into the true essence of Nocturna's teachings."

"Sova, The Master of Black Magic!" Evie sang in an opera-like voice, then burst into laughter.

"Hey, it's fine to joke about it. I'd hardly call myself a Master," I laughed. "How does one even become a Master Mage, anyway?"

"You have to pass the trial of the goddess of life and death, secure the remedy for the most lethal newfound disease, abolish the world from evil, and create a new moon!" Nilah said, her voice full of excitement, as her eyes ogled at me. "And drink the blood of a bat, while cooking one million mushroom stews!"

I face-palmed. "See, Henrith. Look what you did now."

All of them burst into laughter, and I just chuckled under my palm. I took my cup of coffee and inhaled the pleasant, magically enhanced aroma. On the corners of the glass, I could see equations that conjured a spell that amplified the content's smell. After a sip of the warm liquid, I spoke. "I appreciate what you think of me, Henrith, but it's not just me. All three of us work as a team and that's how we manage to pull through. I would be dead several times since the start of our Academy year if it wasn't for those two lovely ladies."

"I understand why they call you Harmony Enforcers," Henrith said, smirking. "It doesn't take long to understand you guys, as long as you're open minded. Not just Mathsmagica, each country should one day write about the wisdom of this trio. An accurate representation of a union. I accept, Master Astron's perception still far surpasses my own."

"Master Astron? He was your teacher?" Evie asked.

Henrith responded with a nod.

"Woah! That's really cool!" Nilah perked up.

"Though, no matter what he said, I feel like a complete failure. To have such a great teacher yet be on the level I am."

"You'll get there," Nilah said, determined.

I smiled at Henrith. "Don't stop walking. No matter how small, each step gets you closer."

"Thank you, Enforcers. I am really pleased to have been your acquaintance. An honour, nothing less," Henrith said and pulled his chair back, standing up. "Until magic crosses our fates again."

"Light be with you, Henrith."

"Shadows consume you," Nilah spoke cheerfully.

Henrith turned around, a frown on his face. "I presume that's not a curse?"

"Nilah, I think we should leave that for other Shadow Covenants. I don't think people are very comfortable with that phrase," I said, chuckling.

"Oh! Sorry. I meant–"

"She meant to wish you well, Henrith." I said, interrupting Nilah before she said something that would need another explanation.

"May The Flow cruise through you, too." Henrith said and withdrew into the crowd.

"How is your," Evie spoke, and then leaned closer to me, whispering. "Your back? How is it?"

"I'm okay. Sorry you had to see that."

"No, it's okay. I'm just worried about what you're battling with. I have never seen a violet scar like that. Especially one that gleams and bleeds magic like yours!"

"Sovie has always had it. Since we were babies," Nilah said, leaning her chin on the fluffy mushroom.

"But what left that scar? And how come it didn't recover for so many years? It looks like an open wound... but magic. As if magic itself is bleeding out of you."

"I…"

"Oh, forgive me if you're uncomfortable to speak about it. I didn't mean to cross a line," Evie said, pulling a lock of hair behind her ear.

"It's okay. I would be curious, too. Well, I am, in fact." I forced a chuckle.

I saw numbers in the air, floating by a piece of paper. Navigated by magic, it came towards our table. As I reached out, my hand awaited its arrival. The girls frowned in the direction I was pointing when the paper settled softly in my palm.

"Where did that come from?" Evie asked, perplexed.

"I don't know. I just spotted it coming," I said, unfolding the paper. "Let's see."

Nilah and Evie both stood from their chairs and leaned next to me, so they could take a peek at the mysterious letter. I took my eyes off it and looked at Evie, as her sweet perfume endowed my breaths. Her skin seemed even softer from up-close. How could each characteristic of hers look so well defined and perfect? Even the most odd thing on a person's face. The nose. Hers was small and just perfectly symmetric to her face. I've read fantasy books about elves being so well proportioned. *Evie, are you an elf?*

"Sova?" she asked, as our eyes met. *Oh crap. I was staring too long.*

"Ugh, sorry. Something got in my eye," I said, my cheeks burning.

"Is that so?" she asked, and her fingers pulled me by the chin. She stared straight into my eyes. "I don't know. I see nothing unusual."

Evie, are you teasing me on purpose?

"Oh no. What is this!?" Nilah yelled. Evie let go of me and we both glanced at my twin sister. "This must be a prank!"

After reading through the few sentences in the letter, I thought I was having a strange type of déjà vu.

"Another summoning. Could it be another raid?" Evie suggested.

"But why isn't it a global message like last time?"

We finished our drinks and went to the Summoning Hall at the requested time.

The Summoning Hall's carpet invited us in. Director Astron stood next to Master Lethalica, with a grim face, and a man whom I hadn't seen before. He came rushing to us the moment we walked in.

"I am happy you received my private letter," Director Astron spoke, but then paused, taking a few seconds to study each one of us. "I don't know how to say this to you in a way that wouldn't be frightening."

Dressed in a black sorcerer's robe, silvery talismans and rings reflecting light, the man who stood next to the table with scrolls spoke in a commanding, firm voice. "There isn't a good way to send children to war, Astron."

"War?" I asked, my eyes opening wide.

"It's The Pillars. They decided it. I can't protect you from this," Director Astron spoke softly.

"Wait, what in Nocturna's name?" I shook my head, narrowing my eyes.

"What are you saying? I can't understand this," Evie said, with obvious annoyance in her voice.

"Sovie..." Nilah pulled me gently by the sleeve.

"Director Astron, can you please explain this to us in a

way that it would make sense? What war? What Pillars?" I spoke.

"The Pillars, students," Master Lethalica walked in our direction. "They are the supreme mages who have enough power and wisdom to decide our best political approach."

"And we," the black-robed man spoke. "Have had High Arcanists trace your magic frequencies."

"I'm sorry, but who are you?" I asked, frowning.

"Why, with great power comes… monumental ego, I suppose," the man said with a sigh. "I am Pillar Serene Gulip. You can just call me Pillar Serene."

"Pillar Serene, what is it that you really ask of us?" Evie asked.

"Less questions, please. How can we respond if we don't get the chance to do so, child?" Pillar Serene asked and waved with a hand at us.

We walked in and stood in a circle. Pillar Serene pointed his arm forward and a table with chairs manifested out of thin air. "Please, have a seat."

As requested, we settled into the chairs, instantly feeling their luxurious comfort and softness. The smell of freshly cut wood flooded the room. *From the conjuring, I suppose?*

"Now, look at this map. Despite being first years, you should be able to read it, I believe," Pillar Serene said, taking a scroll out of his robe's pocket. A needle of light, yellow magic circles rotating around it, served as a pointer instead of a finger - like people usually do. The equations creating the spell were so tightly wrapped around the needle that I had a hard time distinguishing it. "You can tell this is Loria. You have been here already. When you saved the villagers of Erleen. But further west, at the very border of the country. The city of Rilereth, one of Loria's prospering economics."

The man paused, and his brown eyes studied each one of us slowly.

"It is no more."

A chill went down my spine.

"No more?" Nilah asked.

"The Fog has consumed it. We detected a single momentary peak of magic. It would be an understatement to say it was enormous. After that, our scouts could say there was nothing but fog left."

"But how do you expect the three of us to do something when a flash wiped out an entire city?" I asked.

"You were the only summoned ones at this date, indeed, but have no worry. Two Masters will be with you. Master Lethalica being one of them."

"Plus," Director Astron spoke. "At least a hundred more mages with experience in raids."

"And," Pillar Serene added. "Four Paladins."

"Four Paladins?" Evie asked, her mouth agape. "With all that force, what's the point of the three of us even going there?"

"You are the Harmony Enforcers. Evie Stratovic, your ability in wielding The Light is on a level many would envy. You may try to hide it, but we know about it. Sova Ren, your mana pool is fearsome, even to me. When I meet you in person, I can easily tell. You are born with a gift. Our Arcanists have detected your frequencies and perhaps you don't yet know it yourself, but your control over Black Magic Sorceries would inspire jealousy even in the masters. And, Master Lethalica has told me, your affinity for fire is a rare find. One that could save lives of many..."

"You think too highly of me. I am but a first-year student who has an interest in practicing magic," I said, shaking my head.

"And Nilah Ren. Despite falling short of what your brother has showcased, your control over Black Magic Sorcery is also nothing less than great."

"Sovie is a genius... I am just Nilah." My sister spoke, her voice shaking.

I gulped and put a hand over her shoulder as I stared blankly.

"Some flowers are yet to bloom, child."

Nilah shook her head as Evie pulled a blond lock of hair behind my sister's ear and caressed her cheek.

"Fear not, my students. I will watch over you," Master Lethalica spoke in her normal cool voice. "This will be an experience that will bring exponential growth to you not only as mages, but as human beings. As people."

"I've postponed this event as much as two months," Director Astron spoke in a soft voice.

"What!?" Pillar Serene hit the table with his fists. "Astron, this is urgent."

"And sending these kids more prepared just secures the success of the mission," Director Astron looked Pillar Serene flat in the eyes.

"Astron, are you crazy? We need this mission to begin now! What if it swallows the rest of Loria? It's your own country, goddamnit!"

"And exactly because I've lost so much, I don't want to lose more, Serene. These kids have two months not just to become mages, they need to become survivalists and warriors," Director Astron spoke as a magical glow illuminated his robes. "It's my school. My students. I decide it."

Pillar Serene struck the table, fragments of the wood dancing in the air, obedient to the arcane hum emanating from his fists. He stood up and turned his back. After a brief pause, Pillar Serene stepped along the red carpet towards the exit.

"And it's my country, Astron."

Among the Archives

*"Hair as black as night, eyes deep as the abyss. Lean and fit, she forever remained in his shadow, but also his protection. Her name is only a rumour, yet nobody dares speak it, even if they knew it. For she is His and His alone.
Must've been nice. I imagined the luxury she bathed in. Being chosen as a god's woman appeared to be paradise."*

- "Life in Paradise Castle" Book 1, Page 146

DANIEL STEFANOV GEORGIEV

CHAPTER 19
BATTLE PRACTICE

Like a corpse. Each night, no matter what, I craved sleep.

I wondered if the stress changed me like that, or perhaps something else? At times, I wondered if Nilah or someone else wasn't casting some kind of sleeping spell on me. Weirdest part, each night I awoke in a different place. Often sitting on the bed, other times, standing straight in front of the mirror, or sitting next to the window. Nilah said sometimes I just sleepwalked, but I didn't do any trouble. She had read about cases like this in some book for hypnosis. Why did she even read that? *No clue, but at any rate, she is my sister, so naturally, she's full of surprises.*

Academy days were different. We used to go there with a half-lazy ambition, accustomed to the comfort of a boring class, and then an exciting one with magic practice. But The Pillars changed it. The Harmony Enforcers were now a thing some feared, others praised. But the major change was *the eyes*. All eyes were on us. Not just the students, but The High Arcanists as well. Realising all this almost changed how bright the sun was. The days were darker, looming.

"Students," Master Lethalica spoke. "I will have to attend regular classes today, so you will have to be on your own. My substitute has fallen sick to hypercapnia."

"Hypercapnia? That's odd," I frowned.

"It's when you have too much carbon dioxide in your blood, right?" Nilah asked.

"Yes. It seems she had been doing magic experiments," Master Lethalica said. "There won't be another trainer coming to aid you, but I have tasks for you to accomplish."

"Tasks?" I asked.

"Group up two-against-one. Try to put each other in a tight corner. You don't know how many enemies you will face. So group up, make a few rounds, and then switch. Once you're done with that, I'd like each one of you to practice their most tolling spells. But not against one-another! Use the Absorbius Chamber."

Master Lethalica walked away, leaving us in the undergrounds of The Academy, where large arenas, reinforced with top tier magic barriers kept the outside safe from whatever happened inside. The large bricks constructing the walls reflected the light of the magical torches, spreading their inextinguishable flame. We stepped on solid ground, much like what you would find in an often used pathway in a forest. The lingering smell of ozone revealed the excessive use of Elemental Magic. No student knew of this place to even exist. Apparently, masters and top-tier mages were the ones who used it for training.

"Okay. How about ladies first?" I said, smirking. "You two against me."

"Oh, Nillie, would you look at that?" Evie started roleplaying. "It seems we have a troublemaker."

"Evie, we should punish him for his wrongdoings." Nilah said, her face grim. "What torture should we give to make him regret ever laying eyes on you?"

"Oh my," Evie blushed, chuckling.

"I see you're ready," I said and shaped equations. "Level Three Illumination Magic, Shield of Redemption."

In front of my left forearm manifested an almond-shaped shield. Light Dust floated around it as the magic inside kept shifting about. My ability to cast Illumination Magic wasn't a surprise to them at this point. I snatched away whatever spells I found useful from Evie during this special training we received. She already knew I could copy her healing spells, so I had taken a brave step and went further. Master Lethalica had noticed this, but all she did was smile and observe.

"On the defence already?" Nilah asked, a fireball conjuring in her palm. "Your perception hasn't deceived you, infidel!"

Both me and Evie laughed at her. The act was so good, especially with her sweet pout.

The fireball launched, and my shield splashed the flames across its length.

"Watch out!" Nilah yelled from behind me. *Woah! When did she get there?*

I turned around, blocking another fireball, but as I did, Evie's perfume filled my nostrils. That was enough of a sign for a second shield. A flash of light shaped another almond shape in my right hand. The collision of her Lightforged Sword bore such power, it sent me flying to the side. A burst of mana in the shape of Level Two Elemental Magic - Wind Blow reduced the speed at which I was flying towards the wall. *Evie packs some brute strength. When will I get used to her petite figure having this much force?*

Mana spreading across all my muscles and joints, I back-flipped into recovery. By the time I landed on my legs, Evie's Flash Step left a trail behind her, and as I looked up, she held the Lightforged Sword high in the sky. *Damn, she's scary. But I'm not anywhere near done yet.*

My body burst into darkness as I used Level Three Black Magic - Shadow Step. I dashed to the side, meeting Nilah waiting for me, right in front.

"Sorry, Sovie." She said, her fist reinforced with mana, digging into my stomach. At the moment of impact, some mana toughened my muscles, but the damage was still done, lifting me off my feet. The two shields dispersed into Light Dust, as I lost control of the spells at that moment. I heard the whooshing sound of Evie's flash step, already greeting me with another attack.

"Not gonna happen!" I yelled, mixing the equation of Illumination Magic's Wall of Light and what I've seen Master Lethalica used to generate wind.

A shockwave burst out of me, pushing both of them away and propelling me into the air.

"Level Three Elemental Magic, Thundering Roar," I said, pointing an arm at each of them. Out of my palms sparked lightning, and the thunder resonated into the arena. The ground shattered, throwing dirt in the air.

"Nice one," Evie said, as she lowered her barrier, while Nilah already threw fireballs at me.

My feet back on solid ground, I shadow stepped to avoid each one. Evie swung her sword in the air, each slash shaping an arc of light that came at me at an alarming speed. They kept oppressing me, and I evaded with Shadow Step or conjured barriers on the moment before impact, to conserve mana.

I focused and conjured back both shields. In a burst of

Shadow Step casts, I appeared right next to Nilah and bashed her with the shields. Blinded by light, Nilah somehow struck my legs with a force enough to rotate me ninety-degrees. *Good, she's been tapping into how to reinforce her strength very well.*

In a beautiful twirl, she used her arms to propel herself off the ground and kicked me into the air. Just as I opened my eyes, Evie's feminine features were right before me. She hit me with the force of a collapsing building. Thankfully, the shield took in the damage in my stead. I crashed into the ground, the other shield soaked in that damage.

Just as I was about to rise to my feet, a yellow flash bloomed from the sky as Evie landed on me. The Light-forged Sword's tip pointed at my chin. It slowly turned into Light Dust, as she kneeled closer to my torso.

"You're superb, Evie," I said, gulping.

"Probably not good enough," she said, her face turning from a cold-death-delivering beauty to a heart-warming smiling beauty.

I climbed into a seated position, studying her face from up-close. She gazed at my eyes, and I did the same in silence.

"Er, guys, what are you doing?" Nilah looked down at us. "You should just get a room or something."

"By The Light, what?" Evie blushed and jumped off me. "I just defeated the infidel and was securing his will to fight was depleted!"

"Is that so? I think you were doing something else to the infidel," Nilah said, chuckling mischievously. "Sitting on his lap like that. Maybe the infidel converted you to the side of evil?"

"Nillie, is that a mushroom behind you!?" I yelled, pointing with my hand.

"What!? Where!?" she perked up.

Evie extended my arm to help me get off the ground, and I accepted it.

"You lied to me." Nilah frowned. "There's no mushroom!"

"You asked for it," I shrugged.

"Okay, we should change teams now," Evie said.

"Oh, would you look at that party-wrecker?" I pretended to be angry. "She took all the mushroom drinks to herself!"

"Oh no. I'm alone against you two?" Nilah facepalmed. "But you are monsters, that's not fair!"

Nilah, even if at a high disadvantage, didn't lose in a flash. I imagined her ability to be above the average student. Yet, I lacked the real experience of seeing how other students fought. Our long day of training ended with all three of us practicing lethal magic that wouldn't be wise to use against one another. Despite Nilah's obvious worry, we reassured and encouraged her to venture deeper into these waters. After all, using Black Magic was dangerous on its own. Level Four and Five could lead to a miscast leading to one's death. *I won't show you how worried I am, Nillie. If I do, then you'd lose confidence in yourself. And that could lead to the worst of it all. Shadows be with you.*

It was fear. Nothing else. Pure fear of losing those two girls made me push out of the boundaries I had been putting on myself. During our training days, each spell I saw, I tried to copy its equation. I remembered many of them; I experimented with mixing them. My understanding of magic, I couldn't help but notice, differed from theirs. Even from Master Lethalica's. The way she looked at me as I copied her made me sense some uneasiness about her. I disregarded that and tried to make the best of it. Whenever I went inside the Absorbius Chamber, a magic room where you can cast away all the spells you want and they will just remain in this different dimension, I attempted to cast all the spells I had seen that day.

I fear for what magic really is. The Academy teaches us in separate schools of magic, but it sends shivers down my spine - it's not that. That's dead wrong. My experiments prove that magic is one. At least, to me... it is.

I went out of the shower and put on the first T-shirt I had in sight - a white one with a quill on the front and back. I slipped into my black pants, and sat next to the window. A gentle wind moved my hair as I looked up at the full moon. I sank into thoughts about the true essence of magic. My mind kept flashing back to the tapestry I could see. What was it really? How was it all related?

"Sovie?" Nilah's voice came through the door after a few gentle knocks. "Can I come in?"

"Always, Nillie. Come in," I said in a louder voice to make sure I was heard.

Dressed in a white pyjama, she sat on the bed looking out the window. The moon's reflection danced in her blue eyes. We stared outside in silence for a long while.

"What do you think of Evie?"

"Huh? Where'd that come from?" I asked, startled.

"I can see how you look at her from day one."

"How do I look at her? I appreciate–"

"I know you like her, Sovie. She's the first girl you look at like that," Nilah said bluntly.

My cheeks flushed. *What am I supposed to say to this?*

"Is that... something bad, you think?"

"She's from The Luminari. You know what they used to do to us, right?"

"That's history," I sighed. "We should let go of that. Did Evie ever do something bad to you?"

"No, that's not what I meant," Nilah shook her head. "I was just thinking how Evie is nothing alike the other Luminari followers."

"Ah. Sorry, I misunderstood you at first," I said. "Yes, she is. Maybe that's what I actually like about her."

"I think she likes you, too."

"You think so?" I smiled uncontrollably.

"She looks at you whenever you do your cool, only Sovie-can-do things," Nilah chuckled.

"Ah, just that? I think it's because she's really fascinated by magic. That's all," I sighed.

"No, it's not just that. Whenever we study together, she always takes a while to just look at you. I've seen her do it!"

"Oh? Really!?" I perked up. "I think I do the same."

"Yes, you two are always looking at each other all the time, but avoid to lock eyes together."

"Hey, that's not true! Like today, we were looking into our eyes, but you told us to get a room!"

"Yeah, I think you should," Nilah crossed hands before her chest and nodded confirmingly.

"Hey!"

She straightened up and hugged me. I took her into my embrace and patted her head.

"Is this what's been worrying you? That I might leave you?" I asked.

She responded with a curt nod.

"Don't worry, sis. I'm with you to the grave, and hopefully, beyond." I pinched her cheek, making her frown. "We're family. Nothing will change that."

"Thanks, Sovie." She said and pinched my cheek.

"Ouch!"

"Ha! Now you know what it's like!" Nilah chuckled.

We kept staring into the moon; the wind making it a little more chilly than it was minutes ago, but with her by my side, I didn't mind it. It was wholesome.

"Sometimes at night, you come to me and we talk." Nilah whispered.

"What?" I frowned. *Did I hear that right?*

"No, nothing. I think I was dreaming just now," she stretched. "I'll go sleep now. Happy I could talk to you before bed, Sovie."

"Alright. Sleep tight, Nillie. Shadows consume you," I said, smiling.

"Shadows consume you, Sovie. Nighty, night."

Among the Archives

First, darkness consumed the skies. Everyone looked at where the sun used to be. Light Dust shed and then rays of divine light pierced the darkness.

"You, who delivered death, shall meet the weight of consequence." His voice descended as the light carried Him. He had no wings, yet He flew. People rejoiced, no longer in fear of the enormous winged beast.

"Sovah, you are but a human with a gift. You've let flattery get to your head. The skies have always been dragon territory. You dare float before me? I shall teach you consequence," the beast's wings spread out like mountains.

"Perish." Sovah spoke, and the beast perished.

- "Tales of Sovah, The Legendary Mage," Book 1, Page 213

MATHSMAGICA

CHAPTER 20
REUNION

TWO WEEKS.

There were only two weeks left before we headed out on this absurd mission, tasked to us by The Pillars. For the first time since our training had started, we had a Friday, Saturday, and Sunday to rest. We had this immense desire to just lay at the dorm and do nothing, but with nothing other than a gaze, me and Nilah settled upon a decision.

"You guys be careful, alright?" Evie spoke in a soft voice, the wind waving her hair back, the sunlight bouncing off her pale skin.

"You didn't have to send us off all the way to the border, Evie," Nilah embraced her and sighed. "But thank you for doing it, anyway."

"Oh, you sweet thing," Evie patted her, smiling.

"We'll be back in the evening of Sunday. We can grab a drink at Mushroom Cafe, if you're free," I said.

"I've spent every day morning to evening with you two for the past month and a half. Really, I feel so hollow, knowing you won't be around," Evie sighed.

Nilah let go of her and perked up. "Why don't you go to see your family, too?"

Evie pushed a lock of hair behind her ear and looked to the side. "I'll see."

"Hey, Evie." I said and opened my arms. "Come here."

She smiled and hugged me. *I will surely miss this perfume.* My arms comfortably landed across her and I pulled her into a tighter embrace. Her hands wrapped around my back and she squished her head into my chest. I couldn't help but think how small and fragile she appeared at that moment. *How can a body so petite pack such astonishing power?* I couldn't comprehend it, but I respected her a lot more because of that.

"Hey, how long are you guys going to stay like that? Sun'll set," Nilah pouted.

"I'll see you soon, okay?" I said, pulling slightly back. The absence of Evie's warmth suddenly making me cold. All the reflections in her eyes made them appear even more refined than the most polished crystal. *The Shadow Covenant teaches us not to stare too deep into the darkness, even if it might tempt you, and with practice, I can easily tap out of it. But not with Evie's eyes. They mesmerise me beyond any power in this world.*

My heart warmed up as she smiled, her thin lips a remedy for my perception. "Light be with you, Sova."

The breeze kept playing with Evie's hair each time I turned to see her, as she stood in wait for us to disappear out of sight.

"It feels good, doesn't it, Sovie?" Nilah asked me as we went through Mathsmagica's protective barrier.

"I'd usually ask for specifics, but I think I know what you mean." I nodded.

"Knowing somebody will wait for you. To really come back."

"Yes, Nillie. Now, let's go to him. He has been waiting for far too long."

"Brand will be in delight to see us surprisingly going back home, won't he?"

"For sure. I can see him tearing up and hugging us so tight he'd break his own bones. Talk about ours!" I laughed.

Rays of light beamed between the thin-leaved trees. The Heedsight Fort's magically enhanced stone walls serving us as a grand landmark. Just a few years ago, we would already face Black Arrow spells striking us, but Mathsmagica's construction and the peace treaty rendered the rangers unemployed. They still stood guard on the fort's walls, ready to strike, nonetheless. Nocturnia, despite committing to it, didn't completely trust in the recently signed peace treaty.

For the purpose of peace, when Shapers bent the lands to construct Mathsmagica, they moved a piece of mountain to the side, allowing for a road into the country, to the side of the fort and its walls. Nocturnia felt exposed, but swallowing the risk, bowed head and agreed to the potential tactical disadvantage.

Peeking within the fort was impossible, as the walls were so high, you'd only see the mana reinforced bricks towering above. Throughout the trip, I spoke more to my sister about Evie. I didn't do it quite intentionally. She fascinated me so much that I couldn't help myself but share how she inspired me. The warmth I felt when I gazed at her. My sister kept on smiling at everything I said and agreed that Evie is just that awesome. The time flew by so fast that by the time I stopped talking we had passed around the fort and in just minutes, Heedsight's paved streets greeted us.

My heart beat with unexpected excitement at the sight of the familiar buildings. The typical crescent moon symbol adorning the houses' doors, some pavements, and practically almost everywhere one could lay eyes upon.

The smell of lavender haunted the streets, as it was often used in daily rituals by The Shadow Covenant. I threw a gaze at Nilah to see she was looking at me already. We smiled and nodded to each other, strolling towards the city centre.

"Shadows consume you," some people greeted us.

"Sova! Nilah! You're back!" a familiar childish voice perked up, running at us.

"Rummy Loom!" Nilah bounced and embraced the little guy. He had grey drippy clothes, black eyes, and short hair. The sandals he wore, along with the rest of his body, were covered in mud. "How've you been!?"

"Did you play with the cows again?" I asked, patting him on the head.

"Big bro Sova! You look so badass! So it's true!" Rummy bounced in circles. He was about a head shorter than Nilah, hence the way he jumped was really funny to me.

"Do I now? What's true?" I laughed.

"Other students who pass through here mentioned about the Harmony Enforcers bringing justice to The Shadow Covenant! Your uniforms completely fit the descriptions!" Rummy spoke excitedly.

"Oh yeah. The uniforms," Nilah chuckled, looking at her clothing. "Quite the give-away, aren't they?"

"We didn't take them off as, by Director Astron's order, we must wear them all the time in Mathsmagica. And it would be weird if we went through the bridge and started undressing, wouldn't it?" I crouched to level my head with Rummy's.

"I knew going to Mathsmagica would be awesome! I'll grow up, I'll develop such a *BIG* mana pool, I'll cast Black Magic to everyone who says something about, about, about— Whatever!" Rummy threw his arms left and right, pretending to be shooting magic, engaging against imaginary foes.

"Oh, you sure will, Rummy!" Nilah cheered him.

As much as I concentrate on sensing Rummy's mana, I think it's settled. My eyes don't show a single trace of a magical number on him, either. The harsh truth of the world. Born of the lowest class of commoners, even if you have the brightest ambitions, you will never be a top-class mage. No. You'll never be a mage at all.

"I'll show you some magic trick tomorrow if you come around," I said and walked further. "Just make sure you sleep well or you won't be able to handle it!"

"No!" He yelled, pulling his hair back. "How do you expect me to sleep after you tell me that?!"

I shrugged, laughing. "See you tomorrow, Rummy!"

Nilah also waved at him and caught up to me.

"So news of us has reached here. I'm happy it is *good* news. Many rumours could've spread," Nilah said with a sigh.

"Thank Nocturna. It seems mainly for the best. It would explain why some people we never saw before greeted us as well."

Less than five minutes later it was there, before our eyes, the Heedsight Library. Our home. The old wooden door creaked as I pushed it in, the smell of books and burned wax filling my nostrils. *The smell of home.* I couldn't help but exchange smiles with Nilah as a feeling of nostalgia washed over me.

"Now comes the moment when he sees us and cries. Are you ready for it?" I whispered.

"Let's go!" Nilah whispered back.

A loud bang resonated as a man in his forty-fourth year slammed a book shut on the desk. White locks of hair danced among his brown ones. His dark eyes did a typical peer up so he could see above his glasses' border. Bushy brows frowning at us. Clean black commoner robes fitted his slightly overweight body as he whispered. "Sova? Nilah? Did I sniff too much of that weird dust on that book?"

"In the flesh," I said, presenting Nilah and then me with a courtesy head bow.

"That voice. Eight months. I hadn't heard it in eight months. It sounds the same. Hmm," Brand said in a soft voice. "It's really you, isn't it?"

"Brand!" Nilah bounced and ran to embrace our foster parent.

He jumped off his chair and hugged Nilah. I went next to him, waiting in line for what came in order. My sister moved to the side, and he embraced me into a welcome-home hug.

"You've grown taller, haven't you?" he smiled at me, his eyelids half-closed.

"Brand, it's been eight months. I couldn't have grown taller. And I'm twenty now. I doubt I'll grow more than this," I spoke in a beaming tone, as I measured him still a few centimetres taller than me.

"We're closed!" Brand suddenly yelled and rushed towards the door, pushing some person out so fast, I couldn't even see who it was. "I'm locking this door. My kids finally came to see me. Nobody else is welcome today."

"But that's bad for business," I tried to mimic his tone from just a year ago.

"Screw business. My kids are The Harmony Enforcers!" Brand rushed towards the door behind the office. "Come, come! I want to hear all the stories you have to tell!"

The smell of the freshly trimmed grass of our backyard mixed with the lavender scent where the sky burned orange as the sun set. We didn't even realise how much we had to tell, and Brand, like the perfect support he always was, listened to us. He didn't miss even a single detail of our Mathsmagica adventure. His showing emotion and excitement proved how immersed he was. But as we spoke of the most recent mission we had to attend, he sighed a few times more than anyone should.

"Is there no way you can back out from this?" Brand asked, his voice shaking.

"I'm afraid not..." Nilah sighed. "I'm scared too, Brand. But I must not let this fear take the best of me."

Brand smiled and took her hand in his.

"And would you imagine what that would make of The Shadow Covenants then? If we back out now, it'll be a disaster for Nocturnia's reputation," I said, looking at the white pyramid-shaped crystal in the centre of the table. "I see that rumours of us making a good word for the nation have spread already."

Brand sighed and put his free hand on my shoulder. "You two have grown so much in those eight months. You're like completely different people."

"Brand..." I sighed. "We're the same kids you grew up with. People simply talk things about us."

"Yes, Sova. Do you know what that means?"

I cocked my head to the side as the glow of the pyramid reflected from his eyes. Nightfall had begun, and the magic torches hanging across the yard beamed their light up.

"It means you carry the weight of power. Responsibility."

He let that sink in as he gazed into my eyes and then into Nilah's.

"You two are the only remaining descendants of The Darc family. I beg for your forgiveness that I couldn't provide even a tenth of the life you deserve to have." Brand sighed. "I wish you could walk the street without that being a secret held as deep…"

"Brand, don't feel sorry about it," I said, shaking my head.

"It's not your fault, Brand," Nilah added.

"If only it weren't for those Luminari bastards," he said, hatred fuelling his voice.

"Hey. They're not all like that," I said sharply.

"Oh, but they are. If they knew who you were, they would kill you on the spot. They'd call an army if they had to. All powers in their arsenal. Just to erase you from existence."

"Brand, listen to me." I paused until his vengeful eyes turned back to normal. I could tell he was revisiting events of the past. "A Luminari Faith mage is the third member of The Harmony Enforcers. You know that, right?"

"About that," Brand frowned, sighing. "Watch your backs. At the moment when you least expect, that's when he will strike you. When your demise is undoubtful."

"It's not a 'he.' It's a 'she', Brand," Nilah chuckled.

"And her name is Evie Stratovic," I said, my voice sharp.

"That matters little." Brand clenched his fists.

"But it does." I leaned closer to the table, staring into his eyes. "I have taken a liking to her."

The backyard fell silent as if Master Lethalica had used

her incredibly useful silencing spell on us. Even further, nobody even moved.

"Boy. Please, reconsider. I may not be your father, but I care for you as such."

"Evie has the purest soul a person could ever wear on them, Brand. I understand your concern, but you will meet her one day. Then you'll know." I smiled.

"I like Evie, too. She's the best friend I have ever had. And she's been helping us get stronger, too!" Nilah beamed.

"By Nocturna's Shadows, I beg you, kids. Watch your backs," Brand said, shaking his head.

After a brief pause, Brand drew a heart-warming smile on his face and said, "I won't say anything I'd regret later! I know that people of The Darc Family are the most surprising sort. Even if you think it's impossible, they have the birth-given power to defy that."

"Like this?" I asked, conjuring a shield of light next to my hand. Brand's eyes went wide opened.

"Or this?" Nilah asked, a fireball in her hand.

"My goodness! Exactly!" He yelled, clapping his hands. "By Nocturna's Shadows!"

"Don't worry, Brand. We're learning what it means to be ourselves. And Evie is a big help in that!"

"I," he shook his head. "Believe in your choice."

I know you don't. But it is what we want to hear. I appreciate that. You really are wise, Brand. The best foster-parent we could've had.

"It's almost time for Nocturna's Gaze," Brand said, looking at the white pyramid glowing in the centre of the table. "It's a pity you won't be here for it. I am sure the effects of the ritual would've benefited you on your mission."

"I would've benefitted. I'm not sure if Sovie with his

mana pool would even bother to commit to it," Nilah pouted.

"Hey, I'd do it for tradition if not else. And the ritual increases the Black Magic potency!" I said, pointing at the pyramid.

"You say that, but you didn't even bother doing a glimmer on the pyramid for the past few hours."

"Oh, fine." I said, shrugging. "Level One Black Magic Sorcery, Glimmer."

A tiny black energy thundered into the pyramid, enhancing its glow just barely.

"Happy now?" I asked in an annoyed tone, eyeing my sister.

She perked up, and we enjoyed the comforting glow of the pyramid.

"I think the time has come, kids," Brand said and straightened from his chair.

"Are you going to bed?" I asked.

"No. Sova, Nilah. Follow me," he said and went into the house.

Navigating through the living room and into the reserve storage cache, he stopped at the sight of a drawing hanging on the wall.

"It's Haley," I said in a soft voice. Brand stared into his late wife's drawing, but with a headshake he took the drawing off.

"What are you doing, Brand?" I asked, frowning.

"Nilah, hold this, please." He said, giving the drawing to Nilah. I looked at it again, recalling Haley's beaming smile. She and Brand were more than the perfect couple. Unfortunately, she couldn't have kids. *It's been ten years since she passed now, I think.*

"I always liked how her hair was curly and bright,

despite being brown. Haley inspired me in so many ways," Nilah spoke softly.

"Haley rests in the past. It's not why I brought you here," Brand said and pressed the wall where the portrait used to hang. A gap formed, and the wall shifted with a cracking sound. "The time has come for the past to leap into the present."

"We had a hidden place like this?" I asked, frowning.

Brand pushed it open and a small room with a ladder leading down revealed itself to us. He descended, and we followed. A torch hung next to where the ladder was placed. Brand took it and gestured at it. Equations formed within Nilah's palm and in a second, the torch lit the corridor before us in a warm light.

"As you embark into lands unknown, on a path unwalked." Brand spoke, his voice resonating between the stone walls. "Do it as you were destined."

He opened the door before us and I could instantly feel a magic barrier break. Magic dust glowed in the air as Brand traversed it, thick as if it were fog.

"Sova Darc, Nilah Darc." Brand turned to us, a room with undying ash-flame torches on its corners unveiling the most unbelievable sight. "I present to you The Legacy of The Darc Family."

On the left side of the room, on an altar designed of crescent moons held in the air by hand-shaped metal holders, stood a beauty beyond any I'd seen, even in books.

"The legend speaks of a tale of Sovah The Legendary Mage who defeated the dragon Blakiel Deathwing at a stand-off at Frostcap Peak. When the black-scaled dragon threatened to destroy Dreamholme, Sovah fought it and chased it away up to Frostcap Peak, where he ultimately defeated the magical creature. 'The Devourer' was crafted exactly from that dragon's scales. Lumiel, your father, wielded this sword. Passed down to him from your grandfather. And I find no better moment to let you rightfully claim it as your own."

"The Devourer," I said in a soft voice, grabbing onto its handle. The blade shimmered with a captivating glow. Its hilt was intricately carved with ancient runes that pulsed with a faint blue light in sync with my heartbeat. As I raised it before my face, a subtle hum emanated from the sword, as if it were alive. Faint wisps of dark energy swirled around the blade. Somehow, I knew it craved for me to channel magic power through it. Adorned with a design depicting dragons with glowing runes for eyes, the guard further enhanced the beauty that the black sword already was.

"Its handle isn't ordinary either. Crafted from the concealed essence of ethereal beasts, it'll act as a perfect catalyst between you and the sword," Brand explained.

I looked at Nilah, and she seemed captivated by the other item on the right altar. Dark roots shaped a perfect holding spot for another sight of magical craftsmanship.

"Nilah," Brand spoke. "What you see is what Erica, your mother, wielded in battle - Shadowbane."

She grabbed onto it, and runes across it lit up at the moment of contact.

"A legendary bow, crafted from the first tree the ancient sages of Nocturna had planted - The Shadowtree," Brand said. "The bow's sleek black limbs have runes that glow whenever the wielder touches the string. One exception is when it bonds with its wielder, as it did just now."

Nilah felt up Shadowbane along its length with awe.

"The string itself is made of ethereal silk, enhancing any dark school magic that would run through it," Brand's voice shook. "A perfect fit for you."

I looked at him, only to see that he was smiling and tears had been running down his cheeks for a while now.

Our new weapons were indeed of a legendary grade. With ease, I could *feel* The Devourer's abilities. And judging by how Nilah's bow warped in and out of existence on her whim made me guess the same applied for her. Brand seemed really exhausted after giving us our legacy, so he went to bed. Beaming with excitement to try the weaponry, we both wanted to have a try at something, but realising their potency, we knew that would end in a catastrophe. And as Harmony Enforcers, we couldn't afford to just fool around like before. Both Director Astron and Brand said it right. We have power now. And that brought responsibility.

I went to my old room to notice there wasn't even a single speck of dust in it. *Brand has been constantly cleaning our rooms, hasn't he? Did he think we'd give up and just run back home at any moment?* I smiled, lowering my head. *Probably not. He just missed us, I believe.*

I threw myself in bed and before I knew it; I fell asleep.

Among the Archives

"From this day forth, none shall lay hand on the name. For as holy as I, as holy as it. Those who disobey, be it this decade, the next, or a thousand years later, shall know my wrath," He said, and we all bowed.

- *"Tales of Sovah, The Legendary Mage," Book 5, Page 494*

CHAPTER 21
GAMBLE OF TRUST

LAUGHTER, WARM HOMEMADE BREAD, AND FAMILIAR VOICES. The perfect description of the word 'home.'

The Saturday flew by as fast as a breath. Rummy came over and, as promised, I showed him some spells. His eyes were sparkling brighter than the flames I conjured in my hands. A passion I completely understood, because - what is the world without magic? I inspired him to train and try to grow into the best man he could, and I knew my words struck him hard. He would grow up with my image in his head, thinking 'I can be better!' Or at least, I hoped so.

The early morning sun painted the sky, and we set off on our way to Mathsmagica. Before we went through the door, Brand stopped us, giving a word of caution. "Do not flash your legacy weapons carelessly. Not because else, but some know who they belonged to."

Who would know that taking a break from full-day combat practice would have such a positive effect on the body? I kept thinking, as I felt so refreshed and rested. We arrived at the glorious sight of The Academy hours before what we expected. For the sake of nostalgia, we jumped on the rooftops and dashed from one building to the other. Not the wisest choice, as we were the Harmony Enforcers. Thankfully, our speed was considerately greater than the last time we passed through and people didn't even notice us.

We reached our dorm and opened the doors and windows for some fresh air. Instead of sitting down and studying, Nilah suggested we went out. And where else aside from our favourite Mushroom Cafe?

Our drinks were served, and we talked about how we spent the weekend. Of course, we talked about our legacy and this incredible urge to try it in action came back. It took five seconds to swallow the hot drinks, burning our tongues, and jumping towards the training arena. Greeted by some, and scrutinised by others, we walked past everyone in a rush to reach our training spot. As we walked down the stairs and entered the arena, we saw two men practicing martial arts.

"Your stance is good," Director Astron spoke, observing his student amidst the training arena. "But just 'good' is never enough."

In a blink's time, Director Astron's robes rustled as he appeared at the opposite end of the arena. A gust of wind followed him. "If your stance is masterful, you can easily execute the technique, Henrith."

"My practice proves hardly beneficial anymore, Master. Could it be that I have reached the peak of my realisable potential?" Henrith asked, bowing his head.

"Oh, you have returned." Director Astron smiled, gazing at me and Nilah stepping into the arena.

"Sorry, we didn't mean to interrupt your session," I said. "Please continue."

Maybe we can learn something more about Flow Magic. Or at least, I could copy something.

"Sova, Nilah," Henrith nodded lightly to greet us.

"No, I am done." Director Astron said, walking back from the corner of the arena. *He really dashed that distance in a flash, didn't he? And now he's pretending to be drained. Your appearance doesn't cut it, gramps. I know you're just fine.*

"I thank you for your time, Master Astron." Henrith bowed his head and walked towards the arena's exit.

"I said I am done, Henrith. But Sova and Nilah just joined. Since you will go to war together, it could be wise to have a sparring session together."

"What?" I frowned.

"What? You came to the arena to practise, did you not?" Director Astron raised an eyebrow.

"Hm. Yes, but–"

"Good! Splendid. I will spectate," Director Astron cheered and crossed his legs, sitting mid-air. I cocked my head to the side just to confirm, but yes, there wasn't an invisible chair there. However, the numbers my eyes could see indicated a tangible presence of magic surrounding him. *Does Flow Magic have the ability to defy gravity? How does he do that? Now that I think about it, Henrith also meditated in the mage tower, floating mid-air.*

"As you wish, Master," Henrith said, bowing his head and taking a fighting stance. His right leg extended forward, and his hands held a top guard.

I shrugged, a smile forcing itself upon my face as I realised how this situation escalated. "Okay then. What will be the rules?"

"No rules. Just don't kill each other, kids." Director Astron said.

"Nilah, let me try first."

"Okay, Sovie. I will spectate as well." Nilah beamed and sat next to Director Astron.

Good, maybe you could draw some valuable information from him while he is distracted. Smart thinking, sis.

"Sova," Henrith said and bowed. A custom martial artists always did regarding one another. "Let us do our best."

"Let's enjoy this." I bowed my head and walked over to him.

"The fight has begun, kids. Pretend you're fighting a creature of The Fog!" Director Astron yelled vigorously, and then in a soft thin voice said, "Just please, don't kill each other."

I kept walking at a normal pace towards Henrith, my concentration fully immersed to find a body movement showing an attack. I flooded my tendons, muscles, and joints with mana, ready to respond at any moment.

"Didn't you hear, Sova? The fight has begun. You're a ranged mage. Wouldn't you prefer to keep your distance?"

"How friendly, Henrith. But who brings a gun to a fist-fight?" I asked.

"Hmm. I like him," Director Astron said.

"So be it," Henrith smirked. Numbers exploded from his feet and, following a burst of wind, his leg was about to strike me in the chest. I had prepared a barrier in mind, so I executed the equation, a wall of light appearing before me. At the moment it absorbed the attack, I added an air current to the equation, making it a wall of wind that pushed Henrith slightly off balance. He recovered almost immediately, a grin on his face igniting a thrilling smirk on my face. A blink later, Henrith was already to my right, his fist landing on my right cheek. A series of punches with a finishing kick threw me flying at the wall.

"Sova, your weakness is close-combat. You should either improve your ability, or find a way to defeat your opponents from a safe distance." Henrith spoke, dashing at me.

"Right." I flooded my body with mana, propelling myself at him. Caught by surprise, he flew away as my fist landed on his forearm.

The ground shattered as I threw myself in the air, casting a Black Arrow and shot to miss. The thunder shook the ground and dispersed almost immediately.

"Conclusion!" Director Astron said, appearing between me and Henrith.

"But we're just starting, actually?" I asked, frowning. Henrith bowed his head and accepted his master's words for absolute truth.

"Okay, but who wins?" Nilah asked.

"Henrith, did you learn something from this sparring session?" Director Astron asked, his voice commanding.

"T–that I underestimated my opponent."

"If he were a creature of The Fog, do you think he would've spared your life and missed that arrow?"

"No."

"Good. And Sova, did you learn something new?" Director Astron asked.

"I'm not good enough in fistfights yet to match Celestials," I said, shrugging.

"Yet you tried to best him in his own game. Why?"

"How can I improve if I never try?" I asked.

"Good."

"I am ready to go again, Master Astron," Henrith said, taking the same battle stance as earlier.

"Actually," Nilah said, as she shadow-stepped next to me. Director Astron smirked, and Henrith's eyes went wide open. "Director Astron, we wanted to try something in private. It's *very* private!"

"This arena is not only yours, though. You know that, right?" Henrith laughed.

"Director Astron, it's something that should be kept secret from the public," I spoke quietly so Henrith wouldn't hear. *Director Astron is all about union and people's rights. Surely, he could help us with this.* "And I planned to speak to you about this, anyway."

Director Astron's eyes narrowed into a frown, and then he nodded. "Henrith, we have concluded for today. You may go. We shall talk later. The Harmony Enforcers require my aid."

"Yes, Master," Henrith bowed, putting his palms together. "Sova, Nilah. Until The Flow unites us again."

As Henrith left the arena, Director Astron looked at us with expectation. "Well, what is it?"

My sister and I exchanged stares, and then we sighed simultaneously. "Alright. Easier if you see."

Both of us extended a hand forward and a white sphere of energy radiated for a split second when our weapons manifested. The Devourer and Shadowbane.

My sword revealed its spontaneous hunger for magic as its wisps of dark energy swirled around it. Next to me, my sister held out Shadowbane and touched its string, activating the runes on it.

"By all that is holy–" Director Astron stood with his eyes wide open, staring into the items we gripped so tightly. He glanced at the arena's exit once more and then observed our weapons from up-close. "Where did you kids attain these weapons!?"

"We... Our–" I struggled to put in the right words, surprised by the director's fierce tone.

"It's our legacy!" Nilah yelled.

That's it. We're doomed. Beheaded. Executed, perhaps, on the spot.

Within the director's palm manifested a sword. *Conjuring Magic!?*

He swung at me, and I guarded with my sword. "Director!?"

I shadow-stepped, covering my sister, as Director Astron swung his blade at her. Our blades collided. The Devourer drew mana out of me, as if it heard my desperate plea. Black Magic swirled within its edge, crackling thunder as I swung at Director Astron. He evaded my attack easily, bending his back, and he slapped me with his left hand.

"I trusted you!" I yelled, letting my mana spread free. "Why!?"

Nilah shadow-stepped away from Director Astron and drew upon Shadowbane's essence of darkness, releasing a Piercing Arrow. Three barriers emerged, forming an impenetrable shield around him. The arrow effortlessly shattered the first two, but its force dissipated upon reaching the last barrier.

"No!" I screamed, dashing at him, as his focus was on the next incoming arrow. The Devourer's edge expanded in a pillar of Black Magic as I raised it above my hands. With a downward slash, the arena cracked in two, destroying the barrier that kept the outside world safe from whatever magic happened within.

"Enough!" Director Astron's voice resonated from within the cloud of dust, his glowing silhouette amidst, as he held onto The Devourer's blade with his palms.

Magic Dust glowed as the sound of ten barriers cracking like glass shattered by rocks struck my ears.

In a second, a brawny hand pulled me in, and within

another, my sister was in front of me. Shocked, both of us searched for an explanation of how we had moved so fast. I looked up, Director Astron frowning at the weapons in our hands.

"It really is them," Director Astron sighed. "So you really are their inheritors."

My hands shaking, I hesitated whether to strike him while he was this close.

"I'm not your enemy, Sova. I just had to confirm they weren't fake replicas."

"Director Astron? H-how do you expect us to trust–" Nilah asked, shaking.

Director Astron's presence right now is like that of a monster. His killing intent, I can feel it.

"I will cool down my mana. I had to be serious or this wouldn't have worked." He smiled and all of a sudden let out a hearty laughter. "After all, I could've died from that attack."

"What?" I asked, my jaw dropping.

"You know what your weapons can do, kids. After all," he sighed, looking at the sky. "It should be automatic when they bond with you. At least that's what he said."

"He?" Nilah asked.

"An old friend," Director Astron smiled. "One I regret you will never meet, I'm afraid."

"Is it..." I trailed off, my head low. I opened my hand, and The Devourer went back into whatever dimension it would lie in wait at.

"That's right. I am sorry for the life you two must have led," Director Astron patted us. "Lumiel really was a genius."

"Did you know him? Our father!?" Nilah yelled.

Director Astron smiled, closing his eyes and shaking his head slowly to the side.

"I know why you wanted to share this with me. And you were right. Nobody must know who you are. I can't save you from execution by The Luminari Faith," Director Astron sat on the ground. "It's always been like this. Such a pity. The Flow damned it."

"Director Astron, I am sorry, I don't follow."

"Do you know, kids, why The Luminari executed all Darc family members?"

Better not respond. He could tell us something we don't know.

"It's the gift you posses," Director Astron's eyes pierced us. "I thought about it when you wielded fire aside from Black Magic, but now I am certain. I also saw you use Illumination barrier in your spar with Henrith, right?"

"Director Astron, what is this gift you speak of? You know, but we've lived all our lives as commoners. Thanks to our friendly surrounding and our foster parent we could practise Black Magic without drawing much eyes on us. We didn't–"

"Oh, the pity. Lumiel, forgive me for letting this happen," Director Astron grunted and then sighed.

I crossed my legs just like him and sat in front of him. Nilah sat next to me.

"Your foster parents they never told you about it, did they?" Director Astron asked, then mumbling he responded to himself. "Yes, smart move again. How could they keep you safe, otherwise?"

"Director Astron, I just wanted to ask you... for a way to conceal our weapons' appearance. For others–"

"Your classmates? No. But anyone who participated in the wars or is a Luminari would probably guess," Director

Astron massaged his forehead. "I have a temporary remedy for that. But tell me. I must know."

He placed his palms on our shoulders and gazed with hopeful eyes. "Do you know of The Darc gift?"

"We can... have an affinity for more than one magic," Nilah answered hesitantly.

"No, kids." Director Astron clicked his tongue and shook his head again. "You don't have any affinity."

I couldn't help but laugh. Nilah chuckled, frowning.

"Lets take this to the fundamentals of magic, kids. What does an affinity for magic mean?"

"A person is born with the affinities they will posses until death. Whoever has mana in their body can practise all schools of magic, but they will ultimately excel at the one they have an affinity for."

"Yes. So you have no affinity, as a descendant of The Darc noble-line," Director Astron threw us a serious gaze. "Because you don't excel at a specific magic. You excel at all of them."

"What do you mean we 'excel at all of them?'" Nilah asked in a slow voice. "I have seen Sovie do some things... but he is just a genius."

"Your affinity is for all magic equally. Common-folk don't excel at any magic specifically, and you are the exact opposite. You excel at all of them. That's why, by definition of Magic Affinity, you don't have one."

I did have my thoughts about it. I could copy Evie's spells, I could copy almost anything I saw, but I thought it was because I could see the numbers and equations of the spells, unlike others. But this means that Nilah, too, can perform all kinds of sorceries. She just... has to learn them. Brand told us we probably had more than one affinity. Maybe two or three. He didn't know it was all of them, either. Did he know our father also had an affinity for all sorceries? Or could it be that my father didn't have any interest in learning all of them? On that thought, did he see magic the way that I do? Perhaps, if he didn't, then that's why he didn't practice all types of sorceries.

"What is your foster parent's name? Mr Ren? He was wise to not tell you this. Power is tempting. Magic is mesmerising. And you wouldn't have survived, tempted by it. You would've shown and people would've seen."

"But how come we could use fire magic as Harmony Enforcers and nobody paid attention to it?"

"The Shapers often have an affinity for more than one Elemental Magic. Two affinities are easy to close your eyes to. But you kids have the potential to be the most prime of mages," Director Astron sighed deeply. "We must proceed with caution. Lumiel and Erica will haunt me even in the afterlife, should I fail to handle this situation."

"You really knew them? Our parents?" Nilah asked, her eyes full of hope.

Director Astron nodded slowly, smiling at her.

"What were they like!? Tell us more!"

As he stood up and gazed at the cracked wall, a wistful expression crossed his face, revealing his journey down memory lane. With a slight shake of head, he spoke in a soft tone. "They were the most amazing mages I have ever seen."

"Is everybody okay!?" A knight ran through the arena's entrance and eleven more followed. Their blue capes adorned with magic circles waved as they rushed in, closing us in a circle. "Director Astron! The High Arcanist, and hell, the whole academy, shook!"

"I was just making a demonstration of power to these youths here, you see," Director Astron said, making a dismissive gesture.

"But The High Arcanist—"

"It's fine, my knights. You have done well to react so fast. But I assure you, all is fine. Except we'll need someone to repair the arena. Tell that to The High Arcanist."

"Yes, Director Astron. I shall deliver that message." The Knight waved at the rest of the squad and they all moved out.

"Your potential shall be harnessed," Director Astron spoke softly. "Even if it costs me my life."

Among the Archives

"The mountains shifted.
We knew he'd made a path for his army.
Weapons and spells at the ready; we laid in wait.
His army arrived.
A lone man, walking amidst the shifted mountain."

- *"Tales of Sovah, The Legendary Mage," Book 3, Page 111*

CHAPTER 22
I APOLOGISE

"Tomorrow we depart. Tonight we pray, and in this moment, we enjoy." Master Lethalica said.

I gazed at Nilah and then Evie. Their dumbfounded looks made me frown at our teacher even deeper. "What does that mean?"

"You can go drink, play games, have sex, read books, whatever you favour."

"Excuse me!?" all three of us yelled in unison.

"Today you're just twenty-year-old kids at a magic academy. Tomorrow, you will be in an ultimate game of survival of the fittest. Today might be your last day. Enjoy it," Master Lethalica said and turned her back to us. "At dawn, I will wait for you in the Summoning Hall."

"But–" I started, yet she dismissed me with a hand gesture, leaving the training arena.

"Okay, you two. What do you want to do? Maybe you want to go to your family again?" Evie asked.

"Brand is a whole day of walk away. By the time we go there, we'd have to be coming back. It won't make sense to go," I said.

"Hm. There is something that I want to do, actually." Nilah said, her cheeks flushing pink. "But I have to do it alone. Sorry!"

I frowned. "Alone? That's rare."

"Okay, guys. I'm out! See you later, Sovie! See you tomorrow, Evie!"

"Light be with you, Nillie!" Evie said, waving goodbye.

"Well," I looked at Evie and realised I had no idea how to continue that sentence.

She looked at me, and we stared briefly.

"Sorry, do you mean to go see your family?" I asked.

"No, Sova. I'm not in a great relationship with them," she shrugged. "Do you have plans?"

"I mean, if you're free..." I said, my cheeks burning hot like hell's fire unleashing.

"I am."

"That's great," I smiled. "Would you like to keep me company, then?"

"I would love to," Evie said, smiling.

We went out of the training arena and strolled across Mathsmagica's streets. It was the first time I enjoyed spending a long time just looking at what items each shop had to offer. Perhaps Evie always being in my eyesight made it that much better.

"So what gives with your family, anyway?" I asked.

"Well," she paused.

"Ah, sorry! I don't mean to push you. If you don't feel like telling about it, it's no biggie!"

"Thank you, Sova," she said and smiled. "I'll tell you, but first, do you want to do something really wild?"

"Oh? Where did that come from?" I asked, smirking. "Innocent Evie has her evil moments, doesn't she?"

"I read in a book that said all women are evil by default. Maybe it's true? We just hide it too well," she chuckled.

"Hey, Nilah can definitely be evil, I agree."

"Okay, follow me!" Evie crouched amidst the crowd.

"What are you–?"

A yellow flash appeared where Evie was. I traced it with my eyes to one of the nearby roofs. *Using flashy magic, ain't we?* I used Shadow Step and appeared next to her.

"Alright, now try to keep up with me!" Evie dashed to the next roof.

Dumbfounded, I blinked as she flash-stepped further ahead. "If it's a challenge, then I'll gladly accept it with a smile."

Roof after roof, we travelled across the plazas, chasing one another. She often looked back, her face beaming with joy. I recalled doing the same thing with Nilah recently, but doing it with Evie forced butterflies to race in my stomach.

She's gone. She disappeared!

I panicked, looking left and right. The streets, crowded as they were, lacked her presence. The roofs were clear. *Where did she go?*

"Yoo-hoo!" Evie's voice resonated from above. "I'm over here!"

Her black hair and uniform contrasted with the white oval-shaped roofs The Grand Arcanum Library had. *Oh my. We never went there with Nilah.*

"Coming?" she yelled.

I shadow-stepped next to her and as I did; she flash-stepped to the next higher point. Black and Light flashes followed each other until we reached the peak; a Mage Tower's roof.

"Hey, this is where The High Arcanist is–"

"Shh!" Evie turned. "Just be quiet and follow me."

With a stealthy approach, we hopped onto the balcony. I leaned my elbows on the white fence decorated with gold. The tower was above most other buildings, allowing for a mesmerising sight of magic and nature. The pure beauty of gazing into a distant horizon.

"Their focus is outwards, so if you come here and be quiet, they won't notice you," Evie whispered.

"The High Arcanists? Really?"

"Yup. I do this all the time," she said, chuckling.

We gazed into the horizon for a while, a chilly wind blowing in our faces. "That over there is Loria. You can always guess it by the amount of mountains," Evie said, pointing with a finger.

"And on its left, that's the Shapers' country. Domainia," she explained and leaned over the fence. "And a bit to the left should be your home, too! Nocturnia!"

"So to our right, over there," I pointed with a finger. "Should be Savannah. Your home?"

"That's right," she smiled. "But that's boring."

"Why would you say that?"

"You asked about my family, right?" Evie asked after a hesitant stare at her homeland, then took a step closer to me. "My father owns an extensive business. He makes a lot of money and always makes sure everybody has some in their pockets."

"Oh, so you're a rich girl, aren't you?" I teased her, poking her rib gently. *Oh my, I did it again.*

"Maybe." She poked me back and rested her hand on my waist. With a slight discomfort of leaving my hand hanging freely, I returned her gesture and wrapped my hand around her body. "He's always been kind and loving to me. I always felt safe around him."

"Then why wouldn't you want to go home? Do you live in the Northern Lands?"

"No, no. I'm in less than two days' ride from here," she said and sighed. "It's my mother. She's the issue."

"If your father is such a wide-heart, I'm sure your mother wouldn't be much different, would she?" I asked, recalling Brand and Haley. *Yeah, they were so fit for each other. Kind and burning with passion to strive forward.*

"My mother is Reina Stratovic. Perhaps you have heard of her?" She asked, putting her gaze up to meet mine. She gripped closer to me. Our bodies instinctively turned towards each other, creating an intimate connection. Evie put her other hand on my waist as well. With my free hand, I pulled a lock of hair behind her ear and then caught onto her small waist.

"I'm sorry, I haven't," I looked to the side. *Perhaps she is famous and I don't even know her name. I hope this won't hurt Evie.*

"It's fine, don't worry. She's retired, after all."

"Retired? Is she like, really old or something?"

"No, silly," she chuckled. "Don't make me raise my voice like that. The High Arcanist will hear us."

"I'm sorry," I said in a high-pitched whisper. "But what else did you expect me to think?"

"You're right. My bad," she winked. "As a Luminari Knight, there are three ways to go into retirement."

"I should really study more into The Luminari," I nodded. "So, which are those three?"

"Become a cripple, die, or… do a heroic deed," Evie said. Her eyes sank into the horizon as she spoke the last bit.

"It's a harsh world we live, Evie. I'm sorry your mom–"

"She did a heroic deed."

"Oh, okay! That's amazing!" I perked up. She met my excitement with a grim gaze.

"What, isn't that a good thing?"

"Not when you classify a holocaust as heroic."

"A holocaust? What?"

"Twenty years ago, my mother was involved in a certain specific mission."

"Oh no..." I felt a frigid chill run down my spine as my eyes opened wide. *Twenty years ago... I know the major events and talks of that time... Can it be, really?*

"The Luminari Faith had been on a crusade across the continent because of a sole reason."

No... no, no, no! Don't say it! Please...

I felt my eyes watering.

"To seek out each member of a certain noble family bloodline and its possible descendants."

I already know what you will say, Evie, just please... For the love of all that is good, don't say it!

"She eliminated the last members of The Darc Family. Despite the losses of hundreds of Luminari mages at the hand of Lumiel and Erica Darc, my mother - Reina Stratovic - cast a disruptive spell, altering all magic control in a certain area."

My knees too weak to hold me, I landed on them, Evie looking at me sorrowfully.

"Her plan worked out and when she arrived at the scene Erica Darc had been turned to ash, and Lumiel himself, pale and eaten away by cracks of Black Magic. Their two kids gone to never be found," Evie said, as tears ran down my cheeks. "She claimed Lumiel's last magic must've been so out of control that the babies got teleported to another dimension, as there were portal marks left of two people teleporting away from their bedroom."

My throat ached. Soreness and pain coursed through my body as my muscles stiffened, trying to hold down my cries.

"How–long," I tried to ask, through pants and sniffs, my voice cracking. "Did–you–know?"

Evie's eyes watered and tears fell down her cheeks, too. She kneeled before me and bowed her head, our foreheads touching.

"I know my words are nothing but dust in the wind, but I beg of you. Forgive me and my family for doing this to you. I need to apologise to Nilah as well," Evie muttered in a low, monotonous voice.

"How long did you know?" I asked, this time in a more stable form of speech.

"Since you showed an affinity to Illumination Magic as well. I knew it, then…"

I realised the dangerous position I, and my sister, were. A deep breath helped me sober up just enough to speak normally. "Why didn't you report it, Evie?"

She shook her head to the side. "I don't believe in that, Sova."

"I am of that family, Evie. It's not something to believe in. It's the truth! The way it is! I am Sova Darc!" I spoke, raising my voice. *Fuck The High Arcanist.*

"I know. That's not what I meant. I don't believe what The Luminari did was righteous."

My eyes were fixated on her while I gradually regained control of my breathing.

"I know what people you are. You do what is necessary to protect even the ones who hurt you. That's more than enough reason for me to stand up and be by your side. You're no abomination. You're a blessing!" Evie smiled with watered eyes. "And I don't want anyone to take you away from me."

My heart thrusted against my ribcage to escape. My arms wrapped around Evie as I hugged her and cried, burrowing my head in her shoulder. She cradled me and caressed my hair. The warmth of her body and gentle touch of her skin gave me comfort and a sense of safety. The warning Brand gave us came to my head. His words resonating soundly. *She's not like that, Brand. I'm glad I don't regret the words I threw at you.*

"You are the blessing," I whispered next to her ear as I recovered from my breakdown. "You're not supposed to carry the weight of your parents' mistakes. Forgiven? You were never in the wrong, Evie. You are the kindest person I've ever known."

I looked at her deep eyes and delicate features. Her eyelashes seemed so long and gracious, as if she had a natural eyeliner. I put a few locks of her hair behind her ear and then felt her cheek with my fingers. I trailed her jawline down to the chin and leaned in, pink lips completely irresistible at this point.

"Oi! By The Arcane darkness, what are you doing!?" a man yelled as he opened the door at the back of the balcony. "I'll get you expelled—"

With a shadow-step, contrasting with a flash-step, we leaped to the nearby roofs and descended to the ground, faster than the man could see our faces.

"Ah! It's you guys!" Nilah said, the moment we landed in the crowd. "Were you following me!?"

"Nillie!" Evie leered.

"Sis, what are *you* doing here?" I asked her, frowning.

"What do you mean? This is the main plaza, for shadow's sake..." Nilah frowned and peered closer to me, pouting. "What? Were you crying? Sovie?"

Nilah shook her head. "Evie, did you break this poor loser's heart or something? Wait. Evie!? Did he do something to you!?"

"What–?" I opened my eyes widely. *Did my sister just falsely accuse us both and then side with the enemy!?*

"Oh my, Nillie," Evie chuckled, buying time.

"We're all good, sis. Don't worry," I said, sighing.

"Alright. Now that we are all back together, do you want to go grab a Mushroom Coffee!?" Nilah perked up.

"Sure. Let's do that," I said and nodded at Evie.

"I'm in," she smiled.

Among the Archives

His wings spread across the sky, yet we could still see, as veins of magic glowed underneath. Its melodious voice spoke within our heads. "Fear not, humans. I will cause you no harm, but learn to accept our kind. For we soared these lands long before you walked them."

- *"Stories of Legends," Book 1, Page 64*

MATHSMAGICA

CHAPTER 23
A VERDANT SILHOUETTE

GREEN GRASS TRIMMED TO PERFECTION AT ANKLE LENGTH TICKLED BRIEFLY AT OUR SHOES. Flowers bloomed in a timid height, limited by magic. Amidst this rejuvenated field, Pillar Serene delivered his speech before a gathering of a hundred mages, twelve knights, and two masters.

I looked around to find numbers swirling around people as each one had their own reason for a spell to hover about their body. As The Harmony Enforcers, we stood in the front, behind Master Lethalica. Ten metres away was the other Master Mage, whom I had never seen before. The knights were right behind us, their blue capes nobly riding the waves of the wind, holy swords piercing the ground, as they leaned their hands on their handles.

"In the name of all Pillars of Mathsmagica, I wish you triumph! The only thing each one of you should lose is mana. Should you be scarred, may it be over a glorious victory!" Pillar Serene delivered his long speech as we all stood in wait.

Master Lethalica looked at me over her shoulder and spoke softly, "No matter what, stay close to me."

I nodded in agreement. One of the most powerful mages we'd ever seen offered us protection. *I heard rumours that you were like a goddess of the battlefield, Master Lethalica. With you at our side, no creature would stand tall before us. Not for long, at least. I hope.*

Though it's easy to say the fear of those creatures of The Fog was what shook the entire world into a peace treaty. How would these beasts match in power against Master Mages?

"Master Lethalica," Nilah spoke in a low voice. "Is it true that the creatures of The Fog can eat us alive if we run out of mana?"

"Worry not, little one. Use the spell I taught you should your mana be low," Master Lethalica said. "It will let you consume a potion without even touching it, as long as it's on your body."

"Yes..." Nilah nodded.

"Now, raise your heads high!" Pillar Serene yelled. "Those who embark on battle with a head slumped in the ground are as good as accepting their own defeat!"

"When we get teleported, just stay right behind me. If we get separated, search for my magic and come to me," Master Lethalica faced us and smiled. "I'm sure you would recognise it."

We smiled back, and I looked behind to see if I could recognise any faces. Most of the people I had never met, but at the second line of mages, I could recognise Henrith, and further behind in the rows, Bureaus. As much as I expected to see Arthus, he was nowhere to be seen. *Well, he is a first-year, after all. The Harmony Enforcers are the only ones who haven't graduated in this crowd.*

"Now go," Pillar Serene yelled, and a blue light engulfed the entire field. "And reclaim Rilereth of Loria!"

I opened my eyes, my left hand holding Nilah and my right hand holding Evie. *What? When did I even reach out to them?* The next breath I drew felt half as efficient in replenishing my body with oxygen as the previous ones. After releasing my grip on the girls, I narrowed my eyes to better understand my surroundings.

Master Lethalica was at the front with the other Master Mage. His name was Jethod, yet I hadn't really heard of him before. The knights rounded up on the hill's edge, all of them looking down the hill. I treaded, my feet sinking to the ankle in the dust. By the time I reached Master Lethalica, half of the knights had disappeared with Master Jethod, hinting at a two-point angle attack on the city. *If we attack from one side, and the other half of our men from the other, then we might trap the enemy in an all-out fire with no way out. Simple, yet effective strategies.*

"Are we splitting up?" I asked. "Half of us on one side, the others on another?"

"Yes, but kids, you must stay with me. Master Jethod's men will attack from the other side slightly after we go. We will bluff our numbers to fool the enemy and then surprise them," Master Lethalica explained. "Now let's descend the hill."

We advanced with Master Lethalica at our front, me, Evie, and Nilah behind her, and then the knights, each with a division of mages. In a triangle formation, we stepped down the dust covered hill. Strong wind blew specks of soil, scratching my skin. The knights activated barriers, protecting us. A blue sphere took the shape of our formation as we kept treading slowly, but surely, ahead.

"Sovie... I'm scared," Nilah said softly.

My heart beat at a frantic pace, but I had to appear strong for her. And not only. For Evie, too. I called out Nilah and Evie's names, slowing down my pace so they could see me well.

"Don't worry. I'll protect you," I said, forcing a bright smile.

Both of them smiled back at me.

"What's wrong?" I asked as Master Lethalica stopped.

"The city. Rilereth. It's gone," she said. "It should be here."

We advanced further, raindrops faintly mixing up with the dirt hitting against the magic barriers. It wasn't long before we found the source of the water in the air. Furious waves crashed against the dust-obstructed coastline.

"Where is the city?" Evie asked, but none answered.

"Master Lethalica, if we reached the coastline, then… where is The Fog? Or the creatures that come of it?" Nilah asked.

She turned around, her cat-like yellow irises glowing in the dusty air, as she spoke in a cold, sharp voice. "This *is* The Fog."

"Hey! Master Lethalica, is that you!?" an elderly voice, empowered by magic, yelled from the distance, a hundred metres wide barrier's glow, fighting through the dusty obstruction, approaching us.

"Lower the barrier. It's the others!" Master Lethalica yelled.

The blue glow faded, and the dusty wind scratched at our skin and eyes. I raised my hands to protect my face and eyed the girls to see if they were doing okay. *Evie, you look like a warrior. Eyes narrowed and sinking forever onward, ignoring the damage of the dust.*

Just as the elder man's facial features become discernable, from his chest outwards, he turned to dust, exploding and merging with the soil carried by the wind. One after the other, the knights burst, becoming one with The Fog. Our knights erected barriers, their glow in blue and yellow, merged as they drew a fine-line between us and the other men.

"What's going on!?" I looked left and right, as some of our own exploded into dust.

Master Lethalica studied the event with her eyes jumping from corner to corner. "Evie, Sova, Nilah! To me, quick!"

We gathered next to her, and she expanded her hands to the side. An orb of fire surrounded us and we stood in wait. When the screams of panic and agony faded, Master Lethalica's flames exploded around us, clearing our vision for a brief amount of time.

An object in the sky took my attention, as The Fog gradually recovered. Narrowing my eyes, I could see a green glow, numbers falling off of it like rain, as something crawled through the sky. The silhouette made little sense to me, as I had never seen a bird as big as that, or glowing. The object's glitter ceased as it shrank into a smaller shape, landing in the distance. My body froze in place, as the sensation emanating from that object was deathly chilling. The mysterious object had shrunk down to the size of a human. A silhouette of shadow, walking at a slow pace towards us, its verdant eyes glowing through The Fog.

The same sensation as Master Lethalica... and Director Astron, but... MORE MENACING!

My arms shook, mana pouring out of my body by instinct. The Devourer manifested in my hand, yet despite its power, I had no confidence in facing the approaching menace.

"Everyone's... gone!" Nilah spoke, her eyes opened wide, struck by the insanity of an endless swirl of dust. "They're all gone!"

"Nillie, stay close to me!" Evie yelled, her Lightforged Sword already embodied in her hand.

"Shadowbane!" Nilah yelled, and her bow materialised in her palm. Drawing on its power, she extended an arrow and launched it at the verdant-eyed shadow. The arrow propelled, pulling dust with it, the wind force vacuuming the tiny specks in a swirl.

The magical arrow disappeared, as if reduced to nothingness. The shadow kept closing in, the verdant glow in its eyes peering at us.

"Is... Is this why Mathsmagica was formed?" I asked, my voice shaking. "Is this the power of just one creature of The Fog?"

Master Lethalica expanded her hands in the air, flames mixed with water burst in the shadow's direction. The attack filled our vision with flames colliding with shapes of water-dragons. The onslaught of Elemental Magic ended minutes after.

The verdant eyes glowed beyond the aftermath, and a hand expanded at us. It flickered in green and a moment later; I saw tons of numbers shaping around Master Lethalica.

"Master–" I screamed, but a green chain wrapped around her, its grip forcing cries of pain. She tried to break free, but it was in vain.

"Sova, drop your limits. They're in your hands now," Master Lethalica said, looking at me with a smile over her shoulder.

"What– No!" I screamed, and the girls shouted her name.

In a flash of light, she disappeared completely. I extended The Devourer above my head and released a battle cry, filling it with mana. Numbers swirled into my peripheral vision, a magic circle appearing underneath us. Before I could swing my sword, we were no longer amidst The Fog and whatever creature claimed our army's lives like child's play was nowhere to be seen.

Among The Archives

Many tell their kids, even to this day, stories of dragons wielding magical powers. Some scared the children with the stories, others inspired them. Nobody has really seen a dragon. Did they really exist? If they were so mighty and everlasting, then how come we do not see even a faint trace of them?
Perhaps they really are but a myth. But one should not forget, myths also have origins.

- *"Debates on The World," by Christo Spaceri,*
  Page 12

CHAPTER 24
THE CRYSTALLINE SANCTUARY

Darkness took over.

Bathed in an ethereal glow, columns stretched towards the ceiling of what appeared to be a mystical ruin. The cracked bricks spoke of their timeless age, as the encroaching mould slowly mended them. The moisture of the growing vegetation weighted the air and the aroma it brought made breathing a challenge.

Evie cast Level Two Illumination Magic - Tranquillity of Mind, a spell I hadn't seen her use before. It immediately transitioned my panic into logical thoughts. *Magic really isn't about what level it is, how strong it is, or what mana it requires. It's just how you use it. Good job, Evie.*

"Do you girls have any ideas?" I asked, looking around the buildings expanding endlessly outwards.

"It looks like a castle. Is The Fog actually a means of disguising a kingdom?" Nilah spoke, her steps resonating within the enormous place.

"We definitely got transported somewhere. I don't think we're anywhere near the city," Evie said.

"I think so, too. But this place... it looks centuries old.

Not even the crypts in Algama would match this age," I said, my voice reverberating.

"The Hailing Revenants are reaching out to people hundreds of years ago. You mean to say this place is older than that?" Evie asked, her Lightforged blade taking shape in her hand.

"Look at this. Trees growing out of the walls themselves. A tree this big either fed on magic to grow like this, or is hundreds of years old," I said and then pointed further into the distance where trees as big as buildings had climbed atop of the silvery bricks' red roofs. "And that must be thousands."

"Do you have your teleportation stone with you? Maybe we could just–" she trailed off, looking at the useless piece of rock in her hand.

"Whatever got us here sealed away our means of teleporting out," I said, crouching close to the ground.

"The question is 'why?'" Nilah crouched beside me. With two fingers, I digged into the mouldy pavement.

"Sova, what are you doing?" Evie asked.

"I'm marking our spot," I said, drawing a circle with three dots in it, and then an arrow pointing forward. "If it happens that we're walking in a circle, we'd know we took this road at first. And it was the three of us."

"You think we might be separated later?" Evie frowned.

"I... I feel like this place is familiar to me. I haven't been here, really. Yet I don't know why, but somehow I thought it would be a good idea to make this mark."

"Alright," Evie nodded. "Let's go then."

Voices resonated from the distance.

"Quick," I whispered and leaped behind the nearby building. The ancient streets were rather open, as some buildings lacked over sixty percent of their walls. "Prepare to ambush!"

"I am telling you. All of them turned to frickin' dust! I am so happy my little brother didn't come along. In The Shaper's name, I don't know how we're even alive!"

"We should be thankful for this. And should we find a way out, at least one of us must definitely survive. It might not make sense to us, but there are far smarter people in Mathsmagica than us."

I narrowed my eyes as I leaned out the wall. With a smile, I turned to whisper to the girls. "It's actually Henrith and Bureaus!"

"Are you sure?" Nilah asked, her voice cold, unlike her usual bright tone.

"It might be an illusion of some sort. We should test them out first," Evie whispered.

I looked at them, noticing there weren't any chunks of numbers constructing their bodies, which meant there was no magic covering them. "Believe me. They're real."

"Who goes there!?" Bureaus screamed, throwing a fireball at me the moment I stepped out of the wall.

"Chill, a little, will you?" I smiled, blasting his fireball into a simple barrier. "It's us. You're like a cow in panic, man!"

"The Harmony Enforcers!" Henrith perked up, nodding as he saw us.

"In the flesh."

"How'd you guys end up here?" Nilah asked.

"We got separated from our group earlier and as we struggled to get through The Fog, in a blink of an eye, we appeared here," Henrith responded.

"What was the name of the two Necrotics who raided with you?" Evie lifted her sword at them.

"Oi, what are you doing, Evie!?" Bureaus stepped back, a fireball conjuring in his hand. "We're—"

"Answer the question!" Nilah said, Shadowbane manifesting into her arm, its runes glowing beautifully as she pulled an arrow.

"You better answer, Bureaus," Henrith said, smirking. "You're facing warriors on a battlefield."

"Velarian and Roselia. Okay?"

"Okay," Evie smiled, lowering her weapon. Nilah did the same.

"Bureaus, Henrith. It's important that you are aware of everything and everyone. Just like on a raid," I said.

"Look at you talking all high and knowing. I've got a ton more experience than you with—" Bureaus spoke, but Evie interrupted.

"We should leave them alone. Obviously, it's a higher risk to take them with us than let them be," Evie said in a natural tone.

"How can you be so cold-hearted, dammit!?" Bureaus frowned, scratching his bald head.

"I agree with you. We should leave him behind. Allow me to join your party, Enforcers," Henrith said, bowing his head and clasping his palms together.

"What!? Are you insane, man—"

"You can join us, Henrith. We'll appreciate your combat prowess and disciplined mind." Evie said.

From the eternally expanding ceiling, pillars of white light struck the ground in a perfect shape, surrounding us.

I saw equations forming before Evie and, with a wave of hand, signalled for her to stop.

"Sova?" she asked.

"I somehow... know it'll be okay." I took a step forward

and new pillars of light struck the ground four steps ahead of me. "Follow me."

The pillars hit the ground, navigating us in a pathway across the ancient city. Memories poked me. *I can swear I've seen this before. But at the same time... I can easily tell, I've never been here. How do I know this place? Being led by pillars of light like this. It should be the first time to happen... right?*

"Sovie, have you read about this place somewhere?" Nilah's voice reached my ear, taking me out of my thoughts.

"Maybe? No? I'm not sure," I replied honestly.

"This guy's dodgy–" Bureaus started, but Henrith put a hand on his shoulder as I turned to face him.

"I have a terrible headache, Bureaus." I said, looking condescendingly at him. His very presence annoyed me. "I advise you to be quiet."

He looked at me, eyes opening wide.

"Sova, your eyes... are violet again," Evie whispered, as I turned back.

"I don't know why... Sorry."

"Sovie, do you want to take a break?" Nilah asked, her fingers tightening around my hand.

I patted her, forcing a smile. *Something's calling for me. I must continue on this path of light, no matter what.*

We walked in silence until we reached a white sphere hovering at chest-level. *I touched this before. I need to touch it again. Wait... That makes no sense. I have never been here... This is... It feels right.* I put my hand on the sphere and got sucked into it. Appearing on the other side, I took a deep breath, inhaling the sweet aroma of spring. It drew a stark contrast between where I was just a second ago.

The blue sky above had velvet clouds, crystal raindrops falling from them. Each one crashed into the ground in a rhythm that shaped a melody much too pleasing to the ear.

Rivers flowed into lakes and cherry trees hovered above them, shaping a picturesque view with their blossoms. Brown leaves, meshed up with yellow ones, decorated the sidewalk, navigating me up to the top of the cliff.

The others warped in as well, but I was already too far away to hear what they spoke. Evie and Nilah rushed to catch up to me. I turned to see their faces and smiled at them.

The sidewalk took a sharp turn and ended at the entrance of a building. "I remember it..."

Red-painted timbers stood out of what appeared to be paper-thin walls. The roof had a symmetrical curvature on all sides, unlike any I had seen in my life. Yet, I could still say it seemed familiar. *Did I make this? No... That's not possible.*

Small oak stairs creaked as I stepped towards the entrance of the building. The wooden doors, light as feather, didn't even creak as I pushed them in. A crimson carpet decorated the room and drawings hung on the walls, an attempt to fill the vacant space.

"What kind of culture built this?" Evie asked.

"I could say some motives remind me of Celestial Weavers' ancient scrolls, but it is still far too different. I can't tell," Henrith spoke.

"We haven't got such things in Domainia." Bureaus picked a drawing off the wall.

"They seem to tell a story," I said, stepping into the next room, which also had its walls adorned with drawings. "Winged birds speaking to us."

"Not birds, I dare speculate," Evie said, narrowing her eyes at the drawing I was looking at. "Look at the waves that shape its body. The artist knew these are no feathers. They are the creatures of the legends, Sova."

Pain pierced my skull, forcing a grunt out of me. I grabbed onto my head and whispered, "Dragons."

"That's insane. We all know those are The Luminari Faith's super-mega important ego-boosting texts. No dragons existed. They made them up so they can make Sovah The Legendary Mage an even greater hero than he really was," Bureaus spoke with an annoyed tone.

"I invite you to take your words back, Bureaus." Evie said, her eyes opening wide. "You know nothing of Savannah's culture!"

"Bureaus, did I not ask you politely to keep your mouth shut?" I asked in a low tone.

"Bureaus..." Henrith sighed.

"I should've learned a spell to seal one's mouth," Nilah sighed, pouting.

My mind flashed with memories of a big cherry tree. Somehow my body automatically desired to go through the next door. Yet another room with drawings awaited, a white burning candle in the centre differing it from the previous.

"Is this some sort of ritual?" I asked, shaking my head. "Candles are strongly associated with rituals. What's really..."

Go forth. A voice resonated in my head. It sounded rich and deep, unlike any I heard before, yet so familiar, as if I had been hearing it all of my life.

I pressed my hand against the wooden door and pushed, yet to no avail. *Oh, right? Swipe it to the side!* My mind clicked. *But why? Why do I know and felt silly I'd forgotten about it? I've never really been here...*

At the peak of the hill, the background gentle melody resumed, as velvet crystals rhythmically vibrated upon touching the ground. A subtle wind pushed the big cherry tree before me, spreading its blossoming colours to the ground and some even off the hill. *When did we come so high up the mountain?*

Underneath the tree stood a foggy silhouette of a person. Taking a few steps forward, I could distinguish black armour made as if from a beast's scales. The fog underneath it glowed in a white colour, as it leaked at where the pieces of armour connected. The wind picked up, creating a gentle breeze that made the scales flutter and allowed more light to seep out from underneath.

"I used to carry the burden of flesh just like you," a deep voice resonated from within the armour. "Before coming here, that is. In this world."

The armour stood up from its knee and looked up at the cherry tree. It extended its hand forward with an opened palm, a blossom free-falling into it. "I had always dreamed of magic."

The others stood next to me as we looked at the armour towering at double my height.

"Dreamed so hard... that I came into this world in its purest shape. But I never pictured it as it is." the armour crushed the blossom in its hand. "I never expected it to be worse than the normal life I led."

It clasped its palms together and as it drew distance between them, a red scabbard decorated with cherry blossoms materialised.

"My king built this crystalline sanctuary for me. A sole remnant of true tradition and culture," the armour spoke as it grabbed onto the handle of the Odachi Katana that seemed endlessly long. "After all, he promised me the world I always dreamed of."

The armour took a step forward. The sheer intimidation of its appearance and unwavering movement shook my heart. Accepting a slightly bowed stance, thunder shaped eyes leaked a foggy light, its hands at the ready to draw the blade off the scabbard.

"I, Igreus, The Hollowed Knight, shall lay the foundation for My King's return."

AMONG THE ARCHIVES

Break it down.
Emotionally, spiritually, physically.
But don't kill it.
Or we don't know if He won't perish along with it.

- "Unknown," by Unknown

CHAPTER 25
IGREUS THE HOLLOWED KNIGHT

THE WIND BLEW THE LEAKING FOG OFF IGREUS, AS HE STOOD LIKE A STATUE AT THE READY.

"Draw," Igreus said, and The Devourer manifested within my hand, clashing with the knight's two-metre long Katana. My hands trembled from the impact of our blades. I tried to push him off, yet it didn't work as easily as I hoped. With the Katana right next to my face, I explored its beauty, only adding to its deadly appearance. At the dull back-part of the blade, along the whole edge were engraved the moon cycles from the hilt to the top.

"Level Three Flow Magic, Limit Breaker!" I yelled and pushed Igreus away. *Limit Breaker is taking a toll on one's mana, but I shouldn't have an issue with that. I am thankful that I learned it from Henrith when we practiced a few weeks ago. But I will need one more thing.* "Level Three Flow Magic, Reflective Insight!"

"How can you cast Level Three Flow Magic like that?" Bureaus asked as he conjured a fireball in his hand, then flung it at Igreus.

With a swift swing, the Katana slashed through the fireball and it dissipated into the air.

"How is it possible to cut through fire like it is a piece of bread!?" Bureaus yelled.

"My Soul Eater can cut through souls," Igreus spoke, adjusting the edge in a vertical position before his helm. "And magic is even easier."

The grip of The Devourer somehow sucked my hand in and released a loud metallic shriek. The darkness swirling about it grew bigger. *You're excited, aren't you?* I thought, smirking, as I noticed sweat pour down my forehead.

"Oh he, the Shaper of origin, punish thy fool who dared taint your land. Rich be the shape of your judgement upon my enemies," Bureaus chanted, numbers swirling around him, as the scale of his spell manifested. "I'll end this fast," he muttered.

The spell I had cast, 'Reflective Insight', boosted my body's reflexes and perception. Thanks to it, I spotted the killing intent that came from the very first disruption of Igreus' frame. "Bureaus, watch out!" I screamed, dashing in his direction.

Igreus' palm, like an ultimate tool of death, grabbed Bureaus' head within a blink of time. I swung The Devourer at Igreus, but his long limbs served as advantage, kicking me in the stomach and sending me a few metres back. With a swift spin, he brought Bureaus crashing down onto the ground. The numbers surrounding Bureaus were still there, meaning he was still conscious. I jumped back to my legs. Igreus lifted Bureaus and slammed him back to the ground, a fountain of blood splashing across the black scale armour.

"I need no nuisance," Igreus said, one of his knees resting on the ground. Henrith released a loud battle-cry, roaring as his body struck in The Knight's bloodied hand. A barrage of attacks landed as Igreus slowly stood up. Blood splattered, as Henrith's flurry of kicks and swings was so fast that they generated light. Blood flew left and right as shockwaves blasted off on each finisher of the combos. Henrith's technique was supreme. The way he moved was hard to follow, and the attacks all landed perfectly.

"He's not..." Evie whispered.

With a swift movement, Igreus struck Henrith with his Katana's handle. A loud scream of pain reverberated as Henrith blocked the attack, avoiding a fatal blow. He jumped back, aligning himself next to us as we drew a line facing Igreus. Struggling to catch his breath, Henrith's hands shook, blood flowing out of his knuckles, and an enormous bruise scarred his forearms.

"He doesn't take any physical damage..." Henrith grunted.

"Let's do this as a team," I said, looking at our surroundings. "Henrith, you stay back and offer whatever aid you can. Just don't face him straight on again."

"I know some supportive magic. I'll aid you," he said, nodding.

"Nilah, make good use of Shadowbane. Evie, let's corner him," I said and looked at The Devourer. *You're really excited to be in a fight like this, but how do I go about it? You can feed off my magic to grow stronger, but Igreus' Katana cuts through magic. How do I go about this?*

Igreus swung his Katana to the side, generating a sweep of wind, taking slow steps towards us.

A glow of runes illuminated in my peripheral vision, letting me know Nilah's Shadowbane was about to hit off. Just as the arrow swirled, I leaped next to it, and let it collide with The Devourer. "Feast on this!" I screamed, as the sword's edge extended momentarily almost twice its size.

Igreus parried my attack, granting me open, but Evie's black hair flew right before me, her Lightforged Sword, taking a slice at Igreus' torso. A combo of flashes followed, as her flick of attacks drew a triangle of light. Igreus' hand came at her at incredible speed, but she blocked it with the sword.

Nilah shadow-stepped behind Igreus and shot an arrow at his back. Igreus shuffled to the side, the arrow coming straight at me. Startled at first, I recalled my sword's ability, and let The Devourer feast on it. He absorbed the black arrow; the darkness swirling about it vigorously. Evie flash-stepped, slicing at the black armour's heel. Steel clashed as Igreus' Katana swiftly neglected each attack.

"Level Three Flow Magic," Henrith spoke. "Survivalists of The Tide!"

A magic circle shaped underneath our feet and my breaths felt a lot lighter. *A stamina buff, is it? We'll need it.*

Igreus turned back, facing Nilah, and slowly walked towards her, his Katana extended to the side. *No! Not Nilah!*

"Black Arrow!" I screamed, putting my sword as if it were a bow. It swirled with Black Magic, extending its handle to match that of a bow. It transformed into black thunder, as the power of the sorcery boomed bigger than I had ever seen before. I released the arrow, and it crackled through the air, powered up even further from Shadow-bane's energy. Igreus slashed at it with his Katana, but the spell went through, crashing into his chest.

Light leaked from where the arrow struck as his scale-made armour shivered, as if a living creature had been tortured with fire.

"Hollow Disperse," Igreus said, the edge of his Katana turning into cherry blossoms from the tip to the handle.

The wind carried them as they reflected light, much like a blade would.

"Level Three Illumination Magic, Wall of Light!" Evie yelled, putting a barrier before Nilah, then me and Henrith, and finally before herself.

The petals mixed up with the ones falling from the cherry tree as the wind grew stronger. Igreus waved his Katana's handle and a pink flash ripped the ground all the way from him to where Henrith was. The flash soared into the sky, reaching a height of at least thirty metres. The attack ignored all barriers. Henrith screamed with both his arms hung at the ground, as if burned by extreme fire.

"Feeling lucky," Henrith panted. "I dodged just before it struck me. I was as good as dead."

"Your hands!" Evie yelled and cast a healing spell.

"Thank you, Evie," he spoke, frowning in pain.

The petals returned to their original blade-shape as they got attached back to the Katana's handle. Igreus took a low stance as at the start of the battle, putting the Katana back in its sheath.

"Draw," he said, and a pink arc shredded through the air as the sound of metal resonated along with it. Reflexive Insight aided me, pushing my body back as my knees bent and let the slash go right above my belly.

"We won't last long like this. Sova, should we use... Level Five?" Evie asked.

"Nilah, can you do it?" I yelled, hoping my sister would figure out what I referred to.

Igreus dashed towards me. His Katana came from above and clashed into The Devourer. I pushed him back, cracking the ground beneath my feet. Being hardly at his chest's width, it was hard to reach him. "Level Three Black Magic Sorcery, Beam of Darkness!"

The Devourer expanded, as black shadows swirled a few metres around me. The blade fed on the sorcery and enhanced it. I drew a horizontal slash at Igreus, an arc of darkness crackling at him at inevitable speeds. With a swift swing, he sliced at my attack, but it went through, cutting away bits of his armour. He grunted and acrobatically evaded each slash. I used Shadow Step and appeared behind him, to the side, and constantly changed positions and patterns, making sure I was just close enough to make it hard to avoid the attack, yet be away from his grasp.

Good! I'm actually pushing him back! Hopefully, this will buy time for Nilah and Evie to prepare!

Eighty-six slashes later, I counted. Even I felt my mana reserves lower than they had been in the past years. *The toll of constant shadow-stepping.*

Igreus raised his arm in the sky, leaving himself wide open to attacks. Without hesitation, I overcharged a new set of 'Beam of Darkness' into The Devourer and struck Igreus directly. Black Magic crackled, shaking as if the entire world were in Nocturna's shadows, pieces of Igreus' armour breaking. The foggy essence leaked from the wounds in the armour.

"Eclipse of Grief," Igreus' ethereal voice resonated, and the world sank in pitch-black darkness, an eclipsed moon the only thing visible in the sky.

Where am I? What happened!? I looked at my hands, but they weren't there. Everything was black. A pink flash ripped the darkness, as pain shook my whole being. Across my chest, the uniform torn to pieces, blood spilled like a fountain. I fell on my back, eyes shaking in terror. Igreus' thunder-shaped eyes intimidated me, as his towering figure stood before me. I coughed blood, breathing being a task close to hopeless.

"Little... brother..." Bureaus whispered through his bloodied lips. I had fallen right next to him. "Be..." He drew his last breath.

"Sova!" Evie screamed in agony, as she ran towards me.

"Sovie!" Nilah cried in a high pitch, pulling Shadowbane's string and releasing a barrage of arrows at Igreus. The Knight reflected each one with his blade. Henrith jumped right in front of me, his hair flowing in the air as an aura of magic illuminated around him. A barrage of kicks fell on Igreus, who completely ignored it.

"Level Three Illumination Magic, Flash of Light," Evie cried, her eyes opened wide in horror.

Flash of Light? It takes twenty percent of the caster's mana...

Twice the agonising pain of the slash went through my body, but the wound closed within seconds. I leaped back to my feet and saw Igreus holding his blade in the air. Nilah's arrows struck his armour, apparently doing damage, but it didn't stop the knight. The moons along the Katana's back glowed and then Igreus spoke.

"Eclipse of Grief."

"Everyone move!" I screamed, running in a random direction. I could see nothing, so I tripped and fell. All of a sudden, I felt weightless and bruised by the intense wind. A pink flash sliced through the darkness.

What? I'm falling!? I stabbed the mountain cliff with The Devourer, stopping my fall. *While rolling, I fell off the cliff. Fuck. Oh no! The pink flash! Who did he strike!?* The panic of who I might've lost claimed me, and with a feeling of helplessness, I poured mana into my limbs, propelling myself up to where the cherry tree shed its blossoms.

"Nilah!" I screamed, my legs going completely numb. The wind blew my torn clothes as I shook. Igreus cleared his blade of the blood and then slowly turned to face me. He extended his Katana into the sky again.

"No!"

"Eclipse of Grief," Igreus' voice resonated in the darkness.

An explosion of light shed apart the darkness, sucking it in. "Level Five Illumination Magic," Evie yelled. "Pillar of Light!"

Igreus dashed towards Evie, but The Light pushed him away. He took his Katana before him and used it to pierce through Evie's magic.

"Overcharge!" Evie said in a prolonged scream, the light expanding tenfold, consuming everything.

This is the only chance. Now!

"Self-exiled into darkness, your wisdom holds true. Moonlit ravens gather your soul. Bathed in shadows, with your power, we unite. From the palm of my hand, may your rage be true," I chanted, my voice shaking. *If I don't calm down, I might fail the spell and die. Fuck.* I dismissed The Devourer, afraid of what could happen if it sucked the spell in. My shadow consumed my body, clinging towards my hands. "In the dark, I pledge myself to eradicate the light."

As the spell was complete, and the crescent manifested within my palm, I released it straight into the pillar of light. Where I believe Evie should've been. "Level Four Black Magic Sorcery, Nocturna's Crescent!"

It propelled ahead, cutting away chunks of the earth on its path. Sinking straight into the light, I pulled up a reinforced Wall of Light before me. Calling back The Devourer in my hand, I awaited the culmination. It took seconds for Evie's Pillar of Light to mix with my Nocturna's Crescent. With Evie's downward swing, the whole fountain of light tilted and crashed, light consuming everything in pitch-perfect silence.

As the illumination faded, my eyes had to adapt to the brightness levels. Igreus' body was hard to distinguish. Pieces of his helm were there, a part of his chest, and several scales of his arms. The Katana's blade was nowhere to be seen and only its handle remained.

Evie's Lightforged Sword turned to Light Dust as she held it extended at the knight, who, even on his knees, still seemed tall enough to be threatening. Nilah walked next to Evie, her uniform torn amidst the chest, the same way as mine, yet she had a band of cloth hiding her nudity. *Evie, when did you use Flash of Light on my sister as well?*

"Ah," Igreus released a deep sigh. "Two thousand years I practiced calling him 'My King' and not 'My Lord'. I can't believe I won't get the chance to make him proud."

Evie's sword vanished entirely, and she fell to her knees, Nilah grappling onto her for support.

"I wonder where I will end up now, when this life, too, is over. Will I be a royal servant? Or perhaps I will be king myself," Igreus spoke in a tired voice. "At least I got to witness another beauty of magic. Still, not as gracious as yours, My King."

He lowered his head at Nilah and Evie, the foggy essence dispersing with the gentle wind, mixing up with the cherry blossoms. "But I can still lay a foundation for your return. Behold, for the last time, Hollow Disperse."

The cherry blossoms actively reflected the light and a pink flash, this time slower than before, took shape in the sky and crashed at where Nilah and Evie were.

"Devour!" I said, shadow-stepping at the place of the collision, my sword consuming the attack. I raised it above my head, as rose petals swirled around The Devourer's now glowing white edge, black thunder jumping across its length in a constant flow. "I don't know what magic your king showed you, but I'll let you witness the combination of light and darkness, and your very own colour to it! Begone!" I made a diagonal swing, a burst of magic cacophonously obliterating everything before me.

The light cast a soft glow on the floating chunks of grass, cherry blossoms, and what remained of Igreus' helm. As the thunder's crackle faded, the helm dropped to the ground and rolled all the way to the base of the large cherry tree on the hill's edge.

With a sudden halt to their magical enhancement, the chunks of debris tumbled down and landed on the ground. With the mountain trembling beneath me, I fought to keep my balance, my legs wobbling with each jolt of the shaking hill. The edge of the hill downed in a land-slide along with the cherry tree's cut-off huge roots.

Looking up, I let out a sigh. A beam of light pushed through the gaps in the clouds, casting a warm glow on everything it touched. The air was filled with the delicate sound of falling crystals, creating a requiem that echoed through the land for Igreus, The Hollowed Knight.

Among the Archives

*"...about The Devourer and Shadowbane...
It is a rarity to find tools of such power. Many speak that they could rend through reality itself. The very potency these weapons posses is too big a threat. An immediate report is mandatory, should someone spot these demonic items. For, after all, only descendants of The Darc can wield them."*

"Letter to Reina Stratovic"

MATHSMAGICA

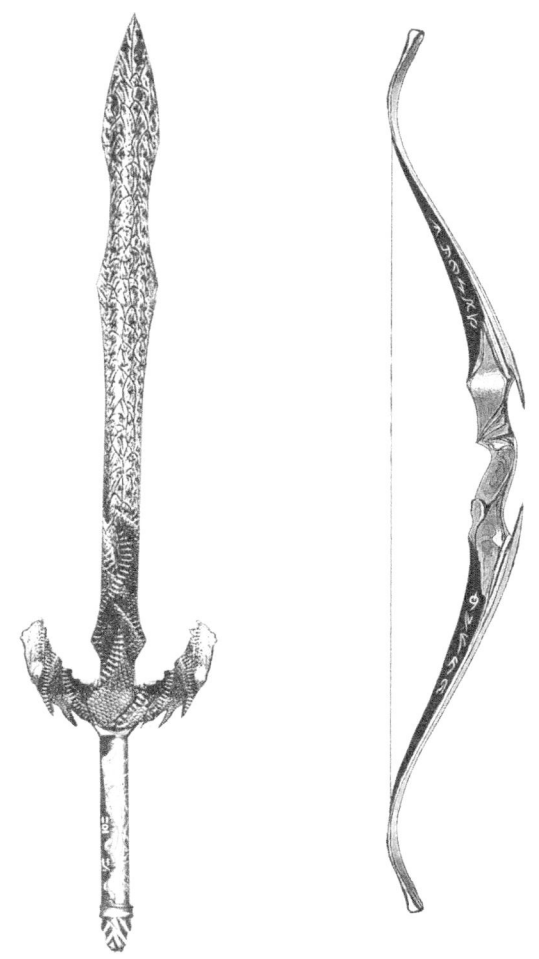

CHAPTER 26
VOICE AT THE TAPESTRY

"Are you girls okay?" I asked, turning around. "Henrith, can you stand?"

Magic circles formed at our feet, and in a second, a light engulfed me. By the time it faded, I couldn't see anyone around. My eyes peered left and right. All the cave walls provided a subtle glow. Each rock covered in numbers. Equations of magic I couldn't comprehend. Oddly enough, brasiers glowed in ash-flame, highlighting a path for me to follow. A mist obstructed the jagged landscape, keeping the endpoint of this lit-path unrevealed.

"Evie?" I yelled, hearing my voice echo in the distance. "Nilah?"

I took several steps forward, inhaling the humid air. "Henrith?"

There were no replies. My steps echoed as I went down the floating brasiers. *If I judge by the echo, it's a large cave. Nobody responding means I'm alone. They can't hear me. So I got teleported far away from them. But if my eyes don't lie to me, they also had magic circles engulfing them. They also got teleported. Were we all split apart? Who is orchestrating this? Could it be that they are confident facing us separately? It is true that we are stronger together, but now I'm even more worried. Evie cast that spell and that will leave her vulnerable for a while, and she already depleted forty percent of her mana by healing me and Nilah. I hope I find them fast.*

The mist got denser with each next step I took. The sound of metal colliding with rock resonated rhythmically, as if I were in a mine. I ceased my movement and held in my breath. A loud shriek came from behind. I turned, The Devourer taking shape in my hand while I already swung at whatever beast ambushed me. Walking on countless legs, its body was like a platform that served for its head and spear-shaped limbs. Red scales acted as its defence against blunt attacks. A dozen eyes were on the very front of the lower part of its body. I jumped back, frightened by the gruesome sight.

"Level Three Elemental Fire Magic, Fireball!" I said, fire bursting out of my hand, burning the creature alive.

I panted, wiping the sweat off my brow as the smell of burnt meat filled the air. *Is it normal that it smells so good? Or am I that tired that even this might prove to be a tasty meal?*

"Level One Illumination Magic." I pointed my hand at the creature. "Analysis."

White light engulfed the creature and turned into a green hue. I smiled. *Poisonous, of course.*

A sharp pain struck me at the back of my head. I narrowed my eyes, the image of a gate with darkness swirling around it, popping into my mind. *What's with all of these memories? I have never been here.* I walked down the misty path, adhering to my ash-lit guide. My stomach growled for food. I kept walking and walking. Now and then, a bug attempted to take my life. With the idea of avoiding the smell of meat, I sliced them down with The

Devourer. There was a lacking in the sword's grip and I guessed he wanted to feast on magic, not on insects. But I, too, didn't want to face these odd creatures. I craved to see my sister and Evie's face, then to find Master Lethalica and go home. *Rilereth is gone. All that's left is this nightmare I hope to awake from sooner.*

At long last, I reached the black gate. There was no darkness like the image I had lodged in my head. A mist, thick and ethereal, gently floated out of it, obscuring everything.

I stepped past the gate, using the numbers on the walls as the only indicator for where the floor was. As I made the first step past the doorway, an image of Igreus appeared in my mind, a headache striking again. He seemed so small. Like a tiny speck on the ground, yet I could somehow see him bowing, a knee on the floor. As I focused on this 'memory' I recalled his voice. "I will take care of it, My King."

Shaking my head, I pressed on. "I have to find them. These are just illusions. Priorities. Set priorities," I spoke to myself as I treaded at a hastened pace.

A light glowed amidst the mist. When I reached it, a purple sphere floated, pitch-black circles floating inside. According to the shape of numbers on the walls, it seemed this was a dead end, and this sphere was the reason for the mist. Frowning, I reached my hand out to it as the mist cleared around it, inviting me in. "What other option have I got?"

I touched the sphere and the black circles fitted at my fingertips, gently sucking my skin in. The mist dispersed as a shockwave blew it away. A blue glow emanated from the sphere and from the walls emerged spirits. Ten of them, each slightly differing from the other. Their pale semi-transparent bodies were that of bulky warriors. Black stripes marked them. They stood in wait near the cave's walls. Each one could be distinguished by a certain number of stripes they had on their bodies. One of them had one, the other two, the third three, and like that, all the way to ten. The sphere in my hand dropped to the ground and the gate that I walked in through swirled with darkness.

"Um. Hello?" I shrugged. The spirits all pointed fingers at me. I frowned, spiralling in place, trying to understand the meaning of it all.

Magic circles shaped before all ten of them, and a beam of light shot out at me. I crouched, avoiding it, but the beams reflected back from the circles. Flow Magic empowered my body and reflexes, as I acrobatically avoided all ten beams. I threw fireballs, as I couldn't focus enough to use Black Magic at the constant necessity of acrobatic movement. The flames crashed into the walls and vanished, heating up the area. *Is it possible that it's sealed off and I can suffocate myself by burning the oxygen? Nocturna, damn it!*

I struck the spirits, but my attacks went through them like through ghosts.

"Devourer!" I yelled and grabbed the sword in my right hand, splitting one of the spirits from the bottom to the top. It divided into two and then shaped into a new spirit with an additional black stripe on its chest. It pointed at me with a finger and fired a beam out its magic circle. My body spun as a beam almost hit me. The Devourer could consume beams, but the spirits launched new ones.

I felt a gentle blow to my chest as a beam made contact. I stood there, untouched, as the rest of the beams swiftly converged on me. The faceless spirits sang in perfect unison, their voices blending into a hauntingly beautiful choir pitch. The melancholic melody had a touch of tranquillity woven into its notes. I frowned as I found myself smiling. Then I cursed, realising the melody was familiar. A pull from the beams took me back to the centre of the room as I tried to escape through the gate I had come in from.

"Stop!" I screamed, disrupting the magic of the music. "What do you want from me!? Let me out!"

They ignored me as I kept shouting. "So be it."

I stood in the middle and chanted, "Self-exiled into darkness, your wisdom holds true. Moonlit ravens gather your soul. Bathed in shadows, with your power, we unite. From the palm of my hand, may your rage be true. In the dark, I pledge myself to eradicate the light."

My arm extended at a group of spirits in a hope Black Magic will vaporise them. I cursed, seeing the spell hadn't activated at all. The equations were hollow. Frowning, I realised my mana wouldn't reach the brackets where it should be poured into.

"Screw this! What do you want!?" I waved my arms chaotically.

As the melody clung onto me, I rested in a seated position, thinking through the situation for the hundredth time. Without the ability to use my spells and unable to run out, I could only seek the answer within. I closed my eyes and sank deeper into a meditation state.

"There you are... But what do I do now that I am here?" I asked, standing before the tapestry that Master Lethalica had taught me how to reach.

"Ah, that melody. It's been awhile since I heard it," a deep voice spoke within the room. The tapestry basked in many colours, flames, water, and magical entities sliding through it, like pages unfolding.

"Who is that?" I asked, looking around, yet nobody was to be found.

No reply followed. I walked around the tapestry,

searching for someone hiding, but the whole place shifted as if I was still standing on the front.

"I am stuck. I need to escape! The others need me!" I said in a loud voice, hoping whatever was listening would hear.

"So am I, Sova Darc. We seem to be in the same situation."

"How do you know my name? And my family name as well?"

No reply followed again. I waited and sat before the tapestry, gazing into it.

"A fascinating tapestry, isn't it?" the voice asked.

I nodded in response, though I had no idea if the voice could see me.

"One thing Nocturna was correct about."

"You know Nocturna? So you are from The Shadow Covenants? Who are you?" I asked.

"She hid in the shadows because she knew about it. The Tapestry of Shadows."

"The Tapestry of Shadows? Right... That's what it's called." I jumped back to my feet and approached it.

"Do you sense her, Sova Darc? Nocturna is staying right behind it. Right in its shadow."

Something about the tapestry seemed different. It tempted me to interact with it. Without a hint of how to, my hand acted on its own. I reached to touch its surface. My fingertip marked it, and a large violet eye with its tall irises peered down at me. I fell to the ground, startled by the abrupt change of the tapestry's shape. I shook in fear, as I could feel a presence far scarier than any I had felt before. Far more dominant, and endlessly more menacing. What I had felt from Master Lethalica was just a fraction compared to this one.

The tapestry returned to normal, and I crawled back, not taking my eyes off it. It resumed its magical folding sequence. The voice then spoke again. "I will lend you a hand, Sova Darc. I will let you find them. But there will be a catch. Something I want from you."

"What would that be?" I asked, panting, as a fearsome aura bathed over me.

"You just have to *allow it*. But I guarantee you this, you will reach the others," the voice spoke and then deepened even further. "That, in my nobility, I offer a promise."

"You're noble?" I asked, but no reply followed.

I waited for hours, asking questions, but the voice no longer responded. My body shook every time I thought of touching the tapestry again.

"Fine! I allow it. Help me save them," I whispered.

"So be it, Sova Darc."

I opened my eyes to the real world. The spirits were gone. My back itched with a pain hard to put to words. The scar had been timid for a while, but now it made up for the time it was silent. I struck my back into the wall and attempted to scratch it. A satisfying feeling washed over me as I felt something release from it, unlike before. The sphere I had touched that summoned the spirits floated into the air, shaking vigorously. Cracks formed on it, and suddenly, it crashed into small pieces of glass. The wall behind me cracked next to my ear, and I jumped forward. All the walls splintered and crashed into glass pieces.

I pushed it all out with a shockwave by combining the wall of light from Illumination Magic and simple air magic.

"At long last," a voice spoke from behind me. "The time has come for me to lay a foundation for My King."

Among the Archives

"I need not waste time writing. For each page I write, I could save hundreds of lives. Words are better remembered rather than written and forgotten."

    - *"Tales of Sovah The Legendary Mage,"* Book 2, Page 30

CHAPTER 27
THE VOID HAS AWAKENED

A SHALLOW LAKE SPREAD BEYOND THE HORIZON. Spheres of energy motioned through basic geometric shapes as they floated mid-air. Some radiated in a yellow light, others blue, and third ones in red. Above, the sky stretched out in a cloudless canvas, adorned with vibrant spheres that painted a star-filled picture. The crystal clear water reflected the light, illuminating the area in a rich image.

I turned to see who spoke behind me. It was but a small child. Her pale-white skin seemed as soft as a newborn. Ear-long white hair, cut in a perfect line, gave only a slight glimpse of her blue left eye and red right eye. Her height reached only my chest. A black gothic-styled dress marked her petite frame.

"Did you get lost?" I asked. *Surely it wasn't her saying anything about some king just now.* "I will help you find the way out. I am searching, as well."

"Human, you dare pity me?" the girl said, her voice as childish as she appeared to be.

"Human?" I smirked. *Okay, this couldn't get worse. Now I*

have to fight a child? "Do you define yourself as something else, then, creature?"

"Of course. I am a Noble Orchidea. One of the few left. All because of your stupid species!" The girl clenched her small hands, shaking fists at me.

"It's the first time I hear of you. How could you blame me for vanquishing something I don't even know existed in the first place?" I asked in a calm tone.

A sudden memory clashed in my head. The image of this same girl, but smiling at me. The headache devoured at my brain. *Why is this happening?*

"Oh. It's been forty years since I saw that happen," she smirked. "I will do my best to make way faster."

"Who are you and what are you talking about!? What forty years ago? I am only twenty, for Nocturna's sake!" I yelled, holding onto the back of my head.

"You needn't know," she said, looking at the triangle shape bursting into a square as it floated by her face. "But I am Genie. Named after my generosity, apparently."

"Okay, Genie, and what about these forty years ago?" I noticed numbers shaping barriers all around the area. *So I am sealed into this place, aren't I? But why?* "What do you want with me, and why do you hate humans? Have you seen Evie and Nilah? Henrith?"

"Hmm, dunno. If I take too long, Aetherial will punish me, so I'll keep it short," Genie said, and her feet ceased touching the ground. She floated amidst the spheres in the air and spoke. "My kind lived a peaceful life in perfect harmony with nature. We gave offerings to it, and *she* gave offerings back. One day, a man came to our village. He said he meant no harm, and even though frightened, we believed him. Such is our kind, you see?"

I opened my dimensional ring inventory and pulled out

a mana potion. Even if I didn't mean to take one, everyone said it's necessary to take mana potions when you go on a dangerous mission. *I didn't expect to actually need this.* I drank from the potion as I kept listening to Genie's story. *She also completely ignored me about the others.*

"The man's appearance was identical to your own. His name, though, is forbidden for a Noble Orchidea to speak. He lived with us for a week. Studied us, we believed. Something about him was really off. That's why, despite him showing an affinity to nature, such as our own, we still held a distance."

"He was human, right? So what did he do to make you hate him?" I asked. *The mana potion isn't working. Maybe something within this barrier is sealing all mana regeneration. I can't recover.*

"He left the village. A year later, he came back with more humans. They all wanted to learn about our traditions and study how we lived. It wasn't long after when nature began repelling us. Something was terribly wrong. We couldn't find out what. All the questions we threw at *her,* she wouldn't respond. Then one day, months later, we saw it."

She touched her belly and patted it gently. "A Noble Orchidea carried the seed of a human. Tempted by the human's charm, a friend of mine allowed herself to become his. Nature hated us. And we hated the humans. Corrupting our nobility. When it was heard, soon after, others did the deed, as well. We were divided. Those who held nature dear and wanted to cleanse ourselves from the humans, and those who believed their newborns will drain the powers humans held and mix them with our own."

"So it was a mistake that happened out of love, Genie.

Do you think it's fair to put all the blame on two people who found solace in each other?"

"It is not love, human. Don't dare say that word again," Genie frowned and spoke in a sharp tone. "You serve your primal urges and nothing else."

"I understand your frustration. But that's a grudge you seem to hold on for a long time, isn't it? Despite your youthful appearance, I can guess your age is far greater."

"My age speaks wisdom beyond numbers. I was too generous to tell you this story. As I should have expected, humans will never change."

"Listen, Genie," I sighed, feeling exhaustion washing over me. "I ask forgiveness for the sins my species have committed to you. My journey has separated me from those I hold dear and I just want to find them and go home. Could you tell me how? Then you would no longer need to see a human's face in a long time."

"A tempting offer, human. Yet I am not here out of my own volition to bare witness to your kind," Genie spoke as she levitated towards me. "I have come to lay a foundation for My King's return."

Her face up close now caused an even greater headache. Images of greeny forests, small white-haired children running about, playing in the grass, picking up blooming flowers, and sheltering themselves in houses beneath the roots of tall trees.

"What is this that I'm seeing?" I muttered to myself.

"Look into my eyes, human," Genie spoke, picking my chin up as she gazed into me. "Now make way for My King."

My strength faded at an unspeakable rate. Exhaustion flooded my body, and I sank my knees into the shallow lake. I took long deep breaths, my eyes inviting me into a dark slumber.

"Endariel, My King, hear my voice," Genie whispered as she put a hand on my forehead, pulling my hair back. "The time to awaken has come. We are all waiting for you."

"Who's... Endariel..." I mumbled, my body going completely numb. *I need to push her away.* My arms had no strength left. I had to resort to magic. An equation took shape, but as I tried to fill it with mana, nothing went in there. *My mana... is gone. This place was draining me of mana all the time. She just bought time for it.*

A desperate feeling took over me, yet my conscious self couldn't react to it. Deep inside, I was in a panic, but there wasn't any power left inside me. *Is this the end? Am I going to collapse in this Noble Orchidea's mind-twisted talk about some king and this Endariel guy? Come on! Evie! Nilah! I need to reach them!*

I need to wake up! Evie and Nilah need my help!

The lake's water kept beaming with colours, yet now it seemed brighter, mesmerising even, filled with my mana.

"Fall to slumber, Sova Darc," Genie whispered in my ear.

The ceiling, pierced by a ray of light, shattered. All the magical floating spheres dispersed, going into the real night sky above. Evie and Nilah leaped in, water splashing as they landed metres away from me and Genie.

"Let Sova go!" Evie raised her Lightforged Sword forward.

"Let my brother go, you kid!" Nilah yelled, drawing an arrow from Shadowbane, its runes lighting up in the reflections of her azure eyes.

"Evie... Nilah... Where is... Henrith?" I mumbled, opening my eyes to a blurred vision of them. If it weren't for the stark contrast of their hair colours, I wouldn't tell them apart.

"You dare disturb The Ritual?" Genie frowned at the girls.

A metal whirring sound resonated, as a flash of light illuminated my eyesight. Genie's head fell in the lake before me, as my head still seemed to be resting in her lap. *Is this an illusion?* I wondered, as I could feel Genie's hands still caressing my hair.

"Do you see now, human? The aggression. The remorseless slaughter?" Genie asked, only her red eye shifting to look at me.

The whole scenery changed into a green forest. A waterfall splashed in the distance, and the comforting sound of a river ran close by. A gentle wind shook the leaves of the large trees, sunrays shedding through in a dance with shadows and light.

"Is it an undead?" Nilah speculated.

"If it was, The Light would've burned it," Evie said.

"And, human," Genie spoke, her head already back on her shoulders. "What do you think I felt back then, when I saw my kind kill each other, because of the human lust? Should you experience it? Perhaps you'd understand then."

"No... Don't do it, Genie. Please," I whispered, lifting my gaze to meet hers. Unlike what I expected, she smiled.

"Noble Orchidea are better than humans, human."

"Then you will not harm them?" I smiled in relief.

She looked down at me, with only her red eye opened, her grin widening. A chill went down my spine and I tried to push myself away, but my body was too weak.

A string whizzed in the air, and Evie blocked it. The sound of the clash was like an enormous hammer had crashed into her sword.

"Nilah, watch out!"

Strings danced about as the girls evaded, blocked with

barriers, or Nilah struck with a precise arrow. Rising in numbers, Genie's string attacks started getting through.

"Oh, there we go. The taste of human blood," Genie spoke softly.

The strings had made minor cuts across their bodies. The girls persisted in their oppressive fight against Genie's magic strings.

"It's just a waiting game," Genie patted me on the head. "Oh. It's almost ready. We should move."

Genie opened both her eyes, and the greenery scenery disappeared. We descended in a spiralling motion, whereas me and Genie seemed to be floating in the same position, as if an invisible cloud carried us down. The means of transportation were unlike anything I had ever seen before, but my groggy and painful state made it difficult for me to comprehend what was truly unfolding.

As we landed, I could see a red carpet extending forward, going down some stairs before a plaza. On the pavements, there were engraved magic circles, yet they seemed inactive. Evie and Nilah were charging in my direction.

"Now then. Your time has come, I believe, Human." Genie said.

A brutal thud vibrated as a kick sent Genie flying back while Evie spun right above me. Landing, she picked me up and carried me on her back down the stairs. Nilah shot arrows at Genie, though I couldn't see the result of that. Evie placed me on the ground and poured a mana potion into my mouth.

"Sova, your eyes... They are violet again," Evie whispered.

"How did you recover from that spell...?" I asked. *Last*

time she used that Level Five spell, she was drained completely. How did she recover so fast?

"Like I said, you're not the only one with surprises, right?" Evie smiled at me. "I will help Nilah take care of that doll and I'll come back to you."

She cast a healing spell, but the equation was cancelled out. Shaking her head, she sighed.

"Evie, wait." I said, pushing myself. "Help me sit."

Her arm supported my back, and I managed a seated position. I gazed into her dark eyes for a while, then I studied her smooth skin and sharp chin. Using all the strength that was left in my hands, I touched her cheek and then pulled the few locks of hair from in front of her face back behind her ear. My fingers fitted the back of her head as if by biological design, and then I pulled her gently towards me. I closed my eyes and sealed my lips into hers. Time stopped. Her taste, her breath, her touch - I loved every bit of it. She kissed me back and her hand held onto my cheek.

I released her from the kiss, looking at her eyes, passionate, yet surprised. Evie's cheeks flushed pink.

"What the hell are you two doing!?" Nilah yelled in the background.

"If I lose you forever," I said in a low voice. "I don't want to have any regrets."

"Sova," Evie whispered and kissed me again.

A loud ringing of metal resonated next to us, as Nilah shot an arrow at the string that would've claimed our lives.

"End this," I smiled as she let my back go and I rested on the ground.

With a nod, Evie stood up, blocking the incoming string attacks, without even looking at them. With a flash-step, she turned into light, propelling into combat.

Alright, with that off my chest, I can try to...

My thoughts faded. The magic circles just a few metres ahead of me captivated my being. I couldn't help but crawl to them. Focused on them, I could tell it was a big magic circle, consisted of many small ones. It pulled me in, just like the violet crystal a few months ago. My head bashed with memories, I couldn't make sense of. Images of cities from high above. Mountain peaks, armies looking at me. People and creatures in different attires all bowing in respect.

The runes activated in a violet glow, starting from left to right, until all circles were well alight. I roared, as a pain like none I had experienced before, clawed at my back. Twitching and twisting on the ground, I tried to fight this surge of whatever leaked from my scar. In abrupt motions, my body shifted into a kneeling position. My screams kept on as I bashed my fists into the ground.

"At last," Genie said, her head hanging in Evie's hand. "My King has awakened."

My body went stiff, and all my veins burned as they emitted a violet light. From my back's scar, a piece of flesh emerged, high in the air. In my agony, I looked to the left to see an enormous wing coming out of me. Aside from the scales covering the bone structure, the wing had a violet hue of magic shuffling through it.

"Wh–" Suddenly, from the right, another wing appeared. I felt them light as feathers, yet my body seemed to be ripping apart.

With each breath, I could see myself exhaling violet coloured gas. Tears ran down my cheeks as the pain kept devouring my very essence.

The wings, uncontrollably, spread out, and I hovered into the middle of the magic circle, the violet magic in the wings humming. The walls of the room turned into crystals that reflected my image perfectly.

"What—" I raised my glowing hands before my face. "What is all this!?"

In response to my desperation, the deep voice from the tapestry spoke through my very own mouth.

"The void has awakened."

Among the Archives

"Ruptures await. The armies are united. We await Endariel's return."

- *"Letter to Lethalica Chillgrip," From 'A friend'*

CHAPTER 28
HISTORY LESSON

ENDARIEL'S POINT OF VIEW

I SPREAD MY WINGS. Violet light bathed everything in the void's energy as it coursed through my body. At a slow pace, I descended to the middle of the magic circle underneath me. My wings built up in a narrow shape upwards, and I landed on the red carpet. Each step I took forced a crackle of void under my feet.

A portal of void opened where Evie held onto Genie's head. The magic expanded between them, pushing Evie and Nilah to the side.

"A rather pitiful sight to greet your king in, isn't it?" I asked, my voice deeply resonating.

"Sova, is that you?" Evie asked.

"No! That's not my brother! That is... something else!" Nilah yelled, her face in horror.

"I apologise, My King. I am ever grateful for your return," Genie bowed, her head popping back to where it belonged. "Welcome back."

With a grin, I looked at Evie and Nilah.

"Bring back my brother!" Nilah screamed, pulling Shadowbane's string.

"Oh? Would you dare? This is your brother's body, after all," I said.

Nilah released the string, a magic arrow flying at me, its darkness swirling in the air. I snapped my finger, a wave of void magic rupturing the entire distance between us, splitting space-time apart. The arrow disappeared into the void, and thus the rupture closed, violet dust sparkling where my spell had been.

The noise of rumble blasted in my ears as the ceiling collapsed. I smiled at the falling debris; the void expanding in a violet thunder, vaporising each object falling in my direction.

"And they say I was late," I smirked. With the entire building levelled to the ground, two enormous creatures spread their wings in the sky as they hovered gracefully behind me. Bodies as big as cities. They performed their landing with such precision that their reptile-like heads would be just metres behind me. As they descended, their radiant glow lit up the surroundings, highlighting the billowing clouds of dust that were kicked up from the ground.

One of them, covered by basil-coloured scales, and a verdant energy coursing under its wings. Spikes went across its nose, making it even further threatening. Extending from the back of where its eyebrows would be, if it had such, were two long horns. The creature had feet that were both powerful and deceptive, with scales that failed to fully conceal their muscularity. Its five-toed feet were adorned with claws that emitted a vibrant, verdant glow. Its cat-like pupils glowed with the same green hue.

The other one, scales made of black ice, eyebrows

burning in fire, as its whole back all the way to the end of the tail, had pillars of never-fading flame. All the claws of the beast emitted shuffling colours of light, starting from yellow to blue, white, and orange. The colour that coursed in its wings was a deep azure.

"Aetherial," I spoke, turning to the verdant coloured one. "You have done well."

The beast released a low-toned growl in response.

"Lethalica," I spoke to the other one, "Your hard work and efforts were undoubtedly unmatched."

I walked closer to the centre between them, and they both got their heads in my range. Their colossal size made me look like an ant compared to them, but that didn't matter at the moment. I wanted to touch them. My left hand caressed Aetherial's green scales, while my right hand caressed Lethalica's black ice.

"My King, I welcome you. It has been twenty years," Aetherial spoke, his voice slightly louder than a human's yell.

"Long twenty years, Aetherial. And you have kept The Fog splendidly under control."

"I do not mean to rush you, but the others are waiting in the capital. I will get rid of the remaining nuisance, while you can complete your transformation," Aetherial said, his eyes narrowing at where Evie and Nilah stood.

"Look at the poor girls shaking in fear, Aetherial. Do you not feel pity?" I asked with a smile.

"For humans, never, My King." Aetherial raised his head.

"Everyone has awaited my awakening for so long. A few more hours wouldn't kill them, for sure," I said, the void crackling underneath my wings as I walked back over to where the girls and Genie were.

"My King, it is urgent," Aetherial said, magic equations appearing everywhere above Evie and Nilah.

With a spontaneous turn, I looked at him over my shoulder, a hundred thousand void spheres opening above his enormous body. "Dare you disobey me, Aetherial? You have been in charge of the armies in my absence, but did that help you forget who I am?"

"The King of All Dragons, Endariel Voidcaller. I could never," Aetherial said and bowed his enormous head to the ground.

I advanced towards Nilah and Evie, spreading my wings freely to the side. "I will deal with the humans as I see fit. There are weapons in everyone here. We just have to learn how to use them."

SOVA'S POINT OF VIEW

DARKNESS. My body existed, yet it did not. I could tell I was standing. My eyes, perhaps blind to see, failed to provide me with sight. I walked, yet I knew not where I went. Despite that, I kept walking. I spoke, yet in a language I didn't know. Well-woven speech left my lips, yet I knew not what I said. Was anyone listening at all? Yes. I was listening. But what was I hearing?

"Sova," a male voice echoed around me. "You are not alone."

I ceased my aimless strode. "Who is that?" I asked, yet the words that came out of my mouth were in a different language.

"Come to me. I am here," the voice said, echoing from all three-hundred-sixty degrees around me.

"I can't see, and I can't pinpoint your voice's location! How can I come?"

"See, Sova, but not with the eyes."

My heart thudded in that moment.

"See with magic," the voice said.

"I can't. My mana is sealed. All of it drained away by some strange kid-witch and—"

"See with magic, Sova," the voice said and as I pushed myself to draw upon my mana, I failed. "Magic is but a canvas. Find the brushstrokes."

For what I thought to be hours, I kept failing. My mind shifted through ideas about what the brushstrokes might actually be, but I couldn't comprehend it. Evie kept appearing in my mind. Falling to my knees, I felt tears go down my cheeks. "I just kissed her. I didn't want to die. No regrets, my ass. I wanted to hold her and share so many things with her. God damn it! Why did I have to die!?"

A warm spot on my forehead pulsed. The Light coursed through my body, flooding me with a sense of hope. It leaked from my skin, and I could finally see again. The sight of a man with blond hair, blue eyes, a handsome face, and a Harmony Enforcer uniform.

"You... you are a copy of me," I said, looking up to meet the man's eyes. He stood before me, his finger distributing warmth through my forehead. "What is the meaning of this?"

"You're not dead, Sova. At least not yet," he said and chuckled. "Sorry, but I think that's a false accusation as well. *You* are a copy of me."

"What do you mean? You look like me, you sound like me, and you even wear the same clothes," I said, accepting his hand to pick me up.

"Wait till you hear my name," he said and looked to the

side. His eyes shifted from deep blue to a golden glow, and the darkness was no more. The familiar sound of flame, water, and other magic splashing filled my ears. The man opened his palm and from nothingness, a wooden chair appeared for him to sit in. He made one for me and I sat as well. We stared at each other in silence for a while and then we gazed into the endless shifting of magic - The Tapestry of Shadows.

"Judging by how you look and that joke you made, let me guess. Your name is also Sova?" I suggested, raising an eyebrow.

"That's quite close," he said. "Just one more letter in it."

"So—"

"Sovah. Yes," he said.

I looked at him for a while, my mind going completely blank.

"As in the man of legends?" I shook my head with a small laugh.

"They *did* write legends, indeed."

"I am confused. Am I in some self-delusional hell after I died to whatever claimed my body?"

Sova pointed at the tapestry, and with a swipe of his hand, all the magic ceased its movement. A page unfolded, revealing a violet-scaled dragon in sleep.

"That's who claimed your body, Sova."

"A dragon? I did grow wings, but what the hell? Dragons really exist!?"

"Only three of them."

"Only three? I must be lucky. What are the chances that one of the three existing dragons would claim my body somehow? What kind of sorcery made this happen?"

"My sorcery," Sovah looked at me casually.

I jumped from the chair and grabbed him, pulling his face close to me.

"Why did you do this to me!? Fix this–"

"Sova," Sovah said, and a wave of relief washed over me. "Calm down."

"Fuck! You're using spells to control my emotions, aren't you!?" I jumped again.

Sovah smiled at me and said, "You really are my kin."

"I'm not sure if that's a compliment. If you really are Sovah The Legendary Mage, you'd never put anyone through this path. You'd never put a fucking dragon inside me! Inside anyone!"

He looked to the side, and I felt pity and regret in his eyes. *He's not controlling my emotions for this now, is he?*

I let him go and sat back in the chair.

"It's not like I wanted this to happen, Sova. You know, I am only human, right?" Sovah asked.

"At least that's what the legends say about you! Hell if I know."

"Hell if I know, too," Sovah said, squeezing his eyes. "I always thought I was human. I must be, right? Yet, throughout all of my life, I kept wondering if I really am one."

With a frown, I shook my head at him. "What... are you getting to?"

"When I was younger, my village was attacked by a dragon. Unlike the others, I could see the spell's maths equations and copy them on the spot. Without any real education in magic, at the age of five, I killed the dragon with its own spells against it. My village and my parents were killed in the process."

"That's indeed a heroic deed. You avenged your village at five... What the hell?"

"No, Sova. At that time, I didn't understand it, but the dragon was attacking only those who were mages with any mana pool above average. But it was confused."

"The dragon was confused?"

"Yes. That a five-year-old boy like me would have so much mana. Not believing it, the dragon started killing others, sparing my life. It thought someone was hiding their presence and using a spell to make me seem like the one with abnormal potential."

"But it was actually true...?"

"Indeed. In fear of losing all my friends and family, I copied the dragon's spells. All of them were of what modern mages would consider Level Four spells. And you know what's really important concerning those spells, right?"

"Their potency and danger?" I asked, frowning.

"You can overcharge them. I poured my entire mana pool into a single spell. The dragon, along with the village, and everything surrounding, vaporised. I killed them all."

"Oh..."

"So I walked and spoke a language I didn't understand. The equations for the spells. I kept repeating them. Just like you did. Without a goal, unaware of where to go. And somehow I survived and reached the next city. People looked after me and I learned to survive on my own. With the idea to repent on my mistake, I studied magic and learned how to control it. Whenever I found someone in trouble, I tried to help. Though this grew on me far too much."

"How come?"

"When I was your age, I was already considered a miracle. I single-handedly slayed the dragons and united the lands. Towns and villages into countries. I shaped them and gave them boundaries. I wanted everyone to be happy, so I moved all religions and cultures to their own haven."

"So that's how the five countries came to be. Close to what the legends say." I scratched my chin.

"Five?" Sovah smiled. "Can you name them for me?"

"You seem aware of modern spell definitions, yet you don't know your geography?"

"I have only some insights into the current world."

"Savannah, Algama, Loria, Nocturnia, Domainia, and most recently, Mathsmagica. Though, Mathsmagica is an artificial city that has its own laws, so it counts to be a country," I said.

"How many continents can you name?"

"How many? Sovah, there is only one," I said, shrugging.

Sovah sighed and looked at the tiles on the floor.

"What?"

"There are a lot more than that. I suppose this is the dragons' handiwork," Sovah said.

"What? So there are more people out there?"

"I can't really be sure anymore," Sovah spoke, shrugging. "So not everything is put to waste, perhaps."

"But wait... Why did you think you're not human? Because of all the revolutions you sparked?" I asked.

"No. Anyone could do that if they had the power and desire. I was too good."

"Too good? Is that a boast or?"

"I allowed the dragons to live alongside humans. My hand shook that of Endariel Voidcaller, their new king. I killed his father and after multiple attempts to avenge his death, Endariel bowed his head to me and asked for peace."

"But... why? How do you even imagine dragons to live alongside humans?"

"They can shapeshift. Easily, they can look like any other human. Do not mistake their beastly nature, Sova. They are more intelligent than humans, and their lifespan is far beyond ours. They are magical creatures that harvest wisdom all their lives."

"So you thought they would—"

"Yes. Most of the magic you have come to know nowadays originates from the knowledge the dragons passed down to our kind," Sovah spoke.

"I didn't see this coming," I said, my mouth going agape. "You really are a man of legends. You did the unthinkable!"

"But that was my biggest mistake, Sova." He looked at me with grief in his eyes.

"Why? Magic is the best thing this world has to offer," I said, raising my hands in the air.

"Because humans gained affinities, and some dared to challenge dragons in battle. They broke the rules. I told you there are only three dragons left, right?"

"Yes, you did."

"There were hundreds of thousands."

"But how do you know there are only three now?"

"Because I could glimpse into Endariel's new memories that he gained through you."

"That makes little sense to me, but then what happened to all the other dragons?"

Sovah placed his hand on his forehead and pulled his hair back. "After my *passing,* the humans, out of fear, I presume, created cults and slayed the majority of dragons. The dragon hunters kept going at it until, at the end, there were only three left."

"So Endariel is one of those dragons. The one who is in my body, right?"

"Endariel Voidcaller, Aetherial Wrathblaze, and Lethalica Chillgrip. Those are the–"

"Wait, what did you say? The last name?!" I jumped from the chair, a chill running down my spine.

"Lethalica Chillgrip. Someone you know?"

"My Master in Elemental Magic at The Academy has that name..."

Sovah smiled. "Red hair and yellow cat-like pupils?"

I gripped onto my head and pulled my hair back, as my eyes almost bulged out.

"Is that why I had this weird feeling about her?"

"What you felt wasn't the fact she is a dragon. The aura she has comes from her potency as a mage. When you reach a certain level, your mana pool expands into an aura that others can feel as threatening, or just uncomfortable. Said simply, it's because they feel the sheer power you poses. As I look at you, I could say some people probably experience that feeling emanating from you as well."

"That's a relief... And not. But what is the dragons' goal, then?"

"Since Endariel is in your body now, it means he picked you as his vessel twenty years ago."

"Twenty years ago... That's slightly after my birth. When my parents died," I said, frowning. "He killed them? But Evie said it was–"

"When I sealed the deal with Endariel and we signed peace, Endariel didn't trust us. He trusted me specifically because he could sense it inside me. But he didn't trust humans as a whole," Sovah explained. "But that's where my greatest mistake was. *I trusted the humans.*"

"What... did you do?"

"I created a spell that in the case of Endariel dying, he would be able to reincarnate into someone's body. That way I secured if humanity would turn against the dragons, Endariel would be able to stop that movement. Because, you know, everyone would want to kill the king first, right?"

"So you made Endariel even more immortal than he already was?" I shook my head. "Just because you believed humans were good!?"

"Naïve, right?" Sovah smiled at me.

"Sovah, these dragons will wipe humanity off the planet, for sure! Their thirst for vengeance must be beyond belief!"

"I figured as much," Sovah said with a sigh. "That's why I'm here."

I frowned, "Wait what?"

"I improved the spell I cast on Endariel and cast it on myself," Sovah smiled.

"What? So... you're going to take me over, too? What the hell– Everyone taking turns on my body!"

"Not exactly. The spell slightly backfired. It seems the Shadow Veil of mana and the Abyssal Eyes cost a lot of time."

"What do you mean? What are those things?"

"Shadow Veil is the gift of this enormous mana pool you have. And the Abyssal Eyes are what let you see and copy spells like nobody else. These two gifts are the reason why I became who I was. But, that being said, they cost so much that it took two thousand years for me to manifest into one of my kin. So yes, Sova. You are the first person I get to talk to besides your sister."

"Wait, what!? You spoke with Nilah!? How!?"

"I'll let you know about that some other time." Sovah stood up and walked in front of The Tapestry of Shadows.

"They are in danger. I think we should intervene before Endariel kills them."

I stood next to him and looked at the tapestry.

"And I think our sync is almost ready. I will take your body for just a few minutes, alright?"

"Sovah! Wait! The dragons... What will you do with them?" I whispered.

"We really are the same," Sovah said softly, as he smiled.

AMONG THE ARCHIVES

"Noble Orchidea - a species we just recently learned about. They seem to grow no more than a hundred forty centimetres in height. What they truly are and how long they live, we do not know. The people who had seen it believe they live a minimum of a few hundred years."

> *- "Letter to the Research Department," from Director Astron.*

MATHSMAGICA

CHAPTER 29
SOVAH, THE MAGE OF LEGENDS

I RESIDED WITHIN MY BODY, YET I PLAYED THE PART OF A MERE SPECTATOR.

Endariel swiped my hands horizontally. With each thrust, the void ripped through the air, cracking time and space. Evie and Nilah evaded the attacks, but somehow, perhaps because I was conscious of Endariel's actions, I knew that he wasn't even trying. He wanted to let them tire out completely and make them... *taste despair.*

My limbs went numb and Endariel froze mid-air. The wings' violet glow dimmed, and the void coursing through my veins subsided. Plummeting to the ground, Endariel shuddered.

"No!" He screamed, his voice loud as a dragon's roar. The ground shook, all of his power leaving him in a single moment.

"It's been a long time, Endariel Voidcaller. I'm glad to see you are still doing well," Sovah spoke through my lips.

The strangest feeling ever. Two people conversing through my body and I am powerless to do anything about it. Just watch. Yet, thanks to Sovah's... presence? Aura? Magic? I feel so calm.

"This can't be!" Endariel roared, crashing my hands against the ground. My knuckles bled as there was no magic to protect them from the rocky surface.

Evie took a stance, ready to slice at me. I commended her bravery and determination.

"Endariel, what's wrong!?" Lethalica asked, shapeshifting from the giant dragon of the elements into her human form with red-hair and mage robes. *So it's really true.*

"Master Lethalica!? What's the meaning of this!?" Evie and Nilah yelled in confusion.

"Endariel! My King!" Aetherial shifted into a human form as well. He was a two-metre tall man, with green cat-like pupils. He was in silver-coloured armour, covering his large muscles, that shaped the body of a warrior whom alone left the impression to be capable of wiping out an army single-handedly. With his smooth skin and neatly groomed hair, Aetherial easily passed for someone in their twenties, but the commanding presence and sturdy frame added a sense of maturity to his demeanour.

"They aren't humans..." Nilah said, and drew her bow. "Stay away from my brother!"

She shot arrows relentlessly.

"Become dust," Aetherial spoke, and all the arrows turned into small specks, their darkness dissipating.

Master Lethalica erected an enormous wall of ice between us, yet her profound mastery made it transparent. Through it, I saw Evie standing before Nilah, carefully guarding her. Genie had already come next to me, kneeling and sobbing.

"Endariel, My King, what's wrong?" Genie asked between sobs.

"How can you be here!?" Endariel asked with hatred in his voice.

"What do you mean? I was here before you. Did you not see?" Sovah asked, forcing a smile onto my face.

Wings burst to open as Endariel forced my body to stand up. "Aetherial, use your Singularity Magic. Devastate this body. I'll find another vessel!"

"But, My King, it's another twenty years–"

"Do it, Aetherial!" Endariel screamed with a dragon's roar.

My limbs shredded into small particles of dust, exactly like the army of mages whom The Fog claimed.

"Now what will you do, Sovah?!" Endariel laughed maniacally.

A ray of light burst out of my mouth and eyes. My veins filled with magic that I could feel and perhaps even control. The Light pulled back the particles out of the air and reassembled my body into its natural state.

My hands reached out to Aetherial and Lethalica and with a sigh, they both crashed into the ground. After the dust that kicked up in the air dispersed, the two dragons shook, staying with one knee on the ground. The equations that my eyes revealed were so complicated that I couldn't exactly comprehend. Sovah used magic to force them into the posture they were.

Aetherial clenched his teeth, pure hatred gazing at me under his frown. Lethalica's head kept low.

"It has been a good two thousand years, my fellow dragon friends. I am happy to see you are alive and well," Sovah spoke, and through my being, I could feel he was sincere.

"Curse you, Sovah. Curse you and your species!" Aetherial roared, his dragon voice bursting in my ears.

"Sovah, we attended your burial. Exactly two thousand sharp cuts through your body. We thought it was the dragon hunters behind it. How come... How come you are here now, and I really feel and know it's you?" Lethalica asked, her voice shaking.

"Aetherial, I just had a debate with my wonderful descendant on this topic. What makes you think I am human?" Sovah asked.

"I can smell it. I can feel it. You are human," Aetherial said. "My hatred for you confirms it."

Sovah turned my right hand to the side and conjured a chair in it. The ground flattened into a perfectly smooth surface where he placed the chair and comfortably sat in it, putting my right leg on top of my left one.

"I wonder, Aetherial. But you're a dragon. Originating from The Tapestry of Shadows itself. You must be right," Sovah said.

In a sudden outburst, Endariel claimed my body and leaped through the ice wall, the void destroying it. My hand smashed into Nilah's forehead and began to turn into small particles as the void leaked from it.

Evie kicked me to the side, but Nilah flew away with me.

"Let her go!" Evie screamed, flash-stepping and kicking me away.

Sovah reclaimed my body and let go of my sister. Her eyes glowed violet instead of the typical azure.

"Look what you've done, Endariel. And I just wanted to talk to you three in peace," Sovah said.

"Sovie..." Nilah whispered and fell unconscious.

My hands covered her eyes, and a ray of light glowed from it. Evie grabbed me by the shoulders and attempted to throw me off. Sovah made my body as heavy as a mountain.

"Child of Light. I believe your name is Evie, am I

correct? This must be confusing for you, but I am healing my descendant from Endariel's pollution," Sovah said, piercing Evie with a sincere gaze.

Shards of ice, along with pillars of flame, and tides of ocean water bashed in our direction.

"Stay here," Sovah said, and Evie agreed with a nod, as if under hypnosis. *Sovah cast some spell on her just now. I saw for but a moment the equation on her.*

Taking a slow step towards the incoming surge of Elemental Magic, Sovah clasped hands together, and then opened them wide. The water wave split to my left and right as if by the force of an enormous gravitational pull. The ice spikes melted when Sovah simply looked at them. Then, the flame pillars shaped golems of fire.

"Genie, you just observe from here," Sovah said, and a sphere of light engulfed her.

Sovah clapped twice and, with pointing and middle fingers extended, he reached towards the sky. The ground underneath shifted as it shaped an island that propelled into the air.

"Now that's more aesthetic, I believe," Sovah said with a smile.

"Curse you, Sovah!" Aetherial charged. Sovah moved my body effortlessly to block every single attack. At the moment before collision, I could see complicated equations taking shape. *That's... barriers? He's making top-notch defensive barriers with such speed and precision?*

"Your Devastation Magic won't work on me, Aetherial. What are the odds for you?" Sovah asked, as an attack propelled me into the air.

"You're just borrowing the kid's body, Sovah. There's no chance that you're at your peak power. You'll just fade and then Endariel will take over!" Aetherial said, as he kept an oppressing rain of blows.

Lethalica, in her dragon form, flew towards us, shooting out a breath of fire.

"You're right," Sovah said, with a sorrowful expression. "But I don't need to be at my peak. My time has long ago passed."

The flames out of Lethalica's mouth were blown to the side, and as if god's hand grabbed onto her enormous dragon body, she was flung to the side, disrupting her flight control.

"I promised my descendant only a few minutes. I've been enjoying our reunion for too long." Sovah closed his eyes, a burst of light blowing Aetherial away, burning his skin.

With a deep inhale, Sovah enriched the air with mana in my lungs. He spun my body graciously into the air and the floating chunk of land cracked into six pieces. Equations emerged all over them, setting them on fire. With the speed of a meteorite, each one collided into Lethalica. Exhaling, Sovah landed us next to Evie and Nilah.

"Enough," Sovah said, his voice resonating like that of a god.

The dragons roared in the sky and charged at us, but he stood tall, shaking his head in disappointment.

"I said, 'Enough.'"

Aetherial and Lethalica froze mid-air, hundreds of spikes piercing through their bodies. The glow of their wings rained down like blood from the wounds. Sovah looked at them with a threatening gaze I didn't know my body could even produce.

"I still hold you dear in my heart," Sovah said and plummeted the dragons in to the ground with gravitational magic. They shape-shifted into their human forms and were forced to their knees, Sovah's equations wrapping tightly around them.

"Why!? Why has the tapestry done this to us!?" Lethalica cursed, tears falling down her cheeks. "How can a mere human do this to us!?"

So dragons can cry, too. "I apologise for my kind's rebellion against you. Forgive me, but I cannot undo that."

"What do you want, Sovah!? We can't even have our king back! You captured him in your playful spell-weaving for eternity! You were supposed to bring peace, yet you took him prisoner!"

These words hurt Sovah. I could feel it. He watched the dragons bowing their heads by his force.

After a sigh and prolonged silence, Sovah walked over to the two dragons. My knee touched the ground, and a tear ran down my cheek.

"I will find a solution," Sovah spoke, and about a thousand magic circles manifested around Aetherial, and another thousand around Lethalica.

"I won't give up on our treaty. I will personally watch over it. This two-thousand-year long story is nowhere near done," Sovah said. With magic's aid, the wings sticking out of my back ripped off and fell to the ground. Blood spurted out of my back, splashing around. A ray of light sealed the wound. The pain subsided immediately. "I shall no longer see wings."

The magic circles all collided into one and shrunk into Aetherial and Lethalica's bodies. "I forbid you to reveal your true forms. Not unless I allow it."

"Who are you to dictate the rules!? You're not our king!" Aetherial roared.

"Yes, I am your *God*." Sovah spoke in an otherworldly

voice. In Aetherial's widened pupils, I could see the golden glow emitting from my eyes. "Lethalica, give me the runed-coordinates to Mathsmagica."

With noticeable hesitation, she opened her palm and the equations for the teleportation magic appeared on it.

"Thank you."

Sovah walked over to Nilah and Evie. The barrier surrounding them faded, and we all teleported at the coordinates given to us.

We stood at the outskirts of the city, The Academy's spires piercing the sky. Sovah inhaled deeply and smiled. "It really is magical."

"Who... Who are you?" Evie asked, looking up at me.

"You are from the Luminari Faith, aren't you, child?" Sovah asked.

"Y–Yes," Evie nodded.

"Then you should know already," Sovah smiled and then gazed at Mathsmagica again. Soft air blew the scent of magic into my nostrils and I could tell he enjoyed it.

"But... Where is Sova? And the other..."

"You're right. I shouldn't get greedy. After all, I asked only for a few minutes. Wouldn't want my grand-grand-grand... well, grand-grandchild to be angry at me, now would I?" Sovah chuckled. "And don't worry about Endariel. Him and I will have a great long talk in the chamber of The Tapestry of Shadows."

"The Tapestry of Shadows?" Evie asked.

"I'll let Sova explain that to you. Now then, before I leave. Thank you for being by those two's side. And take it from me. You have nothing to fear about Sova anymore. I am happy you found each other at this age."

Evie's eyes opened wide, and she put a hand over her mouth. Evie's eyes held a reflection of my own, with a golden glow subsiding from my pupils as I stood still and reclaimed my body.

Lifting my arms before my face, I enjoyed the freedom of movement.

"I... I'm back," I said.

Evie's legs gave out and her knees fell in the green grass. I leaped to support her.

"It's really you, isn't it?" Evie looked at me, her eyes watering.

"I think so," I said, Sovah's calming aura still holding onto me. "I am me."

"Are you sure?" Evie asked.

"Yeah," I pulled her closer gently.

"What's our favourite cafe?"

"The Mushroom Cafe, of course. Does it even need asking?" I chuckled, as she stared into my eyes, and slowly closed in. I stared back for a few seconds until she was too close for me to focus.

Evie's hands wrapped around my neck, and her lips instantly landed on mine. She closed her eyes, exposing her lengthy and gorgeous eyelashes. I closed mine and allowed myself to sink into the power of the kiss. As my arms wrapped around her, the warmth of her body stuck to me. Evie's tongue reached into my mouth, deepening the kiss into something far more intimate. With her hands gently gripping my neck, the softness of her touch took my breath away as her fingers ran through my hair. A heat most chilling went through my body as Evie's grip tightened and her breath washed over me. At a hesitant pace, she pulled away from me. The tantalising taste of her tongue lingered like an addictive elixir, one I was reluctant to part with, even for a fleeting moment. As I blinked, she gazed at me with a passion I could easily drown in. With a prolonged stare, her cheeks burned red and Evie's eyes looked to the side in shame. I caressed her hair and smiled, pulling her in for a hug.

I looked at the grass a few metres to the side where Nilah was. As our gazes locked, she, with one eye opened, motioned for me to keep quiet by placing a finger in front of her lips. *This time you won't ask what we're doing, huh?* I smiled.

On the side, I could see Henrith deeply asleep in the grass, his body completely healed. *Sovah, you did all this and even healed everyone. You really are The Mage of Legends.*

EPILOGUE

THE AIR HUMMED WITH MAGIC, the smell of ozone filling my nostrils. I glimpsed at the corners of the room and from each one; I conjured ice spikes, crashing them into the centre of the training arena. Evie stood at the entrance and watched as I practiced.

"I don't really get it. How can this really be useful in combat?" Evie asked.

"It's not about combat, actually."

"But you've been practicing this for hours. When do I get to know why?"

"You'll find out eventually," I said, crashing the spikes for the hundredth time this hour. "Hopefully, soon."

"Hey, guys, we have to go to the meeting with the Pillars. It's time," Nilah came through the entrance and said with a sigh.

"Just two more attempts and we're going, okay?" I spoke, ice shards flying by me.

"Don't you get bored with him doing that?" Nilah looked at Evie, rolling her eyes.

"I would usually get bored, but seeing Sova practise magic is a sight I could enjoy endlessly," Evie said.

"Oh my, you're really in love, aren't you?" Nilah poked her, chuckling.

I walked over to them, concluding my practice for the day, and saw Evie's cheeks flushed pink.

"Stop terrorising my girlfriend, sis." I squeezed Nilah's cheeks and wiggled her around.

"Okay, I won't, I promise," she pouted in pain.

"Good." I smiled at her and then offered Evie my hand.

"Thank you, Sovie," Evie said, and I tugged her in close, making a quick spin, that I concluded with a kiss. She smiled at me as we sank into each other's eyes.

"You two are just lovely," Nilah said and pulled me. "But we'll be late!"

Pilar Serene stood at the centre of the round table, Master Lethalica to his left, Director Astron to the right, and three of us opposing of them. I held Evie's hand, resting on my left knee. Nilah was to my right, and next to her sat Henrith.

"My humble apologies for the good people we lost. Yet, I must commend the people who returned to this table," Pilar Serene spoke, his hands clasped together. "I really prefer we'd had this talk on an open field or arena where every survivor could hear, but unfortunately, we don't need such space for the amount of survivors we have."

"The mission was a success, yet at an enormous price, indeed." Director Astron bowed his head.

"Master Lethalica has already briefed us on what happened. It is a miracle that the four of you navigated yourselves through enemy territory, and even emerged victorious," Pilar Serene said, his eyes looking at the map on the table. "Aside from clearing the city of The Fog, we received reports that some of the coasts noticed subsiding of The Fog's influence. I believe that to be related to your success."

"As the lethality of this mission was so severe and you pulled through, I am ready to announce Sova Ren, Nilah Ren, and Evie Stratovic as graduates. You can join the ranks of any squad you want, any army you desire, and any raid you seek interest in." Director Astron motioned his hands at us.

"We are really grateful, but personally, I still have so much to learn!" I said.

"Me too!" Nilah lifted her hand.

"I want to educate myself, as well," Evie spoke softly.

Henrith smirked with his eyes closed.

"Well, Astron, it is as you said. These kids really won't accept the graduation gift," Pillar Serene laughed in an elderly fashion. "That's why I prepared something else for you."

"Dear students," Master Lethalica spoke. The moment she opened her mouth, her voice sent a cold sensation creeping down my spine. Yet I knew Sovah didn't want me to speak up and say who, or what, she really was. "From this point on, you will have access to absolutely all classes you want to attend. Anonymously, without the public's notice, you'll be able to take private classes, or propose suggestions on how to improve our teaching."

"That being said, there still is another surprise in wait for you. But you will learn about it later," Director Astron whispered.

"And for what I think most students would rejoice about is," Pillar Serene spoke, leaning over the table. "You get one month of vacancy. You can go home to your countries, or stay at the dorms and rest, or focus on your own experiments. There won't be any duties for you to perform aside from a few small things... But we'll talk about them later."

The meeting finally ended. Henrith bowed in respect to us and said he had already graduated, so none of those really applied for him. But the amount of money he got from the mission would allow him to work on a private project he had, so he was happy about it.

Nilah said she had something to do, so she left me and Evie alone. We climbed up the roofs and leaped onto the same Arcanist Tower as before. Unlike last time, we whispered to each other, so no High Arcanist would interrupt us.

"So, what really happened to Sovah and the other guy?" Evie asked.

"They are still here," I whispered, putting a hand on my heart. "In me."

She sighed, lowering her head. "Does that mean they can still take your body at any moment?"

"I don't know, honestly. But I don't feel like before. I am somehow... free now."

"But Sovah is so powerful. Why didn't he just kill all the dragons? He really is like what the legends say." Evie frowned.

I grabbed her hand and put it on my chest. "Do you feel that?"

Evie nodded, blinking in confusion.

"That's why he didn't. Because he's just human. Good at heart."

"So he didn't kill them... out of pity?"

"The legends speak of his unlimited power. They dehumanised him. He became like a god. No. He became a God! So much so that Sovah himself began doubting his humanity," I whispered in excitement. "Yet what I believe his biggest power was, it wasn't his magic. It was his ability to see the good in everyone. The vision of unity. The same vision that you and I share."

"But the dragons are evil! They want to kill us all! I can't believe Master Lethalica was just sitting with us at that table like nothing happened! The version she said to the director and the pillars probably had nothing to do with dragons..."

"Because, Evie, it's you. I know you will understand," I said and looked at the setting sun, a gentle wind blowing locks of hair before my face. "I feel sorry for them, and I, too, believe in Sovah's dream. Whatever it takes, I will make it come true."

"What *is* Sovah's dream?"

I gazed at her; the sun illuminating her beloved face, and smiled.

"It will take a while, but I will tell you the truth about Sovah's story."

ALSO BY DANIEL GEORGIEV

The White Phoenix: Birth of An Angel

Godwalker: Ashes of Destiny

Makiya - a fantasy novel on Meganovel.com

Acknowledgments

You, who holds onto this book, I'd like to have you know I appreciate you. I am certain that since you reached this part of the book, you really wonder if we will get to see the rest of the magical journey. The answer is yes. This is the start of the series and I have so much stories to tell here!

An honest plea - share about this book with your book-loving friends! Reaching out to others is what helps me as an author the most!

Reinstriver! R.S. Marinov, from the start of my writing journey, you have been there to guide, inspire, and help me improve. We are all looking forward to your books!

Met with unwavering support by my proof and beta readers, along with the whole community revolving around me, I managed to pull through and stay motivated to finish this book! To those who privately reached out to me after reading my books, I also sincerely appreciate you! I always respond to any messages and emails I receive, so don't hesitate to reach out to me.

Living with a guy who's so work obsessed is probably the greatest challenge. The biggest thanks to my fiancé, who supports me through all my projects and ideas in her own special way.

I have to give my big thanks to Skyreach Creative Media© for all the marketing work and advice given. Our partnership keeps proving to be long-lasting, warm, trustful, and kind.

The book's cover art and all illustrations inside were made by Boyan Petrov. His dedication to the "Mathsmagica" project was fascinating from start to finish. All this eye-candy we owe to him!

Many thanks to the editing team and all who provided insight on the overseen small things!

Dear reader, when you first opened this book, did you notice? It was the light of many that engulfed you. The hard work of each person involved. We appreciate you let your mind and soul bask in our Light.

JOIN THE COMMUNITY

For all those of you who want to get in touch with me, or like-minded people, you are invited to join our growing community of creative souls.

We are supporting each other in our creative endeavours and boost the positive energy!

I also urge you to leave a review whether you liked the book or not! That is a huge help not only to me as the author but also to other readers who might enjoy the book!

I am mostly active on my Facebook page, but don't be afraid to contact me anywhere else, or directly by email. I always respond =]

danielgeorgievofficial@gmail.com

- facebook.com/danielgeorgievofficial
- instagram.com/danielgeorgievofficial
- tiktok.com/@danielgeorgievofficial
- goodreads.com/danielgeorgievofficial
- youtube.com/@DanielGeorgievOfficial

About the Author

Daniel Stefanov Georgiev, also known as Blentkills, is an emerging multi-genre author. This is Daniel's third self-published book and fourth book in total.

Born in Bulgaria, at the age of fifteen, Daniel made his first attempt at exploring the fantasy worlds in his mind and the idea of "Makiya" was born. The web novel grew strong as a top trending book on the exclusively contracted web platforms: Goodnovel and Meganovel. The success with "Makiya" drove him into confidence, inspiring many of his musical pieces, and further enhanced his ambition to write new stories.

"The White Phoenix: Birth of An Angel" released on 20/11/2023 as his first self-published book. Daniel received many messages on social media from his fans in an attempt to get to a signed copy personally from him, to which he responded with unmatched positivity. The book grew his following, as many of the thousands of readers from "Makiya" immediately leaped over for Daniel's new release. That trend kept going with the release of "Godwalker: Ashes of Destiny" putting a heavy weight of responsibility on Daniel as now he has three series started and people wait for the next book in each one.

When Daniel doesn't write or edit his works, he likes to spend time interacting with fans on his social media, fly drones, do photography, play video games, or sing songs with his guitar in hand.

Printed in Great Britain
by Amazon

55612154R00195